The

MYSTERY
WOMAN

AMANDA QUICK

D1313069

PUTNAM

G. P. PUTNAM'S SONS
Publishers Since 1838
Published by the Penguin Group
Penguin Group (USA) LLC
375 Hudson Street
New York, New York 10014

USA • Canada • UK • Ireland • Australia
New Zealand • India • South Africa • China

penguin.com
A Penguin Random House Company

ISBN 978-0-399-16986-1

Printed in the United States of America
1   3   5   7   9   10   8   6   4   2

Book design by Gretchen Achilles

The

MYSTERY
WOMAN

G. P. Putnam's Sons

New York

For Frank, with love, always and forever.

The

MYSTERY
WOMAN

One

The heel of one of her high-button boots skidded across the stream of blood that seeped out from under the door. Beatrice Lockwood nearly lost her balance. She caught her breath and managed to grab the doorknob in time to steady herself.

She did not need her psychical senses to know that what she would find on the other side of the door would haunt her forever. Nevertheless, the gathering storm of horror ignited her other vision. She looked down and saw the violent energy in the footprints on the floor. There were more darkly iridescent prints on the glass doorknob. The paranormal currents seethed with an unwholesome light that iced her blood.

She wanted to run, screaming, into the night, but she could not turn her back on the man who had befriended her and provided her with a lucrative and respectable career.

Shivering with dread, she opened the door of Dr. Roland

Fleming's office. The gas lamp inside had been turned down quite low but there was enough light to reveal the man who lay bleeding on the floor.

Roland had always prided himself on cutting a fashionable figure with his hand-tailored suits and elegantly knotted neckwear. His curly gray hair was trimmed in the latest style, the sideburns and mustache artfully designed. He had given himself the title of doctor but as he had explained to Beatrice, he was, in reality, a showman. His charismatic personality and imposing presence ensured that his lectures on the paranormal were always well attended.

But tonight his finely pleated white linen shirt and dark blue wool coat were drenched in blood. His gold-framed eyeglasses had fallen to the floor at his side. Beatrice rushed to him and opened his shirt with trembling hands, searching for the source of the blood.

It did not take long to find the deep wound in his chest. Blood gushed from it. The color told her it was a mortal injury. Nevertheless, she pressed her palms firmly over the torn flesh.

"Roland," she whispered. "Dear God, what happened here?"

Roland moaned and opened gray eyes that were dull and unfocused with shock. But when he recognized her, something that might have been panic briefly overrode the tide of death that was sweeping down upon him. He clamped one bloody hand around her wrist.

"Beatrice." His voice was hoarse with the effort it took for him to speak. There was a terrible rattle in his chest. "He came for you. I told him that you were not here. He didn't believe me."

"Who came for me?"

"I don't know his name. Some madman who has fixated on you for some reason. He is still in the building, searching for something that will lead him to you. For God's sake, run."

"I cannot leave you," she whispered.

"You must. It is too late for me. He wants *you*."

"Why?"

"I don't know, but whatever the reason, there is no doubt but that it will be terrible. Do not let me die with that on my conscience. I have enough to repent. Go. Now. I beg you."

There was nothing she could do for him and they both knew it. Still, she hesitated.

"You know that I can take care of myself," she said. She used one hand to hoist her skirts high enough to allow her to reach the stocking gun she wore in the holster strapped to her thigh. "You were the one who taught me how to use this, after all."

"Bah, I fear it will be of little use against the man who did this to me. He moves with great speed and he is utterly ruthless. Run."

She knew that he was right about her little stocking gun. When he had instructed her in its use, he had emphasized that such small weapons were not accurate over distance. They were designed for close quarters. Across the width of a card table or in the confines of a carriage they could be deadly. But beyond that, they were little more than toys.

"Roland—"

He tightened his grip on her wrist. "You have been like a daughter to me, Beatrice. My dying wish is to try to save your life. Honor me by fulfilling it. Leave this place now. Use the bolt-hole. Take your pack and your lantern. When you are away from here you must never return. He will search for you. To survive after this night, you must remember everything I taught you about going on the stage. Rule Number One is the most important."

"Become someone else. Yes, I understand."

"Do not forget it," Roland gasped. "It is your only hope. Leave now, for my sake. Lose yourself and, whatever you do, stay lost. This monster will not give up easily."

"I will miss you, Roland. I love you."

"You brought light into my lonely, misspent life, my dear. I love you, too. Now, go."

Roland coughed again. This time blood filled his mouth. Beatrice became aware of the utter stillness of his chest. Fleming's heart was no longer beating. The dreadful red flood from the wound slowed to a trickle.

And in the terrible silence she heard footsteps on the stairs at the end of the hall.

Pistol in hand, she rose and hurried to the wardrobe on the far side of the room.

In all the time she had worked for him, regardless of where they set up the Academy, Roland had always had a bolt-hole. He had explained that there were two reasons for taking precautions. The first was that when business was brisk, they took in a fair amount of money that might attract villains intent on robbing them.

But the other, more important reason, he claimed, was that, by the very nature of their careers, they sometimes learned secrets that put them in personal danger. People tended to confide in paranormal practitioners, especially in the lucrative private counseling sessions where clients sought advice. Secrets were always dangerous.

She braced herself for the squeak of metal when she opened the wardrobe door and breathed a tiny sigh of relief when there was no sound. Roland had kept the hinges oiled.

She hiked up her bloodstained skirts and stepped into the wardrobe. Once inside, she pulled the door shut and groped in the darkness for the lever that operated the concealed panel.

The inner door slid aside with only the faintest of muffled sounds. Damp, dank night air wafted from the ancient stone passageway. There was just enough light slanting through the crack in the outer doors to reveal the small, shielded lantern, the package of lights and the two canvas packs on the floor. She returned the pistol to her stocking holster and scooped up the lantern and the lights.

She slung her pack over her shoulder and glanced at the dark mound of Roland's pack. It was too heavy to carry in addition to her own burden, but there was money stashed inside. She would need it to survive until she found a way to reinvent herself.

Hurriedly she unfastened the second pack and rummaged around. In the shadows she had to go by feel. Her fingers brushed against some spare clothing and the hard shape of a notebook before she found an envelope. Assuming the emergency money was inside, she opened the envelope. But it proved to be filled with photographs. She stuffed the pictures back into the pack and tried again. This time she came up with a stack of letters bound together with string.

Frantic now, she reached back into the pack. She found a soft leather bag filled with money. She seized it and thrust it into her own pack.

She was about to light the lantern and move into the deep

darkness of the tunnel when she heard the killer return to Roland's office. Unable to resist, she took a quick peek through the crack in the wardrobe doors.

She could see very little of the man who stood over Fleming's body, just a slice of heavy leather boots and the sweeping edge of a long black coat.

"You lied to me." The voice was freighted with a thick Russian accent. "But you will not defeat me by dying on me, you miserable old fool. I found the wigs. I found the costumes she wears onstage. I will find her. There will be something here that will tell me where she is. The Bone Man never fails."

The figure in the black coat crossed the room and moved out of Beatrice's line of sight. She heard drawers being yanked open and knew that it was only a matter of seconds before the killer tried the wardrobe door.

"Ah, yes, now I see," the intruder hissed. "You are here, aren't you, little whore? You stepped in his blood, you stupid woman. I see your footprints. Come out of that wardrobe now and I will not hurt you. Defy me and you will pay."

Her footprints. *Of course.* She had not been thinking.

She could scarcely breathe. She was shaking so terribly that it was all she could do to close and lock the heavy wooden panel that formed the back of the wardrobe. When Roland had installed it he had assured her that both the lock and the panel were quite stout. Sooner or later the Bone Man would get through the inner door but with luck she would have the time she needed to escape.

A fist pounded on the rear panel of the wardrobe.

"You cannot hide from me. I never fail."

She lit the lantern. The glary light illuminated the stone passage in hellish shadows.

She hitched the pack higher on her shoulder and fled into the darkness.

She was certain of one thing—she would never forget the terrible energy that seethed in the footprints of the Bone Man.

Two

ome months later . . .

S "Dreadfully warm in here, isn't it?" Maud Ashton re-
marked. She fanned herself vigorously with one gloved
hand and used the other to raise a glass of lemonade to her lips.
"It's a wonder that the ladies do not faint dead away on the dance
floor."

"Yes, it is quite warm," Beatrice said. "But the dance floor has
the French doors that open out onto the garden. The dancers have
the benefit of the cool evening air. I expect that is why they are
not collapsing from the heat."

She and Maud, both hired companions, were ensconced on a
banquette in a quiet alcove just off the ballroom. The bitterness
embedded in Maud's voice was unmistakable. Beatrice was not
unsympathetic. She had spent only a short time in the other
woman's company tonight, but that was long enough to hear a
great deal of Maud's unhappy story. It was a sad tale but not an

uncommon one among those who were condemned to careers as paid companions.

Maud had made it clear that she had suffered a fate worse than death—a catastrophic loss of social status due to her husband's bankruptcy. Following his financial crisis, Mr. Ashton had sailed for America to make his fortune in the Wild West. He had never been heard from again. Maud had found herself—alone and middle-aged—saddled with her husband's debts. There had been no choice but to become a professional companion.

Maud's world had once been very different. Her marriage to a wealthy, upper-class gentleman had given her entrée into the fashionable crowd that she was now obliged to watch from afar. There was a time when she, too, had worn elegant gowns, sipped champagne and waltzed until dawn beneath glittering chandeliers. Now she was forced to content herself with a position on the fringes of Society. Professional companions accompanied their employers, who were often widows or spinsters, everywhere—soirées, country-house parties, lectures and the theater. But, like governesses, they were virtually invisible to those around them.

The world could be a harsh place for an impoverished woman who faced it alone. There were very few respectable options when it came to employment. Maud had every right to be resentful of her fate, Beatrice thought. But on the other hand, evidently no one had vowed to hunt her down for unknown reasons. No one had murdered an innocent man in the process of that hunt.

"I vow, this ball is interminable," Maud grumbled. She checked the watch that dangled alongside a small bottle of smelling salts from her chatelaine. "Dear me, it's only midnight. We'll likely be here until three. And then it will be on to another ball until five.

It's enough to make you want to jump off a bridge. I believe I'll just have another nip of gin to liven up this dreadful lemonade."

She reached into her satchel and took out a flask. When she started to pour the gin into the lemonade, however, the glass slipped from her fingers. The contents splashed over the dull gray skirts of Beatrice's gown.

"Oh, dear," Maud said. "I am so sorry."

Beatrice stood quickly and shook out the heavy folds of her gown. "Quite all right. No harm done. It was an old dress."

She owned newer, more expensive and far more fashionable gowns, but she reserved the oldest dresses in her wardrobe for those times when she was on assignment from the Flint & Marsh Agency.

"How clumsy of me." Maud whipped out a handkerchief and made a fuss, trying to blot the damp patch of the gown.

Disaster struck in the blink of an eye. The unnerving tingle on the back of Beatrice's neck was the only warning she got that something had gone badly awry.

She whirled to survey the dance floor. Daphne Pennington had vanished.

In other, more normal circumstances, the situation would not have been unduly alarming. It certainly would not be the first time that a reckless young lady had slipped out into the gardens for a few stolen kisses.

But tonight the circumstances were anything but normal. What made the situation a thousand times more ominous was that the man with the cane and the scarred face had also disappeared.

She had become aware of him a few minutes before when she had sensed that she was being watched. She had immediately searched the crowded room to see who might be looking at her. No one *ever* looked twice at a paid companion.

She had locked eyes with the scarred man leaning on an ebony-and-steel cane. It was a nerve-shattering encounter because deep down she had experienced a strange, intense sense of recognition. But she was positive she had never met him in her life.

He was not the sort of man a woman could forget. It wasn't the violent slash that had destroyed the left side of his fierce, sharply planed face or the fact that he used a walking stick that made him so memorable. Rather, it was the impression of power that emanated from him. She was quite certain that there was a steel core inside the stranger and implacable promise in his eyes. She could easily envision him with a fiery sword instead of the cane.

For a heartbeat or two, during which she could not breathe, he had regarded her with a steady, focused gaze. Then, as if he was satisfied by whatever he had seen, he appeared to lose interest. He had turned and moved off down an empty hall. It was clear from the hitch in his stride and the stiffness in his left leg that the cane was not a fashionable affectation. He depended on it.

She had started breathing again but her senses remained unsettled. Her intuition told her that she had not seen the last of the man with the cane. The realization was deeply disturbing but not nearly as unsettling as the knowledge that some part of her *wanted* to encounter him again. She told herself it was because she needed to know what it was about her disguise that had caught his eye. Her objective, after all, was to remain invisible.

But in that moment she had to stay focused on her assignment. Daphne and the scar-faced man were not the only ones who were now missing from the ballroom. Daphne's dance partner, Richard Euston, a handsome young gentleman who had been introduced to Daphne by a friend of the Pennington family, was also gone.

The situation was deteriorating rapidly.

"Excuse me," Beatrice said. "It appears Miss Pennington has taken herself off to a withdrawing room. Perhaps she tore her gown or wore a hole in her dancing slippers. I must go and see if she requires my assistance."

"But your dress," Maud exclaimed anxiously. "It will be ruined."

Beatrice ignored her. She picked up her satchel and went swiftly along the hall.

A ruined dress would be a disaster for most paid companions whose wardrobes were extremely limited, but it was the least of her concerns tonight. It was time for her to earn the excellent salary that the Flint & Marsh Agency paid her. She prayed she was not too late.

Daphne and Euston had been dancing near the French doors when she had last seen them. It was likely that they had slipped out of the room via that route.

Daphne's grandmother, Lady Pennington, was on the far side of the ballroom chatting with three other ladies. There was no way to get to her to tell her what had happened without wasting precious time forging a path through the crowd.

Beatrice had studied all of the exits from the ballroom an hour earlier when she and Lady Pennington and Daphne had arrived. At the time she had concluded that if someone was intent on compromising Daphne, as her grandmother feared, the villain would most likely lure his victim out into the night-shrouded gardens.

At the end of the dimly lit hallway Beatrice opened the door she had noted earlier. She stepped out into the summer night and paused briefly to orient herself.

A high wall surrounded the extensive gardens. Colorful lanterns illuminated a section around the terrace, but she stood in an unlit area near the gardener's shed. The gate that opened onto the narrow lane behind the grounds was not far away. Anyone attempting to abduct a young lady would no doubt have a closed carriage waiting. The ballroom terrace was some distance away from her position. If she moved quickly she could get to the gate before Daphne and her abductor reached it.

If she moved quickly and *if* she was correct in her conclusions. So many ifs. It was quite possible that she was mistaken. Perhaps Daphne was at that very moment enjoying a light flirtation with the very attractive Mr. Euston, who intended no harm.

But that did not explain the disappearance of the scarred stranger. Her intuition told her that it was not a coincidence that he, too, had vanished.

She set her satchel beside the step, whisked up the hem of her gown and removed the small stocking gun from the dainty holster strapped just above her knee. She hurried toward the gate along an aisle formed by two rows of tall hedges. Her gray dress helped her blend into the shadows.

When she neared the gate she heard the muffled sound of a horse stamping a shod hoof in the lane on the other side of the wall.

She came to the end of the twin hedges and stopped. In the moonlight she could see that the gate was partially open. As she feared, a small, fast carriage stood waiting. There would be a second man with the vehicle.

At that moment she heard the soft thud of rapid footsteps coming toward her through the garden. Whoever had taken Daphne would arrive in a matter of seconds. She could not deal with two villains simultaneously. It occurred to her that if she managed to close and lock the gate, the man with the carriage would not be able to come to his associate's assistance.

She rushed toward the gate and got it shut before the driver of the carriage realized what was happening. She slammed the lock into place and whirled around just as Richard Euston burst out of the shadows.

Euston did not see her at first because he was concentrating on keeping a grip on Daphne, who was struggling valiantly. Her hands were bound in front of her and there was a gag in her mouth.

Beatrice aimed the small gun at Euston. "Release Miss Pennington or I will shoot. At this range I cannot miss."

"What the bloody hell?" Euston stopped abruptly. His astonishment turned to anger. "You're just the companion. What the devil do you think you're doing? Open the gate."

"Let her go," Beatrice said.

"The hell I will," Euston said. "She's worth a fortune. Drop that silly little gun. We both know you won't pull that trigger. You're a paid companion, not a bodyguard."

"I never bluff," Beatrice said.

She cocked the pistol and aimed the barrel at Euston's midsection. He seemed stunned that she actually intended to shoot him, but he recovered quickly and yanked Daphne in front of himself to use as a shield.

A shadow emerged out of the darkness behind Euston, who never saw the black-gloved hand that wrapped around his throat and tightened briefly.

Unable to breathe, let alone speak, Euston released Daphne and struggled to free himself. But it was finished in seconds. He collapsed, unconscious, to the ground.

The crack of a whip sounded on the far side of the high wall. Hooves clattered and carriage wheels rattled on paving stones. The vehicle took off in a frantic rush, the driver evidently having realized that something had gone very wrong with the abduction plan.

Daphne rushed to Beatrice's side. They both watched the man with the ebony-and-steel cane move into the moonlight. Beatrice kept the weapon aimed at him.

"Is it common for paid companions to go about armed?" he asked. His voice was dark and low and stunningly calm, as if he was accustomed to confronting pistols. As if he found her an interesting curiosity.

"Who are you?" Beatrice asked. "If you think to take over where Euston left off, you had better think again."

"I assure you, I have no intention of abducting Miss Pennington. You are the one I wish to speak with."

"Me?" Shocked, she could only stare at him, something akin to panic sleeting through her.

"Allow me to introduce myself," he continued in that same calm, controlled tone. "Joshua Gage, at your service. We have mutual friends in Lantern Street."

She experienced an almost overwhelming surge of relief. He was not referring to her days with Fleming's Academy of the

Occult. This was about Lantern Street. She forced herself to concentrate, trying to remember if she had encountered anyone named Gage in the course of her work for Flint & Marsh. She came up blank.

"Whom do you know in Lantern Street?" she asked warily.

"Your employers, Mrs. Flint and Mrs. Marsh, will vouch for me."

"Unfortunately, neither is conveniently at hand to provide introductions," she pointed out.

"Perhaps this will do." He reached into the pocket of his coat and took out a card. "I realize you cannot make this out in the moonlight, but when you return to the ballroom you will be able to read it. If you take it around to Lantern Street in the morning, Mrs. Flint and Mrs. Marsh will recognize the seal. Tell them Mr. Smith's Messenger sends his regards."

"Who is Mr. Smith?"

"My former employer."

A strange feeling whispered through her, stirring her senses. She suddenly got the disturbing premonition that taking the card would change her life forever in ways she could not begin to imagine. There would be no going back. *Ridiculous,* she thought.

She took a few cautious steps across the damp grass and plucked the card from his fingers. For an instant both of them were touching the crisp, white pasteboard. A tiny shiver of awareness arced across the back of her neck like an electrical spark. She told herself that it was her imagination, but she could not escape the intuitive certainty that her world had just turned upside down. She should be worried, perhaps frightened. Instead, she was unaccountably *thrilled.*

A thrilled idiot, she thought. After all, there was no doubt in her mind that Mr. Smith's Messenger was a very dangerous man.

She glanced at the card. There was a name on it—presumably that of the mysterious Mr. Smith—but it was impossible to decipher in the moonlight. With her ungloved fingertips, however, she could feel the raised imprint of an embossed seal. She hesitated and then slipped the card into the pocket of her dress.

"Morning is a long time off and there are decisions to be made tonight," she said, trying to sound authoritative.

She sensed that the balance of power was shifting between herself and Mr. Gage. That was not a good turn of events. One misstep and she knew that he would take full control of the situation, assuming he had not already done so. This was her case and Daphne was her responsibility. She had to stay in command.

"Very true, but detailed explanations will take a good deal more time than we have to spare," Joshua said. "You must return Miss Pennington to the ballroom before there is any gossip."

He was right. Daphne was her first priority. The mystery of Mr. Gage would have to wait. She had to make a decision and she had to make it immediately.

"I suppose your acquaintance with the proprietors of Flint and Marsh must serve as a character reference tonight," she said.

"Thank you." Joshua sounded amused.

She uncocked the pistol and turned away to discreetly whip up her petticoats. She returned the little gun to the stocking holster and lowered her gown.

When she straightened she saw that Daphne was staring at her, fascinated. Joshua was watching also, his hands stacked on the hilt of his cane. His expression was unreadable but she got the odd impression that he found the notion that she went about armed rather charming.

Most men would have been beyond shocked, she thought. They would have been appalled.

She concentrated on removing Daphne's gag and untying her hands.

"Miss Lockwood," Daphne gasped when she could speak. "I do not know how to thank you." She turned to Joshua Gage. "And you, sir. I have never been so terrified in my life. To think that Grandmother was right all along, someone did, indeed, intend to compromise me. I never dreamed it might be Mr. Euston. He seemed like such a fine gentleman."

"It's over now," Beatrice said gently. "Do you feel faint?"

"Good heavens, I'm not going to faint." Daphne's smile was shaky but determined. "I would not dare succumb to such weakness after watching you defend me with a gun. You are an inspiration, Miss Lockwood."

"Thank you, but I fear Mr. Gage is correct," Beatrice said. "We must return to the ballroom immediately or there will be talk. It takes so very little to shred a young lady's reputation."

"My gown is in good condition but I fear my dancing slippers have been ruined," Daphne said. "They are soaked through and there are grass stains all over them. Everyone will know that I have just spent a great deal of time out in the gardens."

"That is precisely why paid companions who accompany young ladies to balls make it a point to bring a spare pair of slippers," Beatrice said. "They are in my satchel. Come, we must hurry."

Daphne started forward and then paused to look down at Richard Euston's unconscious figure. "What about him?"

Joshua moved slightly in the shadows. "Do not concern your-self, Miss Pennington. I will deal with him."

Daphne stiffened in alarm.

"You must not have him arrested," she said. "If you do there will be a great scandal. Mama and Papa will pack me off to the country and I shall be obliged to marry some fat widower old enough to be my grandfather. That truly would be a fate worse than death."

"Euston will not be telling any tales to the police," Joshua said. "He is going to disappear."

"But how can that possibly happen?" Daphne asked. "He moves in Society."

Joshua looked at Beatrice. "Don't you think that you and Miss Pennington should be on your way?"

She did not care a fig if Euston disappeared forever, Beatrice thought, but the fact that Joshua was confident he could make that happen was more than a little unnerving. Nevertheless she had other problems at the moment. Saving Daphne Pennington's reputation was currently at the top of the list.

"You are quite right, Mr. Gage," she said. "Come along, Daphne."

She urged her charge toward the side door of the house.

"Later, Miss Lockwood," Joshua Gage said quietly behind her.

She could not decide if the words were a threat or a promise.

A SHORT TIME LATER she stood in an alcove with Lady Pennington, a small, elegant, gray-haired woman, and watched Daphne take the dance floor with another young gentleman. In her new dancing slippers, her eyes sparkling with mystery and excitement, she was ravishing.

"Look at her," Lady Pennington said proudly. "One would never know that less than twenty minutes ago someone tried to abduct her in order to compromise her. She came within a hair's breadth of being ruined."

"Your granddaughter is a very brave young woman," Beatrice said. "Not many gently bred young ladies could endure such a close brush with disaster and manage to go straight back out onto the dance floor as though nothing at all had happened."

"Daphne takes after my side of the family," Lady Pennington said with an air of cool satisfaction.

Beatrice smiled. "I do believe she does, madam."

Lady Pennington peered at her through a gold-handled monocle. "You saved my granddaughter tonight, Miss Lockwood. I am forever in your debt. Your employers in Lantern Street assure me that you are well paid for your services, but I wish you to know that tomorrow I shall send around a small, personal gift that I trust you will accept as a token of my gratitude."

"Thank you, but that is unnecessary."

"Nonsense, I insist. There will be no more discussion of the matter."

"You must give much of the credit to yourself, madam," Beatrice said. "If you had not become suspicious and contacted Flint and Marsh, there would have been a very different ending to this affair."

"It was just a feeling that I got a few days ago," Lady Pennington said. "Nothing I could put my finger on, you understand."

"I believe that sort of thing is called a woman's intuition, madam."

"Whatever the case, I *knew* Euston was not what he appeared to be, but he certainly managed to conceal his true nature and the state of his finances very well, indeed. Daphne's parents were completely fooled by him. My granddaughter is a great heiress. If Euston had managed to compromise her there would have been a terrible uproar."

"But you control the purse strings in the family," Beatrice said. "From what little I have seen of you in recent days, I do not believe that you would have insisted that Daphne marry Richard Euston, even if he had succeeded in his plan."

"No, of course not." Lady Pennington shuddered. "Euston was clearly only after her money. I was married for similar reasons, and I assure you, I would never put my granddaughter through such a hellish experience. I can only be thankful that my husband had the decency to get himself killed in a racing accident some years ago. Nevertheless, Daphne's reputation would have been in ruins if Euston had been successful tonight. She would have been obliged to drop out of Society."

"She did appear to be alarmed by the possibility of being sent back to the countryside. She was worried about the prospect of having to marry someone she described as an overweight widower who was old enough to be her grandfather."

"Lord Bradley." Lady Pennington chuckled. "Yes, I have done my best to terrify her with that threat in an effort to get her to be careful here in town. She is a very spirited young lady."

"Obviously she takes after you in that regard, as well, madam."

"Yes." Lady Pennington stopped smiling. Her mouth pinched into a grim line. "But I will not see her life ruined because of her lively spirit. Are you quite certain that Euston will no longer be a problem?"

Beatrice took the calling card out of her pocket and examined it again. The name on the card was simply Mr. Smith. The raised seal was an elegantly embossed image of a heraldic lion.

She thought about the certainty in Joshua Gage's voice when he had assured her that Euston would disappear.

"Something tells me that Richard Euston will not trouble you or your family ever again," she said.

Three

Joshua gritted his teeth against the flaring pain in his left leg and hauled the groggy Euston up into the carriage.

Henry, his face shadowed by a low-crowned hat and the collar of his heavy cape, peered down from the box.

"Ye sure ye don't want some help, sir?" he asked.

"Where were you when I had to carry the bastard out of the garden and down the lane a few minutes ago?" Joshua asked.

"Didn't know we were going to have to get rid of a body tonight, sir. Like old times, eh?"

"He's not dead. Not yet, at any rate. And no, this is not like old times."

"Whatever you say, sir. Where we taking him?"

"To a nice, quiet place near the docks where he and I can have a private conversation," Joshua said.

"Ah, so he'll be going for a late-night swim after you finish talking to him, eh?"

"Depends on the answers I get from him."

Joshua dropped his burden onto one seat and lowered himself cautiously onto the opposite leather bench. Another jolt of pain shafted through his leg when he reached out to seize the door handle.

"Damned leg," he said aloud. But he said it in a whisper.

He was losing focus again. He inhaled slowly and pulled on his years of training to distance himself from the nagging pain. When he was back in control he tightened his grip on the door and pulled it shut.

Euston groaned but he did not open his eyes.

Joshua gripped the hilt of the cane and used the stick to rap the ceiling of the cab twice. The vehicle rolled forward.

He considered whether a scarf mask was required and concluded that it would not be necessary. The interior carriage lamps were unlit and the curtains were drawn across all but a narrow slice of one window. What little light entered the cab would fall on Euston's face, not his. He had learned long ago how to remain in the shadows.

He sat back and contemplated the manner in which his carefully laid plans had been overtaken by events, in particular the unanticipated actions of Miss Beatrice Lockwood.

He had not set out that evening with the intention of assisting in the foiling of an attempted abduction. Beatrice had been his quarry from the start. But matters had taken a decidedly unexpected twist.

He pondered what he had learned about her in the course of their very short meeting. He had only spoken to her for a few moments back in the garden, but he had always been rather good when it came to assessing the character of others in a short span of time. In the past his life had often depended on his skill in that department. His intuition in such matters was certainly not infallible. The bad leg and the scar were proof that when he did fail he did so in a rather spectacular fashion. No halfway measures for the Messenger, certainly.

But he was quite sure of at least one conclusion about Beatrice Lockwood: She was going to be a much more complicated problem than he had anticipated.

He kneaded his sore leg absently while he thought about her. His initial impression could be summed up in a name, he thought. *Titania*. Like the fairy queen of myth and legend and Shakespeare's *A Midsummer Night's Dream*, Beatrice was a force to be reckoned with.

The lagoon-blue eyes, delicate features and the air of fragile innocence had not fooled him for a moment. Nor had the unfashionable gown. He had long ago been trained to look beneath the layers of a disguise. Beatrice was an excellent actress—he gave her full credit for her playacting talents—but she had not deceived him.

She had, however, succeeded in surprising him. He was not sure how he felt about that singular fact. It was certainly not a good thing, but for some reason he felt the stirring of something that had been locked in ice deep inside him for a year. Anticipation. He was looking forward to the next encounter with Beatrice Lockwood.

But first he had to finish the business that had arisen so unexpectedly tonight.

Four

Shortly after two-thirty in the morning the Pennington carriage stopped in front of a small town house in Lantern Street. A single lamp glowed at the top of the steps, next to the front door. A footman handed Beatrice down from the cab.

"Are you certain you wish to be set down here?" Lady Pennington asked. She eyed the door of the office through her monocle. "The Flint and Marsh Agency is closed. The windows are dark."

"Mrs. Flint and Mrs. Marsh live above their offices," Beatrice said. "I shall wake them."

"At such a late hour?" Daphne asked.

"I promise you, they will have a great interest in what occurred this evening," Beatrice said.

"Very well, then," Lady Pennington said.

"Good night, Miss Lockwood," Daphne said. "Thank you, again, for saving me from Mr. Euston."

Beatrice smiled. "You owe your thanks to your grandmother. She is the one who suspected that something about Euston was amiss."

"Yes, I know," Daphne said. "One more thing before you go. Do you think that perhaps you might teach me how to fire a small pistol like the one you carry? I would so love to have a gun of my own."

"What on earth are you talking about?" Lady Pennington asked sharply. "What is this about a pistol?"

"It's a long story," Beatrice said. "I shall let Miss Daphne tell you the details," Beatrice said.

She went up the steps of the discreetly marked door of the Flint & Marsh Agency and raised the knocker. It took a couple of raps before a light came on somewhere in the depths of the town house. Footsteps sounded in the hall.

Mrs. Beale, the middle-aged housekeeper, opened the door. She was dressed in a chintz wrapper, slippers and a lace nightcap. She did not look pleased.

"It's three o'clock in the morning, Miss Lockwood. What are you doing here at this hour?"

"You know I would not awaken Mrs. Flint and Mrs. Marsh unless it was important, Mrs. Beale."

Mrs. Beale heaved a great sigh. "No, I don't suppose you would. Come on in, then. I trust no one is dead this time."

"I did not lose a client, if that is what you mean."

"I knew it. Someone is dead."

Beatrice ignored that. She turned back toward the carriage and gave a small wave to indicate that all was well before she went into the front hall. The elegant Pennington equipage rolled off down the quiet street.

Mrs. Beale closed and locked the door. "I'll go upstairs and wake the ladies."

"No need to awaken us," Abigail Flint said from the top of the stairs. "Sara and I are on our way down. Who died?"

"No one died," Beatrice said. "At least, I don't think so."

Sara Marsh appeared on the landing. "Is our client's granddaughter safe?"

"Daphne is fine, but it was a near thing," Beatrice said.

"What'll it be?" Mrs. Beale asked, sounding resigned. "Tea or brandy?"

"It has been a very long night, Mrs. Beale," Beatrice said.

Mrs. Beale sighed again, in a knowing way this time. "I'll fetch the brandy tray."

A SHORT TIME LATER Beatrice sat with her employers in front of a small fire. They all had glasses of brandy in their hands. Abigail and Sara were in their nightclothes, bundled up in robes, slippers and nightcaps.

"Obviously our client was right to trust her instincts when Mr. Euston began to display such a keen interest in Daphne," Abigail said. "Lady Pennington might not have much in the way of psychical talent but there is nothing like a grandmother's intuition when it comes to that sort of thing, I always say."

Abigail was a tall, thin, angular woman of a certain age. She was endowed with sharp features that included a formidable nose and a pointed chin. Her black hair was rapidly going silver. Her dark eyes had a curious, veiled quality that Beatrice was certain concealed old mysteries and secrets.

Abigail's temperament could only be described as dour. She was inclined to take a pessimistic view of the world and of human nature in particular. When Sara chided her because she went about expecting the worst, Abigail invariably pointed out that she was rarely disappointed.

Her companion in business as well as in life was her polar opposite in both appearance and temperament. Sara Marsh was of a similar age but it was difficult to spot the gray in her blond hair. She was pleasantly rounded in a manner that men—young and old—invariably found attractive. She was cheerful, optimistic and inquisitive.

A keen, self-taught amateur scientist, she was fascinated by the various kinds of evidence left at crime scenes. She maintained a well-equipped laboratory in the basement of the town house where she examined everything from fingerprints to samples of poison brought to her by Flint & Marsh agents.

Mrs. Beale frequently declared that one day Sara would accidentally set off an explosion or unleash poisonous gases that would be the death of everyone in the household.

Both Abigail and Sara possessed what they referred to as a sixth sense. In their younger days they had operated a bookshop that had catered to those with an interest in the paranormal. But a few years ago they had closed the shop in favor of launching what proved to be a successful private inquiry business. The firm of Flint & Marsh attracted wealthy, upper-class clients who wished to commission discreet investigations.

The volumes from the bookshop days now lined the walls of

the parlor from floor to ceiling. Many of the books were infused with energy. Beatrice was aware of faint currents stirring the atmosphere of the room.

"Excellent work, my dear," Sara said. "You mustn't blame yourself for what happened out in the garden."

"Euston nearly managed to abduct her and it was my own fault," Beatrice said. "I allowed myself to become distracted by the spilled lemonade. And when the man with the cane vanished from the ballroom at approximately the same time that Daphne disappeared, I worried that he was involved with the abduction."

"All in all, a bit chaotic there at the end, but all's well that ends well," Sara said.

Abigail snorted. "Doesn't sound as if things ended well for Mr. Euston. Not that I am overly concerned with his fate. I am very curious about the gentleman who came to your assistance, however, the one with the cane and the scar. That part of your story is extremely worrisome."

"Yes," Sara said. "Tell us about him."

Beatrice struggled to find the right words to explain her reaction to Joshua Gage. "He appeared first in the ballroom. He was only there for a short time but I knew that he was aware of me, that he was watching me." She hesitated. "Studying me, might be more accurate."

Abigail frowned. "He should not have taken any notice of a paid companion sitting in the corner of a large ballroom."

"I know," Beatrice said. "But he did. What is more, after he introduced himself in the garden and offered to get rid of Mr. Euston he used you and Mrs. Marsh as character references. He then announced that he wished to speak with me tomorrow." She glanced at the clock. "That would be today, actually."

"Well, I think that clarifies things," Sara said. "If he knows about Flint and Marsh and if he is aware that you are one of our agents, he must be someone who was involved in a previous case. That's a perfectly reasonable explanation."

Abigail's eyes narrowed. "But neither of us recognizes his name."

"Most likely because we never actually met him," Sara said patiently. "But he obviously knows one of our clients."

"There was something quite . . . unsettling about him," Beatrice said.

Abigail frowned. "You say he wishes to talk to you in the morning?"

"Yes. He also said that Euston would no longer be a problem. He was quite clear on that point. To be honest, I am somewhat concerned that Euston might end up in the river."

"Euston might deserve such a fate but the policy here at Flint and Marsh is to avoid any sort of scandal," Sara said uneasily.

"Nonsense, bodies turn up in the river all the time." Abigail brushed the matter aside with a wave of one long-fingered hand. "Euston's will be just one more."

Beatrice winced and exchanged a glance with Sara, who gave a long-suffering sigh. Abigail was often inclined to take the pragmatic approach to problems.

"You know very well, dear, that the bodies of gentlemen who move in Society do not turn up all that often in the river," Sara said. "Euston was not a highflier, but he was known in certain circles. He obviously had some connections. That is how he managed to get himself introduced to Daphne Pennington by a respectable friend of the Pennington family. If he is found dead under mysterious circumstances there will likely be a police inquiry. We all know that Flint and Marsh cannot afford to be connected to that sort of thing."

"You are right, of course." Abigail drummed her fingers on the arm of the chair. "We can only hope that this Mr. Gage will take great care to make certain that Euston's disappearance will not cause any problems."

Beatrice cleared her throat. "He did give the impression that he had some expertise in such matters."

Abigail brightened. "All the more reason not to worry about Euston."

"I would remind you that Euston was alive when I last saw him," Beatrice said. "It is possible that Mr. Gage did not go to extremes tonight."

"What concerns us at the moment," Sara said, "is his interest in you, Beatrice. You are certain you do not recognize him from your days at Fleming's Academy of the Occult?"

"Quite certain." Beatrice drank some brandy and lowered the glass. "Believe me when I tell you that he is not a man that one would be likely to forget."

Abigail raised her brows. "The scar is that bad?"

"It's not the scar that makes him memorable," Beatrice said. "Or the limp, for that matter. You're sure you do not recognize his name?"

"Quite certain." Abigail pursed her lips. "Although I suppose he could be a customer from the old days when we owned the bookshop. We had hundreds of patrons over the years. We cannot possibly remember all of their names."

"I almost forgot, he gave me a card," Beatrice said. She set aside her brandy glass and reached into the pocket of her gown. "I believe the name on it is that of his former employer. He seemed to think you would recognize it."

Sara took her reading glasses off the table and propped them on her nose. "Let me see it."

Beatrice handed her the card. When Sara looked at it her expression abruptly tightened in shock. She traced the lion seal with the tip of one finger.

"Mr. Smith," she whispered. "But it's not possible. Not after all this time."

"Mr. Smith?" Abigail scowled. "There must be some mistake. Let me see that card."

Sara handed the card to Abigail, who studied it in mounting disbelief that swiftly changed into openmouthed astonishment.

"Good heavens," she whispered. She touched the seal. "Do you suppose he really is alive?"

"We always wondered about those rumors of his death," Sara said.

Beatrice searched Sara's face and then looked at Abigail. "Who is this Mr. Smith?"

"Damned if we ever knew," Abigail said. "We never met him, of course. We dealt with his Messenger."

Her ominous tone did not worry Beatrice nearly as much as the fact that the card was trembling in Abigail's fingers. It took a great deal to make Abigail Flint shiver. She tended to live up to her surname.

"I'm sure Smith was not the Lion's real name," Sara said. "But that name and the seal were all we knew of him. As Abby explained, when he had dealings with us, he sent his Messenger."

"Mr. Gage asked me to tell you that the Messenger sent his regards," Beatrice said.

"Oh, dear," Sara whispered. "This situation is growing more odd by the moment."

"Can you describe this Messenger?" Beatrice asked.

"We can't give you a physical description," Abigail said. "When we met with him it was always in a location of his choice and he was always deep in the shadows. We never saw his face in the light." She paused. "But I'm quite certain he did not walk with a limp. What do you think, Sara?"

"There was certainly no indication that he used a cane," Sara said. "I remember how it always startled us when he spoke to us from the darkness of whatever place he had selected for a meeting. We never heard him arrive and we never heard him leave. It was as if he, himself, was a shadow."

"Hmm," Beatrice said. She thought about Gage's halting stride and the way he leaned on his cane. "Well, accidents do happen. And I imagine that a man in his profession would attract a large number of enemies."

"Very true," Abigail said.

"You said this Messenger person worked for Mr. Smith," Beatrice said. "I don't understand Smith's role in all this. Why did he require a messenger?"

Sara and Abby exchanged glances. Then Sara turned back to Beatrice.

"Abby and I long ago concluded that Smith was a player in the Great Game, as the press and the novelists like to call the business of espionage."

"Do you mean to say that he was a spy?" Beatrice asked.

"A *master* spy," Abigail said. "The Messenger assured us that his employer was in the service of the Crown and we have no reason to doubt that. From what we could deduce, Smith's reach extended throughout England, across Europe and beyond. But you know how it is with legends."

"One never knows the whole truth," Sara added.

"Hmm," Beatrice said. "I expect that worked out very well for both Mr. Smith and his messenger. People always fear the unknown more than the known."

Sara made a face. "Actually, in the case of Mr. Smith, what sensible people feared was his Messenger, the man Mr. Smith dispatched to hunt down traitors and foreign spies in our midst. The Messenger foiled any number of plots and conspiracies, some quite bizarre."

"And we assisted him on occasion," Sara said. There was a touch of pride in her voice.

"I don't understand," Beatrice said. "What do you mean by bizarre?"

"When Mr. Smith sent his Messenger to investigate a conspiracy or an act of espionage, one could rest assured that the threat was far from ordinary—not the sort of case one expected Scotland Yard to handle. There was invariably a paranormal twist."

Abigail gave a short, humorless bark of laughter. "Not that the Messenger ever allowed that there was even the possibility of a paranormal explanation in the cases he investigated, you understand. He didn't believe in psychical energy. That always struck me as amusing because it was obvious he possessed some talent himself."

"A great many people dismiss the paranormal side of their natures," Sara pointed out. "They come up with other explanations when confronted with their own abilities."

"What was the nature of the Messenger's ability?" Beatrice asked.

"He appeared to have an absolutely uncanny talent for finding people and things," Abigail said. "If he set out to track down someone or something, he was invariably successful."

"You speak of both the Messenger and Mr. Smith in the past tense," Beatrice said. "What happened to them?"

"No one knows," Abigail said. "About a year ago the rumors of Smith's death began to circulate. They were mere whispers at first, but the whispers grew louder. Eventually Sara and I concluded they were likely true."

"The Messenger vanished at the same time," Sara explained. "Which is why we assumed that he was dead, as well. He certainly has not contacted us in all these months. To tell you the truth, I have missed him."

"Rubbish," Abigail said fiercely. "He was a very mysterious individual. He made me uneasy whenever he came around." She paused. "I will admit that he paid quite well for information, though."

"The thing is," Sara said wistfully, "in spite of his opinion of the paranormal, he understood the value of a scientific approach to the investigation of crimes. He always respected my opinions, unlike certain inspectors at Scotland Yard I could name who never paid any attention to my advice because I am a woman."

"Just because the Messenger respected your scientific talents does not mean that he was not extremely dangerous," Abigail said.

"Yes, I know," Sara said. "But I must admit I quite enjoyed analyzing the various bits and pieces of evidence he sent to me."

Abigail looked at Beatrice. "We assumed that the Messenger was killed by whoever or whatever killed Mr. Smith. It was the only theory we could come up with to explain why they both vanished at the same time."

Beatrice considered that for a moment. "What if Mr. Smith and the Messenger were one and the same man? That would explain why they both disappeared simultaneously."

Abigail and Sara glanced at each other.

"It's a possibility," Sara admitted. "But I'm inclined to doubt it. We always had the impression that Mr. Smith managed a far-flung empire of spies and information gatherers. The Messenger, on the other hand, appeared to focus entirely on investigations here in London."

"He had connections that ranged from the most exclusive gentlemen's clubs to the criminal underworld," Abigail added.

"Obviously the man I encountered tonight wants you to believe that he is the Messenger you once knew," Beatrice said.

Abigail stiffened abruptly. "Perhaps he's an impostor. That would explain a great deal. Maybe someone has reasoned that since the real Messenger is dead, it is safe to assume his identity along with his perceived connections."

"I don't think it's that simple, dear," Sara said. "Why would anyone do such a thing?"

"The Lion's Messenger was greatly feared in certain quarters," Abigail said. "He must have known many deep secrets, some of which no doubt could have brought down some very powerful people. There are those who would kill to acquire his reputation because with it would come the ability to intimidate and control others."

"What, exactly, was the nature of his reputation?" Beatrice asked. "Aside from being rather dangerous, that is."

"As Abby told you, he always found whatever he set out to find," Sara said. "His other hallmark was that his word was his bond. Everyone who had dealings with him knew that if he made a promise, that promise would be kept. In addition, he was relentless. If you met him you simply *knew* that the only way he could be stopped was by death."

"Which, we presumed, was exactly what finally did stop him," Abigail said.

"Excuse me," Beatrice said, "but how, precisely, did the two of you come to have a connection with the Messenger? You said something about assisting him on some of his cases."

Sara glanced at the leather-bound volumes that lined the walls of the parlor. "It was the bookshop that brought him to us in the beginning. We catered to a clientele that was interested in psychical matters. Regardless of the fact that he, himself, put no credence in the paranormal, he was often in the business of investigating crimes with paranormal elements."

"Whether he acknowledged that or not, we certainly recognized the psychical connections in most of those cases," Abigail said. "He used our bookshop for research initially. Then he discovered Sara's interest in scientific investigation techniques."

"One thing led to another and the next thing you know, Abby and I became his occasional assistants," Sara concluded.

Abigail raised her brows. "He had a great influence on us, actually. It was the business of assisting him that eventually persuaded us to open our own investigation firm. One could say that if it weren't for the Messenger, we would still be squeaking by on the income of a small bookshop."

"In other words," Beatrice said, amused, "I owe my present post as a Flint and Marsh agent to the Messenger."

"That is certainly one way of looking at it," Sara agreed.

Beatrice winced. "There is definitely an element of irony involved here."

Sara squinted in a thoughtful expression. "Not irony."

"Coincidence?" Abigail asked, clearly troubled.

"You know I do not believe in coincidence," Sara said. "No, what is going on here appears to be a confluence of small events that all have one thing in common."

"What is that?" Beatrice asked.

"A paranormal element. Only consider the obvious ingredients in this brew—your previous career at Fleming's Academy, your work here with us, the reappearance of the Messenger after all these months, his unusual talent and the fact that he often investigated cases that had a paranormal factor." Sara shook her head, troubled. "I do not pretend to comprehend the pattern yet, but there is one, of that I have no doubt."

"But what on earth can he possibly want with me?" Beatrice asked. "And how did he find me tonight at that ball?"

"There is no knowing why he has focused his attention on you," Abigail said uneasily. "But as to how he discovered you at the ball tonight, that is easy enough to explain. I thought I made it clear—the Messenger always finds what he sets out to find."

Sara's eyes were shadowed. "Obviously he was looking for you, dear."

Five

The traffic was thin and the streetlamps were now set far apart. The smell of the river was strong on the night air. They had arrived at their destination.

Joshua used the cane to prod the finely dressed lump on the opposite seat.

"Wake up, Mr. Euston. You have been a great inconvenience to me tonight. I do not wish to spend any more time in your company than is absolutely necessary."

Euston groaned and opened his eyes. There was just enough light coming through the partially covered window to reveal the bewilderment on his handsome features.

"Where am I?" he mumbled. "Benson? Is that you?"

"Sit up," Joshua said.

"Huh?" Euston managed to lever himself upright in the seat. He tried to focus. His bewilderment metamorphosed into alarm. "You're not Benson. Who the devil are you?"

"You do not need to know my name. All that is necessary is that you understand the instructions that I am going to give you."

"Bloody hell, what are you talking about?"

"By tomorrow morning you will no longer be accepted in Polite Society. Your name will disappear from the guest lists of every hostess in town. No club will allow you through the front door. My advice would be to sail for America or take a tour of the Continent at the earliest possible opportunity."

"How dare you threaten me?" Euston hissed.

"Let me be clear: I am not threatening you. I never threaten. I give you my word that by noon tomorrow everyone who matters in your world will be aware that you are a fortune hunter and a fraud."

"You can't prove that. The girl's family would never allow you to go to the police, in any event."

"I'm not going to take this to the police," Joshua said. "There is no need to do so. We both know that Society does not demand proof before it pronounces judgment. The Polite World is more than happy to gorge on rumors and whispers. I promise you that the news that you have been exposed as a fortune hunter who is trying to find himself an heiress will be all over town within a few hours and, no doubt, in the press."

"You can't do this to me. You're bluffing."

"You will discover tomorrow that I am not bluffing."

The carriage halted. Joshua opened the door. Fog wafted into the cab, bringing with it another dose of the odor of the river. A single gas lamp glowed at the end of the street but the mist consumed much of the light before it could radiate more than a few feet. Warehouses loomed in the shadows.

"This is where you get out, Euston," Joshua said. "Go quickly before I lose my patience. It has been a long night and I am not in the best of moods. You interfered with my own plans for the evening. I do not take that sort of thing well."

Euston looked nervously out into the waiting darkness. "I'm not familiar with this neighborhood. It is obviously dangerous. How will I get back to my lodgings?"

"There is a tavern on the far side of that warehouse. I expect there will be one or two cabs waiting in the street. But you might want to take care to walk quickly. You are correct. This neighborhood is home to all sorts of thieves and cutthroats."

Euston did not move.

"Go," Joshua said. He spoke very, very softly. "Now."

Euston jerked as if he had been struck by the lash of a whip. He lurched out the door and half stumbled, half jumped down to the pavement. Turning, he paused to look back into the cab.

"I do not know who you are, you bastard," he said, "but I will make you pay if it is the last thing I do."

"I'm afraid you will have to stand at the end of a very long queue."

Joshua pulled the door closed and rapped the roof of the carriage twice.

Henry opened the trapdoor. "Where to, sir?"

"Saint James."

"Aye."

Henry closed the door, slapped the reins and drove off into the fog.

Joshua pushed aside one of the curtains and looked out into the night. The sharp pain in his thigh had subsided to a dull, throbbing ache. He consoled himself with the knowledge that there was some excellent brandy waiting for him when he got back to the town house.

Nothing had gone right tonight.

It would be more accurate to state that nothing had gone right since the start of this affair, he reminded himself. And that was precisely what made it all so interesting.

A fortnight ago he had been at his country house sinking ever deeper into the quicksand of the excruciatingly dull routine that he had established for himself. His mind-numbing days started with morning meditation followed by what limited martial arts exercises he could still manage with his bad leg. The exercises were followed by a few hours devoted to overseeing business matters. He managed the family fortune for his sister, his nephew and himself. Late in the afternoon he took his daily halting, often painful, walk along the cliffs above the restless sea.

His nights were more often sleepless than not. When he did sleep his dreams were all variations on the same recurring nightmare. He relived the explosion, saw Emma's body lying on the stone floor and heard Clement Lancing shouting at him from the other side of the wall of flames. *You did this, you bastard. She's dead because of you.*

All the dreams ended the same way, with Victor Hazelton watching him from the shadows, silently accusing him of failing to save Emma.

He was well aware that recently in the course of his afternoon walks he had begun to spend far too much time standing precariously close to the edge of the cliffs contemplating the mesmerizing chaos of the wild surf far below. It would be so very easy for a man with a weak leg to lose his balance.

But he had responsibilities that he could not escape. It was the knowledge that his sister, Hannah, and his nephew, Nelson, depended on him that made him turn away from the sight of the swirling waters at the foot of the cliffs every afternoon.

His carefully orchestrated life had come to a crashing halt, however, when he had received the telegram from Nelson.

Please come to London immediately. Mother needs you.

There was only one force still powerful enough to pry him from his own private hell, Joshua thought, the same force that made it impossible for him to seek oblivion in opium or the sea— his responsibility to his family. For the first time in nearly a year he had a mission to carry out.

He had planned to spend a week or two in London dealing with the problem and then retreat once again into seclusion. But the case, which had appeared simple and straightforward at the start, was proving to be far more complicated and infinitely more intriguing than he had anticipated. In spite of his aching leg he felt invigorated and refreshed. Finding Beatrice Lockwood tonight had acted like a tonic for his spirits.

He had set out to snare a shady little adventuress who obviously had a history of living by her wits only to discover that she was not entirely what she seemed. The stocking gun she had used to stop Euston was only one of several intriguing and unexpected surprises tonight.

By the time he had tracked her down to the agency in Lantern Street he had been well aware that the appearance of fey innocence that Beatrice affected was a tribute to her talents as an actress and no doubt served her well in her new career as a Flint & Marsh agent. But he knew that whatever innocence she had once possessed had long ago been stripped away. As a woman alone in the world she was solely responsible for her own safety and survival. In such situations one did what was necessary. He understood and respected that. He certainly did not blame her if she had slipped off the pedestal now and again. He admired the fact that her spirit was still a bright, fierce flame.

Her survival instincts were obviously very much alive, which only made her risky defense of her client tonight all the more astonishing. True, he knew that the paid companions supplied by the firm of Flint and Marsh were an unusual lot. Mrs. Flint and Mrs. Marsh were, after all, an unusual pair. Nevertheless, one did not expect a woman like Beatrice—a female who, among other things, had pursued a career as a fraudulent psychical practitioner and then proceeded to blackmail some of her clients—to come to the rescue of others. When there was danger afoot, most intelligent people—male or female, regardless of their backgrounds—managed to make themselves scarce. It was not as though Beatrice had not done exactly that on a prior occasion, he thought. She had vanished from Dr. Fleming's Academy of the Occult following the murder of her employer.

All of which raised new questions about what had really happened the night Fleming died. Morgan at the Yard and the sensation press were convinced that Beatrice had killed her employer, stolen the night's ticket receipts and taken off for parts unknown. But Joshua had been unconvinced of the merits of that assumption from the start. Now he sensed that his instincts had been correct. Whatever had occurred on the night of Roland

Fleming's death, the murder had not been a simple, straightforward matter of robbery.

Henry brought the carriage to a halt in front of one of the most prestigious clubs in St. James. Joshua gathered up his cane, hat and gloves. Setting his jaw against the pain he knew was coming, he opened the door of the cab, gripped the handhold and used the iron step to descend to the pavement.

Gone were the days when he could jump nimbly out of a vehicle and land with athletic ease, he reflected. Even Euston, still groggy after the short period of unconsciousness, had managed to alight more elegantly after being tossed out of the cab.

Joshua consigned Euston and his own past to hell and went up the steps of the club. An elderly porter materialized out of the front hall to block his path.

"Can I help you, sir?"

Joshua took the envelope containing one of the old calling cards from his pocket and handed it to the porter. "I have a message for Lord Allenby. Please give this to him immediately and tell him that I will wait in my carriage."

The porter eyed the envelope with suspicion but he accepted it.

"I will give him your message, sir."

The porter's tone of voice implied that he did not expect that there would be a response. He disappeared back into the club and closed the door very firmly.

Joshua limped back to the carriage and climbed the steps into the cab. He sat down and massaged his leg while he waited. *Not much longer now,* he promised himself. *There will be brandy soon.*

The wonderful thing about the gentlemen's clubs of London was that time stood still inside the walls of the establishments.

Change came at an excruciatingly slow pace, if ever. Joshua had always found the predictability and dependability of the members' habits extremely useful. Allenby, for example, took pride in always possessing the latest gossip. And when it came to passing that gossip along, he was extraordinarily reliable.

Allenby, a portly man of some seventy years, appeared on the front step of the club. He spotted the carriage on the far side of the street and started toward it.

"Won't you join me, sir?" Joshua said from the shadows of the unlit cab.

"I say, it is you, isn't it? Smith's Messenger." Allenby clambered up into the vehicle and sat down. "I recognize your voice. Heard you were dead. I suspected someone might be playing a trick."

"Thank you for making time to see me," Joshua said.

"Of course, of course. Old times and all that. I will always be in your debt, sir, for what you did for my son a few years ago. Glad to see you are, indeed, still alive. What can I do for you?"

"As it happens, I would like to request a small favor from you."

"Absolutely, absolutely," Allenby said.

Joshua settled deeper into the corner of the cab. "I have recently learned some disturbing news concerning the character of a gentleman named Euston."

"Euston? Euston?" Allenby squinted. "The young man they say is angling after the Pennington heiress?"

"Yes," Joshua said. "Euston is not quite what he seems, unfortunately. His finances are in ruins and he invented his social connections."

"Hah. Fortune hunter, eh?"

"I'm afraid so. You are acquainted with the young lady's father. Thought you might want to put a word in his ear."

"Certainly, certainly," Allenby said. "Known Pennington for years. We were at Oxford together. Least I can do is let him know there's a fortune hunter after his girl."

"Thank you."

"Will that be all?" Allenby asked.

"Yes. I appreciate your assistance in this matter."

"Of course, of course." Allenby paused and cleared his throat. "I wouldn't presume to inquire why you haven't been around this past year but the porter mentioned a cane."

"I use a walking stick these days," Joshua said.

"Accident, eh?"

"Something like that, yes."

"Well, then, may I say that I am delighted to know that you survived," Allenby said.

"Thank you, sir."

"I'll be off then. Pennington will no doubt be dropping into the club later tonight. I'll make sure he gets the information about Euston."

Allenby lumbered out of the cab and made his way across the street.

And that was that, Joshua thought. By morning Euston would be persona non grata in all of the wealthy homes of London. Gossip traveled faster than a flooded river through the gentlemen's clubs of London.

Six

Half an hour later Joshua climbed the front steps of his small town house. He had purchased the residence several years earlier when he had become the Lion's Messenger. His requirements at the time had been simple. He had needed privacy. A modest address in a quiet street where the neighbors minded their own business had suited him perfectly. None of the respectable people around him had any notion that the occupant of Number Five carried out clandestine investigations for the Crown. As far as they were concerned he was a single man of modest means surviving on the income he received as a clerk employed by a shipping company.

The town house had been closed for the past year but the always reliable Chadwick had done a remarkable job of making arrangements for the hurried move back to London.

Joshua let himself into the dimly lit front hall. He removed his hat and sent it sailing across the small space toward the polished console table. He allowed himself to take some satisfaction when the hat landed precisely where he had intended. His bad leg made it impossible for him to move at anything faster than a halting walk and many of the fluid martial arts maneuvers that had once upon a time been second nature to him were impossible now.

But, damnation, when it came to his hat his aim was as good as ever.

"Impressive, Gage," he said to the man in the mirror. "The next time you get into a hat duel you will most certainly trounce your opponent."

The man with the badly scarred face and the soulless eyes gazed back at him.

He made a note to instruct Chadwick to remove the looking glass in the morning.

He propped the cane against the console long enough to strip off his gloves and peel away his coat. Chadwick would know that he was home. Chadwick knew everything that went on inside his domain. But he also knew that unless he was summoned there was no need to leave his bed.

Joshua set the gloves on the table, gripped the cane and went down the hall to his study. He did not bother to turn up the lamp. His night vision had always been excellent. The moonlight slanting through the windows was sufficient to allow him to see what he was doing.

He unknotted his tie, opened the collar of his shirt and crossed the room to the brandy table.

He splashed brandy into a glass and sank cautiously down

onto one of the leather wingback chairs. He stretched out his left leg. It was throbbing more than usual. He was going to pay a price for hauling the unconscious Euston up into the carriage.

But the cost, however high, was worth it, he reflected. He had found the elusive Beatrice.

Seven

Beatrice opened the door of the pleasant little town house shortly before dawn. George, who worked for Mrs. Flint and Mrs. Marsh as a coachman and general errand-runner, waited in the street with the small, aging carriage until she was safely inside the front hall. She paused on the threshold.

"Thank you, George," she said. "Sorry to bring you out at this hour of the night."

"Think nothing of it, Miss Lockwood." George tipped his hat. "Not that long until sunup. By the time I get home the household will be stirring and there will be coffee and breakfast."

He slapped the reins lightly against the horse's rump. The vehicle rolled off down the street.

Beatrice closed the door and shot the bolt on the lock. The house was very quiet. Mrs. Rambley, the housekeeper, was still abed in her private quarters near the kitchen. Clarissa Slate would also be asleep.

The wall sconces had been turned down for the night but they gave enough light to illuminate the stairs. Beatrice made her way up to the bedroom floor and went along the hall.

The door of one of the bedrooms opened. Clarissa appeared, a candle in one hand. By day she affected a severe appearance. She wore her dark hair pinned into a prim knot and used spectacles to veil her serious amber eyes. Her gowns were always so dark and so strictly tailored that most people assumed she was in perpetual mourning. But tonight, clad in a white cotton nightgown, her hair tumbled around her shoulders, she looked very different—far more innocent and vulnerable.

Of course, appearances were always deceptive when it came to the lady investigators who worked for Flint & Marsh, Beatrice reminded herself. They all had their own secrets.

"I heard George's carriage in the street," Clarissa said. "Why are you coming home at such an hour? Did something go wrong in the Pennington case? Are you all right?"

"Yes, I'm fine," Beatrice assured her. "The case concluded quite suddenly at the Trent ball tonight. Richard Euston made his move. He attempted to abduct Miss Pennington with the intention of compromising her so that she would be forced to marry him."

"He did not succeed, I trust?"

"No, but the situation became complicated and makes for a long story. I promise I will tell you everything in the morning."

Clarissa smiled. "Not much longer, in that case. It is nearly dawn. Try to get some sleep."

"I doubt if I will be able to do that. You know how it is after a case concludes. There is always that edgy sensation."

"I understand," Clarissa said gently. "Perhaps a hot bath and a dose of brandy would help."

Beatrice smiled. "I stopped by the office before I came home. Mrs. Flint and Mrs. Marsh have already plied me with brandy. Go back to your bed. I promise I will tell you every detail in the morning."

"Very well." Clarissa made to close the door. "It's good to have you home safe and sound. I had an uneasy feeling all evening. I was starting to become worried and was about to send a message around to Flint and Marsh to see if all was well. But then the sensation faded."

"Your intuition was not off," Beatrice said. "For a time there was some danger involved for Miss Daphne, but in the end all was well. Unfortunately, there is another rather heavy boot yet to drop."

Clarissa's dark brows rose. "A boot?"

"His name is Joshua Gage."

Eight

Mr. Gage is here?" Beatrice looked up from the morning papers, a shivery thrill of excitement and dread spiking through her. "Are you quite certain, Mrs. Rambley?"

The housekeeper was a formidable woman of some forty years. She was constructed along the lines of a sturdy Greek statue. She made no secret that she was offended by the implication that she might have gotten the identity of the caller wrong.

"That was the name the gentleman gave me." Mrs. Rambley drew herself up and peered down her imposing nose. "He said that you are expecting him."

"Not at ten o'clock in the morning," Beatrice said, exasperated.

She and Mrs. Rambley were alone in the house. Clarissa had left an hour earlier to receive the details of her new assignment for Flint & Marsh.

Mrs. Rambley's irritation changed abruptly into anxiety. Beatrice immediately felt guilty. It was not the housekeeper's fault that Joshua Gage had chosen to arrive at this hour. Mrs. Rambley was still adjusting to her unconventional employers and their unconventional careers. She was worried now that she had made a serious mistake by allowing a gentleman caller into the small household.

"I will tell Mr. Gage that you are not at home," she said. She lowered her voice to a whisper. "He does look quite dangerous. There's a fearful scar on his face and I would not want to know how he came by that limp. I'm sure the story would chill one's blood." She started to turn away.

"Don't bother, Mrs. Rambley. I don't think there's much point suggesting that he leave. From what little I have seen of him, Mr. Gage is not easy to get rid of. Please show him into the parlor. And I do apologize for snapping at you."

"No need," Mrs. Rambley said gruffly. "It is certainly a bit early in the day to be receiving visitors."

"Especially male visitors," Beatrice said. "No need to be shy about it, Mrs. Rambley. I know what you are thinking and I agree with you. This is not proper. The real question here is, what in heaven's name can Gage be thinking?"

Mrs. Rambley's face tightened in concern. "Are you worried that he might be a problem, ma'am? Do you think he might attempt to impose himself on you in some way? I can send for a constable."

"It would certainly be interesting to see how Gage might deal with a constable, but we will forgo the experiment. And yes, I anticipate that Mr. Gage will prove to be a problem, but I'm quite certain he is not a danger to my person."

"If you're sure, ma'am."

Beatrice thought about what she had seen in Gage's footsteps last night. There was good reason to be cautious around him. But she could not summon up any great fear of the man. Anticipation, yes, and curiosity, too. Both emotions made sense. But she could not explain the inexplicable thrill that came from knowing that he was right here, in her home, waiting for her.

"Quite certain," she said.

"Very well, then."

Mrs. Rambley left the doorway and went back down the hall.

Beatrice rose and moved to the door. She listened as Mrs. Rambley showed Joshua into the parlor. The sound of his voice, low and intensely masculine, stirred her senses, just as it had last night. So much for thinking that things would be different in the daylight.

Mrs. Rambley hurried back to the breakfast room. "I'll bring in a tea tray, ma'am."

"I don't think that will be necessary," Beatrice began.

But Mrs. Rambley was already rushing off toward the kitchen.

Beatrice took a deep, steadying breath, drew herself up, straightened her shoulders and went along the hall to the parlor. She deliberately tried to make as little noise as possible in what she knew would no doubt be a futile attempt to catch Joshua off-guard. She wore a plain housedress. There was no street-sweeper ruffle at the bottom to rustle and swish against the floor. The soft leather soles of her slippers muffled her light footsteps.

She paused in the doorway and heightened her senses, opening them to glance at the floor. Dark energy burned in Joshua's footsteps but she saw nothing that made her alter her first impressions of him. This was a man of ice and fire; a man capable of great passions but also of ironclad control.

If a woman were so unfortunate as to find herself trapped in hell, this was surely the man she would want to come for her.

He stood at the window, both hands locked around the hilt of his cane. He had his back to her and gave no indication that he had heard her. She smiled to herself. He knew she was there.

He was well dressed, she thought, but in a quiet, unobtrusive manner. His coat and trousers were of the darkest possible shade of charcoal gray. She suspected that he frequently wore somber colors. They certainly suited him.

"Good morning, Mr. Gage," she said, keeping her tone polite but cool. "I wasn't expecting you for breakfast."

He turned politely toward her as though only now becoming aware of her presence. For the first time she got a close view of his hard, scarred face in the light of day. His raptor eyes were a fascinating mix of green and gold. The flicker of amusement that came and went in the depths told her that he had known precisely where she was at every step of the way when she had made the journey from the morning room to the parlor. She also knew that he was aware that she had tried to keep her approach silent.

Good grief, she thought, *we are playing some sort of cat-and-mouse game with each other. It is as if we find each other a challenge.*

Joshua had never so much as touched her. The closest they had come to a physical connection had been last night in the garden when he had given her his card. Yet there was an unsettling intimacy between them, at least there was on her side, she thought. The sensation stirred things deep inside her and caused her pulse to beat a little faster. All morning she had been trying to convince herself that the sensations she had experienced last night had been generated by the danger and excitement of events. This morning she was no longer so certain. There was something else between them, she thought. Something inexplicable. Something mysterious.

"My apologies for interrupting your breakfast, Miss Lockwood," Joshua said. His tone was as coolly polite as hers. "I'm an early riser myself. I sometimes forget that others sleep late, especially after what must have been a very long night for you."

From out of nowhere one of Roland Fleming's rules came back to her. *Do not take the stage unless you are prepared to take control of it and the audience.*

"I am accustomed to long nights," she said. She walked into the room. "In my profession, they tend to occur frequently."

"That does not surprise me."

"One of the many questions that kept me awake after I finally did go to bed concerned the fate of Mr. Richard Euston."

"Euston will no longer be a problem for Miss Pennington."

"He might be if his body is fished out of the river this morning. Everyone knows that he was spending a great deal of time in Miss Pennington's company. It would be unfortunate if word got around that his suit was rejected and that he took his own life in despair. Some might be led to believe that Miss Daphne is a callous and cruel young lady."

Joshua looked at her for a long, considering moment. She got the impression that he was not accustomed to having his decisions and actions questioned.

"I stopped by Euston's lodgings on my way here," he said eventually. "His landlord informed me that Euston had packed his things and departed for the Continent."

"Fascinating. And how very convenient for all concerned."

"I'm a great believer in convenient answers," Joshua said.

She smiled and sank down onto the sofa. "Nevertheless, I would very much like to know what induced Mr. Euston to leave the country on such short notice?"

"Does it matter?"

"Given my own personal involvement in the situation, yes, Mr. Gage, it matters. Won't you please be seated."

He considered that briefly and then lowered himself into a chair. He propped the cane so that it was within easy reach.

"As we speak, there is considerable gossip going around to the effect that Euston was not what he seemed," Joshua said. "His finances are in a disastrous state and it has come out that he is a fraud who is seeking an heiress to repair his fortunes. Fortunately for all concerned, Lord Pennington discovered the truth in time to protect his daughter from the attentions of a scoundrel."

"Good heavens." Beatrice stared at him in growing wonder. "I assume that gossip is your doing, sir?"

This time Joshua did not answer. He simply watched her. She was certain she detected a little heat in his eyes.

"Yes, of course, you are responsible for planting those rumors," she said crisply. "I must say, I am very impressed."

His brows rose. "Are you, indeed?"

"It is a brilliant solution to the problem. Euston will no longer be able to go about in Society and Daphne Pennington's reputation is unharmed. Her father will get the credit for exposing Euston. As I said, brilliant."

"Thank you," he said drily. "It also has the advantage of being the truth."

"Indeed. Well, then, on behalf of my client, I thank you for your services last night."

Joshua inclined his head a polite fraction of an inch. "You are entirely welcome."

The cat-and-mouse image floated through Beatrice's head again. *I am no mouse, Mr. Gage.*

Tea things clinked and rattled in the hall. Mrs. Rambley was approaching the parlor. There was no help for it, Beatrice thought. She would have to invite Joshua to stay for tea.

"You will have tea, I assume," she said, somewhat ungraciously. "I believe my housekeeper is bringing in a tray."

His mouth kicked up at the corner in a genuine smile of amusement. "Thank you. I could use a strong cup of tea. Actually, I could use a cup of strong coffee. As you said, it was a long night."

"Yes, it was, wasn't it?" Beatrice said. "Oddly enough I was enjoying coffee when you arrived. I'll ask Mrs. Rambley to bring in the pot. There is plenty left, I'm sure."

"There is no need to remind me again that I interrupted your breakfast, Miss Lockwood. I am well aware that I am imposing on you."

Mrs. Rambley appeared, her cheeks flushed with exertion, a heavy tray laden with the household's best pot, cups and silver in her hands. She set the tray on the low table in front of the sofa.

"Shall I pour, ma'am?" she asked.

"It seems Mr. Gage would prefer coffee," Beatrice said. "Would you mind bringing in the breakfast pot?"

"Yes, ma'am."

Mrs. Rambley shot a quick, curious look at Joshua and went out into the hall.

A heavy silence settled on the parlor. When it became clear that Joshua was not going to break it, Beatrice decided she would not speak, either. Two could play this game.

Mrs. Rambley reappeared and made room for the coffeepot on the tray.

"Thank you, Mrs. Rambley," Joshua said.

"You're welcome, sir." Mrs. Rambley reddened and looked expectantly at Beatrice.

"That will be all, thank you," Beatrice said.

"Yes, ma'am."

The housekeeper left. Joshua listened to her footsteps in the hall for a moment. Then he pushed himself to his feet and made his way across the room, cane thudding heavily on the carpet. He closed the door, came back to the chair and sat down again.

Beatrice watched him, her wariness increasing by the second. It was obvious that he did not wish the housekeeper to overhear what he was about to say.

She poured coffee into both cups and handed one cup and saucer to Joshua. When his fingers touched the china she got another whispery tingle of sensation. She released the saucer so quickly it was a miracle that the coffee did not spill. But Joshua seemed unaware of the near-disaster.

"Who taught you how to use a stocking gun, Miss Lockwood?" he asked.

"A former employer," she said.

"Would that former employer by any chance be the late Dr. Roland Fleming, proprietor of the Academy of the Occult?"

For one frozen moment she could not breathe. It was as if the room had suddenly tilted, throwing her off-balance. Her own cup of coffee trembled in her hand. Her pulse beat frantically and she knew a panic unlike any she had experienced since the night she fled the scene of Fleming's murder.

She called on all of her acting skills to collect herself.

"I have no idea what you are talking about, Mr. Gage." She summoned up her stage smile. "Or should I address you as the Messenger?"

"I see you talked to Mrs. Flint and Mrs. Marsh."

"I roused them from their beds early this morning. They were, I must say, quite shocked by the sight of that card you gave me. Evidently you and your own former employer, Mr. Smith, left a memorable impression on them."

"That was a long time ago."

"I believe it has only been a year since they last dealt with you."

"It has been a very long eleven months, two weeks and four days," Joshua said.

She glanced at his scarred face and then at the cane. "You sound like a prisoner who keeps track of time by marking off the days on the walls of his cell."

"That is not far from the truth." Joshua drank some coffee.

"Mrs. Flint and Mrs. Marsh assumed you were dead, but I suppose you are aware of that," Beatrice said.

"To tell you the truth, I had not considered the matter one way or another."

"Is Mr. Smith still alive, as well?" Beatrice asked.

Joshua's eyes went cold. "Our business together does not concern Mr. Smith."

"So he is still alive."

"Retired would be more accurate," Joshua said.

She glanced pointedly at his cane. "Can I assume that you, also, have been in retirement for the past year?"

"Yes," he said. He drank some more coffee.

She heightened her senses and looked at his footprints again. The seething iridescence in the psychical residue told her that retirement had not been a pleasant experience for Joshua. Not surprisingly, given the nature of his injuries, there was physical pain. But there was evidence of another kind of anguish, as well, the kind that cast a shadow on the heart and the senses.

"My employers informed me that you once investigated unusual cases that had a connection to the paranormal but that you, yourself, do not believe in the paranormal," she ventured.

"I have never made any secret of the fact that I consider so-called psychical practitioners to be frauds at worst or deluded at best."

He watched her, waiting for a response.

She smiled and sipped some coffee.

His eyes tightened at the corners. "Have I said something that amuses you, Miss Lockwood?"

"Sorry." She set her cup back down on the saucer. "I'm afraid that the notion of the notorious Messenger—a supposedly brilliant investigator who can find anyone—employing Mrs. Flint and Mrs. Marsh as consultants but never realizing that they both have some paranormal talent is rather entertaining."

"A *supposedly* brilliant investigator?"

"I didn't mean to insult your skills. I'm sure you're very good, sir."

"I found you, didn't I?"

She went cold. "Yes, you did. And if you went to all that effort merely to accuse me of having been a fraudulent practitioner, you have wasted your time. I have been out of that business for some months now."

"I'm not concerned with your talents onstage during your association with Dr. Fleming's Academy. I'm sure your performances were excellent. I always admire skill and competence of any sort."

"I see."

"And while we're on the subject, I do not deny that Mrs. Flint and Mrs. Marsh both possess considerable powers of observation. Furthermore, I have always respected Mrs. Marsh's scientific approach to investigations. But I see no reason to attribute their abilities to paranormal senses."

There was no point arguing with him. As Mrs. Flint and Mrs. Marsh had often observed, those who did not believe in the paranormal could always find alternative explanations for psychical events.

"Where have you been for the past year, Mr. Gage?" she asked.

"I retired to the country and that is where I would have been content to remain had it not been for you, Miss Lockwood."

She set down her cup and saucer with exquisite care. "If you have not tracked me down to level an accusation of fraud, what is it you want from me, sir?"

"The truth would be an excellent place to start. But in my experience that is usually the last place people wish to begin. For the sake of novelty, however, let's try it. I will tell you what I know. You may confirm or deny the facts as I lay them out."

"Why should I cooperate in your game, sir?"

He studied her with an assessing expression. "I believe you will want to assist me because I am looking for a blackmailer, and at the moment, Miss Lockwood, the evidence points to you as the extortionist."

Nine

She stared at him, stunned speechless. She thought she had been braced for almost anything but this was the very last thing she could have imagined. When she finally managed to catch her breath, she shot to her feet, her hands clenching into fists at her sides.

"Accusing me of being a fraudulent practitioner is one thing," she said. "But how dare you accuse me of blackmail?"

He did not seem to be affected by her outrage.

"Will you please sit down?" he asked, sounding almost weary. "If you remain on your feet good manners will oblige me to stand, too, and I would much prefer to remain seated." He paused a beat. "The leg, you know."

"Oh." She hesitated. Unable to think of anything else to do, she dropped back down on the sofa. "Explain yourself, sir."

"There is nothing complicated about the situation. At least, there didn't appear to be any complications when I started. My sister is being blackmailed."

"I'm shocked, of course, but I'm certain I've never even met your sister."

"You're wrong, Miss Lockwood, you have met her, although you may not recall the meeting. Her name is Hannah Trafford."

"I don't know who you are—" Beatrice broke off, suddenly remembering an attractive, well-dressed lady in her late thirties whose psychical prints had radiated anxiety. "Mrs. Trafford is your sister?"

"She attended several performances at Fleming's Academy. She saw you onstage a number of times and was so impressed that she booked some private appointments."

"I do recall the appointments, but there was nothing unusual about them. I certainly did not use anything I learned from Mrs. Trafford to blackmail her."

"Someone at the Academy discovered my sister's most closely guarded secret during the course of a treatment that no doubt involved hypnosis."

"But I never used hypnosis in the course of the private sessions," she said. "Dr. Fleming was the expert in mesmerism. I'm quite sure that Mrs. Trafford never booked any sessions with my employer. She was very specific about wanting to consult with me."

"Which makes you my primary suspect, especially given the fact that Dr. Fleming is dead."

"I don't understand any of this," she whispered, appalled.

"As far as I have been able to determine, there were no other employees at the Academy."

"No," Beatrice said. "At least not at the time that Mrs. Trafford booked her appointments with me. We had a medium for a while who conducted séances. Quite popular. But she ran off with Dr. Roland's assistant. I believe they are now touring in America."

"I looked into that pair. You're right, they are currently in America. It's highly unlikely that they are blackmailing people here in London because the instructions in the extortion note stipulate the location of the first payment—a country house named Alverstoke Hall."

"I've never heard of it," she said. "But, then, the only times I move in social circles are when I'm on assignment."

"Lord Alverstoke is a noted eccentric whose collection of Egyptian antiquities is said to put the British Museum to shame."

She frowned. "What in the world does he have to do with this extortion business?"

"I have no idea," Joshua said. "Yet. But given what I do know about Alverstoke, I suspect he is being used. I'm told he is easily confused these days and has become somewhat absentminded. He has scheduled a country-house party at the end of the week. It is an annual event during which he shows off his collection. Alverstoke and my sister have a passing acquaintance but she has never before been on the guest list for these yearly affairs. She is not fond of country-house parties or Egyptian antiquities. But the blackmailer indicated that she must attend this one."

"Alverstoke Hall will be overflowing with guests," Beatrice said. "All in all, a perfect cover for a blackmailer. So many suspects."

"Exactly. Assuming for the moment that you are not an expert in hypnosis—"

She glared. "I'm not."

"Then let us consider another scenario. My sister tells me that she remembers the appointments with you. When she arrived at the Academy, Dr. Fleming always showed her into a dark room and told her that you would arrive momentarily. She recalls the consultations—"

Beatrice raised a hand to stop him. "One moment, sir. Did your sister describe me?"

"She described Miranda the Clairvoyant. That was you, Miss Lockwood. You used a black wig and a heavy veil in your act."

"In other words, Mrs. Trafford never saw me, did she? She could not identify me."

"No, but I am aware that you were Miranda, so there is no point wasting time trying to deny it," Joshua said calmly. "To continue, at each appointment, my sister was shown into the consultation room. You entered. She talked to you for some time. But now I'm wondering if perhaps on one or more occasions Dr. Fleming returned to the room and put her into a trance during which he learned her secret. Perhaps he gave her a post-hypnotic suggestion instructing her to forget that he had ever come into the room. My sister then left the Academy remembering only that she had consulted with you."

"That's not what happened," Beatrice insisted. "I am very sure that Mrs. Trafford never requested hypnotic therapy. Dr. Fleming never treated her in my presence or otherwise."

"Then how did someone at the Academy learn her secret?"

"*I don't know.*" Beatrice paused, trying to marshal her thoughts. "What makes you so sure that whoever is blackmailing your sister was involved with the Academy?"

"The note my sister received implied that her secret had been discovered by paranormal means at the Academy. I discounted the notion that psychic powers had been involved, of course."

"Of course."

He ignored the sarcasm. Or perhaps he simply had not noticed the ice in her tone, she thought.

"My sister, however, has a long-standing interest in the paranormal," he continued. "Hannah has consulted a number of practitioners over the years and belongs to a small society of researchers. She is convinced that if she did inadvertently give up her secret, it could only have been during the private sessions with you at the Academy."

Beatrice narrowed her eyes. "Why am I the obvious suspect?"

"She believes you to be one of the very few genuine psychical talents that she has encountered in the course of her research. The others are not likely suspects. One currently resides in an asylum. One is a frail, elderly woman who does not practice professionally and does not take clients. Two are recluses who suffer from poor nerves and do not receive visitors. The last makes his living as a gambler. Two years ago he sailed for America because he heard there was a great deal of money to be made at the card tables in the American West. That leaves you, Miss Lockwood."

Beatrice winced. "I see."

"You may be interested to know that there is a new tenant occupying the rooms where you and Fleming conducted business." Joshua finished his coffee and set the cup and saucer aside. "But the landlord was kind enough to allow me to search the premises."

She watched him warily. "What did you hope to find after so many months?"

"Among other things, I found some old bloodstains on the floor of the office," Joshua said. "Very hard to wash out, blood."

She had been about to take a sip of her coffee but her fingers were shivering ever so slightly now. She set the cup back down in the saucer with great care.

"I also found an ancient stone tunnel behind an old wardrobe in the office," Joshua added gently.

She took a deep breath. "You conducted a very thorough search, Mr. Gage. That tunnel was the route I used to escape the night Roland was murdered." She paused, memories returning. "Roland and I kept our emergency packs just inside the tunnel in the event we were forced to flee from robbers or disgruntled clients."

"More likely Fleming was afraid that sooner or later one of his extortion victims might come looking for him," Joshua said. He raised a brow. "Or perhaps he feared that someone else in the same line would attempt to steal his secrets."

"Dear heaven." She was too shattered to think clearly. "I cannot believe that Roland was blackmailing people."

But Roland's dying words came back to her. *Do not let me die with that on my conscience. I have enough to repent.*

"You said that you and Fleming both kept your packs inside your escape tunnel?" Joshua asked.

"Yes. I had to leave his there that night. I could not carry both. But I opened Roland's pack to take out the money I knew he kept inside." She hesitated. "I did notice that there were some odd items in the pack. A notebook. An envelope filled with photos. Some letters."

"You could not carry Fleming's pack," Joshua said. "So perhaps you took out a handful of blackmail items along with the money and left the rest behind?"

Anger whipped through her.

"No," she said. "I took the money but nothing else. I wondered why he kept the items in his pack but I concluded they were all mementos that had some great personal meaning for him. The man who murdered Roland must have found the pack when he forced his way through the back of the wardrobe. Find him and you will have your extortionist, Mr. Gage."

Joshua's eyes burned. "That is precisely what I plan to do. With your help, Miss Lockwood."

Ten

"Y ou believe me?" she asked, still wary.

"Yes," he said.

"You truly don't think that I murdered Roland and started blackmailing his Academy clients?"

"I'm quite sure that you did not kill Fleming."

"Ah," she said, her spirits soaring. "Now that you have met me you don't believe that I'm capable of murder and extortion."

"Everyone is capable of murder under the right circumstances." He paused, evidently thinking about the second part of her statement. "And most likely extortion, as well. As I said, it all depends on circumstances."

She stopped smiling. "You have a very cynical view of human nature, Mr. Gage."

"I prefer to think of it as a realistic view," he said. "But in this case, I am certain you are not the killer."

"Indeed? How can you be so sure of that?"

"There are a number of reasons. The first is that I read the doctor's autopsy report. It was well done because Fleming's death was something of a sensation at the time."

Beatrice shook her head. "All that nonsensical speculation in the press about how he might have been murdered by forces from the Other Side. It was maddening."

"Fleming operated a business named The Academy of the Occult," Joshua said, his tone very dry. "It seems only natural that after he was murdered the press would go wild with speculation about spirits and paranormal forces."

"The press, perhaps, but I expected better of the police," she said. "I will admit they did not attribute his death to ghosts, but they focused their attention on me, instead."

"The missing assistant, yes. You must admit they had good reason to do so. It was only logical to assume that you were the killer. You were the mystery woman in the affair. No one had ever seen your face because of your costume."

"Roland thought the veil and the widow's weeds added a certain drama to the demonstrations," she said. "He also felt I would be safer that way. He said there were always a few strange people in any audience for a paranormal performance. He was afraid I might attract a deranged individual."

Joshua nodded with a very serious air. "A wise precaution."

"In the end, that is what happened. The man who stabbed poor Roland was just such a madman, someone who had fixated on me. Roland died trying to protect me."

Joshua's expression was almost feral. "Are you certain of that?"

"There is no doubt. The man who killed Roland came for me. I heard him vow to hunt me down. That is the main reason why I had to disappear."

"A man with an unwholesome fascination for a woman he be-lieves to have psychical powers kills the man who is in his way and then steals his victim's blackmail stash and proceeds to ex-ploit the secrets?" Joshua thought about that. "It's possible."

"It's the only explanation that makes any sense," she said, exas-perated.

"Huh."

She studied him for a long moment. "What was it in the au-topsy report that convinced you I was not the killer?"

"Roland Fleming was a large man. The wound was high on his chest. The force and angle of the thrust indicate that the killer was tall, powerful and, most likely, an expert with a knife. Either that or he was extremely fortunate in his first attempt. Regardless, you are a rather small and delicately made woman. If you had used a knife, the wound would have looked much different. Actually, you probably wouldn't have taken the risk of using a knife in the first place. In my experience, women prefer more tidy approaches to that sort of thing. Poison, for example."

She was shaken by the cold, methodical manner in which he had analyzed the crime.

"Good grief," she said. She took a deep breath. "Evidently you've had considerable experience with this sort of thing."

He looked at her with his bird-of-prey eyes, not speaking.

"If you had already concluded that I wasn't the killer, why did you try to frighten me with your suspicions?" she demanded.

"My apologies," he said. "I knew that you were not the killer, but what I did not know—and still don't know—is the nature of your connection to the killer."

She froze. "I don't have a connection to him."

"That you know of," he corrected quietly.

"For heaven's sake, why would you think I am linked to a murderer?"

His eyes tightened at the corners. "There is something about this case that makes me think that everything is connected, including you and the assassin."

"Assassin?"

"I believe whoever murdered Fleming was a professional who was very likely working for a fee that night."

"Then there *is* someone else involved."

"I think so, yes. I am looking for two people—the assassin and his employer. But where do you fit in, Miss Lockwood?"

"I have no earthly idea."

"Can you describe the killer?"

"Not physically. But I heard his voice. He spoke with a thick Russian accent." Beatrice paused. "He called himself the Bone Man. I heard him say *the Bone Man never fails.* I also saw his footprints."

Joshua frowned. "Footprints?"

"I know you will not believe me, but I saw his paranormal prints on the floor of the office that night. I would recognize them if I ever saw them again." She shuddered. "So much violent energy."

"Huh."

Her brows rose. "I did not think that you would be impressed with that observation."

He let that go. "Damnation. This case grows more bizarre by the day."

She poured more coffee for both of them.

"How did you come to discover that I was Miranda the Clairvoyant?" she asked.

"Finding people is something I do very well."

"Mrs. Flint and Mrs. Marsh said something along those lines." She searched his face. "What is your secret, sir?"

"There's no great trick to finding that which is lost. One simply looks in the right place."

Mrs. Flint and Mrs. Marsh were right, she thought glumly. Whether he wanted to acknowledge it or not, Joshua appeared to have some paranormal talent for locating whoever or whatever he set out to find.

Feverishly she considered the possibility of packing a bag and booking passage on the next ship bound for America. But even as the plan formed in her head she knew it was doomed. Flight would do her no good. Joshua had found her once. He would surely find her again.

But there might still be a way she could turn the situation to her advantage, she thought. Granted, Joshua had his own reasons for finding the killer, but if he was successful—and given his talent that was a real possibility—she would finally be free of the haunting fear that had shadowed her for nearly a year.

"I do not deny that Roland billed me as Miranda the Clairvoyant during my association with the Academy of the Occult," she said. "But I certainly never blackmailed anyone in my life. The only reason that I am not demanding that you leave this house immediately is because I find myself somewhat in your debt after the events of last night."

He watched her with his unsettling eyes. "And because it has occurred to you that I am in a position to do you another favor.

When I find the blackmailer, he will lead me to Fleming's killer. You will not only have some justice for Fleming, but you will be free of the anxiety you must have been feeling for the past several months. It is hard to keep looking over your shoulder, isn't it?"

It was as if he had read her mind. She fought the impulse to dump her cup of coffee over his head. Really, how could she possibly have found this man attractive?

"You sound as if you have no doubt but that you can find Roland's killer and the blackmailer," she said.

"I always find whatever it is I set out to find," he said.

He was not boasting, she realized. As far as Joshua was concerned, he was simply stating a fact.

"Have you ever failed, Mr. Gage?" she asked, genuinely curious.

"No," he said. He paused. "But once in a while I have arrived too late."

And she suddenly knew beyond a shadow of a doubt that it was one of those occasions—a time when he had arrived too late to save someone—that explained the shadows in his prints and, most likely, the scar and the cane.

He stretched out his left leg and shifted position a little in the chair. She could tell from the almost undetectable tightening at the edge of his mouth that the motion cost him.

"You appear to be uncomfortable, Mr. Gage."

"An old injury. It acts up occasionally."

"Such as after you toss an unconscious man over your shoulder and carry him some distance to a waiting carriage?"

His mouth twisted in a grim smile. "I'm getting too old for that kind of exercise."

"Richard Euston was not a small man."

Joshua acted as if he had not heard the comment. "I stopped by the offices of Flint and Marsh this morning."

"Did you?"

"Mrs. Flint and Mrs. Marsh assured me that you are one of their best agents," he said.

"I'm pleased to hear that they are satisfied with my services."

"I also informed them that I want to hire you as a paid companion," he added coolly.

"What?"

"If you agree, we will set a trap to catch the blackmailer, who will, in turn, lead us to the assassin who murdered your former employer," Joshua said.

"I do not appear to have much of a choice in the matter," she said. "I will help you with your plan."

"Thank you."

"Tell me, sir, as a point of general interest, is this the way you regularly conduct your business?" she asked.

"Sorry. Not sure what you mean."

She gave him a cold smile. "I am merely wondering if you are in the habit of applying pressure and threats when you wish to gain the cooperation of others?"

"I find pressure an effective technique. And I never make threats—only promises."

"There is an old saying. *You can catch more flies with honey than you can with vinegar.*"

"Honey never worked well for me."

Eleven

lement Lancing started the electricity machine and inserted the trailing end of the gold wire into the glass jar filled with the preservative formula. The rest of the long length of the wire was wrapped around the neck of the statue of Anubis that stood beside the workbench.

Small bubbles appeared in the preservative fluid. Clement was sure the chemicals were starting to change color. But when he looked at the statue he saw that the obsidian eyes of the jackal-headed god remained cold.

Still, he dared to hope. The Egyptian Water was frothing now. He watched the dead rat immersed in the chemicals. He was certain he saw small, spasmodic movements of the legs. For a brief moment he thought that he had finally succeeded and that the creature had awakened from the profound state of suspended animation induced by the formula.

It was frustrating to be forced to go back to conducting his experiments on rats but he dared not use humans again. That was what had led to the disaster a year ago. Gage had retired but it was likely that he still had his sources on the streets. If people began disappearing from the poorest neighborhoods again, word would reach him sooner or later. He would recognize the pattern. Gage was very, very good when it came to identifying patterns.

Clement kept the wire immersed in the fluid for a full two minutes, the longest time yet. But when he removed it from the jar the preservative became clear and colorless once more. The rat went limp; utterly motionless. To all intents and purposes it appeared dead.

But it was not dead, Clement thought. There was no evidence of decay. The creature was in a state of suspended animation. It was alive. It had to be alive. He could not bring himself to accept the alternative.

He stared at the rat for a long time before he raised his eyes to look at the other nine jars lined up on a nearby shelf. Each contained a motionless rat preserved in the Egyptian Water. He had prepared the formula with exquisite care, following the instructions on the ancient papyrus precisely, the instructions that Emma had translated.

There was no question but that the Water worked. The problem was with the power source—the damned statue. He had to find the woman with the talent to activate the energy locked in the obsidian eyes.

He looked at the Anubis figure and fought back the frustrated rage that threatened to eat him alive. It was all he could do not to smash the statue with a hammer. It had taken Emma months to find the eyes. As soon as she inserted the stones into the statue, they had both sensed the power locked in the figure.

But power that could not be released and channeled was useless. Emma had been strong but not quite strong enough. Nevertheless, they had been making progress when the disaster had struck.

In the past few months he had conducted innumerable experiments with electricity, hoping that the modern source of energy would overcome the last remaining obstacle. But it was evident now that there was no way around the instructions on the papyrus. *The sleeper can only be awakened by one who possesses the ability to ignite the jewels.*

He had to find Miranda the Clairvoyant.

London was overflowing with paranormal practitioners who claimed to have psychical talents, but the vast majority were frauds or simply delusional. Locating a woman with true talent had been akin to searching for the proverbial needle in a haystack. Nevertheless, there had been a stroke of good fortune. Miranda the Clairvoyant was the genuine article, but she had slipped away and vanished into the streets of London.

Time was running out. According to the papyrus, the sleeper had to be revived before a full year had passed. Beyond that length of time the process was irreversible. There was no option. The paranormal practitioner had to be found, and there was only one sure way to accomplish that goal.

The risk was extraordinary but there was one man who could be counted on to find whatever he set out to find.

Clement pushed himself away from the workbench and crossed the stone floor of the laboratory to the quartz sarcophagus. The coffin had come from the tomb of a high-ranking priest of a small, ancient Egyptian cult. It was unlike any other that had been discovered in that the lid was not made of solid stone. Instead it was inset with a large piece of thick, transparent crystal.

The sarcophagus had been empty when he and Emma had discovered it. Initially they had believed that the mummy that had been encased in the stone box had been stolen by tomb raiders. It was only after Emma had deciphered the hieroglyphs etched into the sides that they had both understood the magnitude of their find.

He stood looking down through the crystal lid. The sarcophagus was no longer empty. Emma lay inside, locked in deep sleep. She was immersed in the Egyptian Water. Her eyes were closed. Her beautiful dark hair floated in the chemicals. There had been no room in the box for the voluminous skirts and petticoats that she had been wearing that terrible day. He had been forced to put her into the sarcophagus attired in her nightgown.

It was Gage's fault that she had died. The bastard was responsible for everything that had gone wrong.

The rage inside welled up once more, threatening to choke him. He clenched his hands into fists.

"It is done, Emma. I have sent Gage to find her. He will not fail. He never fails. Soon she will be here. Until then, sleep, my beloved."

He looked closer and noticed that the fluid level inside the sarcophagus was lower than it had been yesterday. The lid fit snugly but there was always some evaporation.

He went to the shelves on the far side of the room and took down the container that held his supply of the special salts. It was time to prepare some more of the Egyptian Water to refill the sarcophagus.

Twelve

Joshua sat on a hassock in front of the low, black lacquer table and concentrated on the candle that burned in the holder. A small gong suspended from a wooden frame was positioned to one side of the candle. There were no other furnishings in the room that he had converted into his meditation chamber.

There was a time when he had performed the mental exercises while sitting cross-legged on the floor, but assuming such a position now was impossible because of the injury to his leg. In any event, his physical position did not matter. He had been practicing the meditation routine since he was in his teens. He could put himself into a light trance under almost any conditions.

Although he no longer required the flame or the gong to achieve the deepest state, he found comfort in the familiar rituals. This morning he had much to contemplate.

He picked up the small mallet and struck the gong lightly. The low sound resonated in the atmosphere. He slipped into the breathing exercises first. One of his mentor's axioms whispered through him.

Control the breath and you control the rest.

He found the inhale-exhale rhythm and struck the gong again. This time he followed the tone down into the self-induced trance.

In this state his senses still functioned. He could smell the faint scent of the candle and hear the clatter of carriage wheels in the street, but it was as if he was in another dimension. An invisible wall kept the outside distractions from affecting his concentration. In this realm he could contemplate things in a different light; see patterns and connections that were not readily visible when he was in a normal state of awareness.

He meditated on Beatrice Lockwood. He knew that she was critical to the success of his plan. But what he did not understand was how she was connected to all the other factors in the case. She injected a discordant note of chaos into the otherwise clockwork precision of his scheme. As a rule he did all he could to control elements of uncertainty. But sometimes the currents of chaos were precisely what were required to unlock doors that would otherwise remain closed.

Chaos, however, was, by definition, unpredictable. Chaos was energy that, by its very nature, could not be channeled or controlled. It was raw power, and power was always potentially dangerous.

He picked up the mallet and struck the gong a third time. The sound hung in the atmosphere for several seconds before gradually fading.

He went deeper.

Beatrice Lockwood was important and not just because he needed her assistance to find the blackmailer and the killer.

She was important to him in ways that he did not yet fully comprehend.

He was trying to see the patterns in the chaos when he heard the discreet knock on the door. Chadwick would not have interrupted him during his exercises unless there was a compelling reason.

He came swiftly out of the trance and extinguished the flame. Wrapping his hand around the hilt of the cane, he pushed himself to his feet and made his way across the small, spare space.

He opened the door. Chadwick stood in the hall, immaculately turned out as usual. A thin, wiry man of indeterminate years, he wore his formal butler attire with the aplomb of a military officer in uniform. Under fire, he was far more unflappable than many officers Joshua had met. It was Chadwick who had taken on the task of nursing his employer back to health following the disaster that had nearly cost Joshua his leg and an eye. Chadwick had dealt with blood, fever, delirium and the periodic outbursts of his patient's bad temper in a calm, dignified and efficient manner.

"My apologies for interrupting you during your morning meditation, sir," Chadwick said. "But young Mr. Trafford is here. He says it's urgent."

"With Nelson everything is urgent."

"Might I remind you that your nephew is eighteen years old, sir. Young men see no great virtue in patience."

"They may have a point," Joshua said. "Life is short, after all.

Tell him I will be down in a few minutes. Perhaps you could find him something to eat? He always seems to be famished when he arrives on our doorstep."

"He is devouring a muffin as we speak, sir."

Footsteps pounded up the staircase. Nelson crested the stairs and bounded down the hall, moving with a lithe, athletic grace that made Joshua sigh. There had been a time when he had moved with such ease. Like Nelson, he had taken his excellent physical coordination and fast reflexes for granted. The poet was right, he reflected, youth was wasted on the young.

"Did Miss Lockwood agree to the plan, Uncle Josh?" Nelson demanded, shoveling the last bite of muffin into his mouth.

Nelson possessed the dark hair, sharp features and lean build that characterized the men of the Gage family. He was also brimming with a thirst for adventure that Joshua remembered all too well. When he had turned eighteen, he, too, had lusted after excitement, danger and a noble cause. That was before he had discovered that such thrills were too often accompanied by blood, death and betrayal.

But there was no use trying to warn young men like Nelson of the reality of what lay ahead. They would not heed the warnings. Nature made it impossible for them to do so.

I have become far too jaded, Joshua thought. He knew there was no stopping Nelson. The best he could do was to try to keep his nephew from making the mistakes he had made. But just how did one go about instructing a young man on the dangers of trusting others? Some things had to be learned the hard way.

"Yes, Miss Lockwood did agree to assist us," he said. "This

morning I sent word to your mother to let her know that she will be attending Lord Alverstoke's country-house party with a paid companion from the Flint and Marsh Agency."

"Brilliant," Nelson said. Then his face tightened with frustration. "I just wish I could go, too."

"That is not possible. Neither of us can attend the affair as guests as we did not receive invitations."

"Where will you stay?" Nelson asked.

"I have made arrangements to rent a cottage near the estate for the weekend. I'll pose as a painter who has come to the country to do some landscapes."

Nelson frowned. "You don't paint."

"There's no great trick to smearing paint on a canvas as long as one doesn't intend to complete the picture."

"You must be close at hand in case the ladies need you. You cannot expect Miss Lockwood to deal with an extortionist by herself. She is just a professional companion."

"Miss Lockwood has hidden depths," Joshua said. *Not to mention a hidden gun,* he added silently. "But you're right. I certainly do not intend for her to take on the blackmailer alone. If my plan is carried out properly, neither Miss Lockwood nor your mother will come into contact with him. Don't worry, Nelson, I will keep an eye on the women."

"Mother is very worried about your scheme. She keeps talking about how you were nearly killed on your last case. She says your temperament is similar to that of the other men of the Gage bloodline. She worries that you will come to a bad end."

"You know Hannah tends to fret."

"True." Nelson glanced at the cane and grimaced. "But she says she can't forget that she had a terrible premonition shortly after you left London to investigate your last case."

"This is a very different situation."

There was nothing else he could say that was reassuring, Joshua thought. Hannah had good reason for her concerns. She was the one who, at seventeen, had been left to pick up the pieces and care for her younger brother when their recently widowed father, a thrill-seeker all of his life, had died while on a hunting trip in the American West. Edward Gage had been accidentally shot and fatally wounded by one of his companions.

On the heels of the telegram that had delivered the news of Edward Gage's death, she had been forced to confront another disaster, one of a financial kind. After learning of his client's death, Edward's man of affairs had absconded with the Gage fortune.

With the very real threat of the workhouse looming before them, Hannah had taken the only respectable avenue available to her. She had accepted an offer of marriage from William Trafford, a wealthy man who had generously agreed to take his bride's younger brother into his household.

Trafford had proved to be a decent, scholarly man who had treated Hannah and Joshua with kindness. He had been in his early sixties—old enough to be Hannah's grandfather. A widower with no children of his own from his first marriage, he had been thrilled when Hannah had given him a son.

Trafford had succumbed to a heart attack a few years later but not before he had instructed Joshua on the proper management of the fortune that he had left to Hannah, Nelson and Joshua. Overseeing the family investments had proved to be a relatively simple, boring matter for Joshua. The men of the Gage line had a knack for making money.

By that time Joshua had "fallen into the clutches of that dreadful man," as Hannah put it. The *dreadful man* was Victor Hazelton, known in the shadows of the espionage world as Mr. Smith.

Hannah had devoted herself to Nelson, intent on making certain that he followed in William Trafford's staid, scholarly footsteps and not those of his grandfather or his uncle on her side of the family tree. For a while all had been well. Until recently Nelson had been a dutiful son who had tried to please his mother.

But in the past year he had begun exhibiting what Hannah called the wild blood that tainted the Gage line. She feared that he would descend into the gaming hells and dark clubs of London's underworld, just as his grandfather and great-grandfather had done. Just as Joshua had done for a time.

She was right to worry, Joshua thought. Two months ago when he had come to London on a rare visit to take care of some business affairs, he had been obliged to drag Nelson out of one of the worst hells in town. He had arrived just as the manager of the club was sending his enforcers to toss Nelson out into the street. Accusations of cheating were being leveled. Impending violence had simmered in the atmosphere.

A few nights ago he had found it necessary to take time out of his investigation of the blackmailer in order to repeat the exercise.

"Look at it this way, Uncle Josh," Nelson had said, his voice slurred by a great deal of cheap claret, *"I always win."*

"There is no great mystery in that," Joshua had said. *"You've got the Gage luck when it comes to cards. Unfortunately it doesn't apply to much else."*

"Huh. Probably best not to mention this episode to my mother."

"Agreed. I didn't mention the last occasion, either."

Hannah would be horrified if she discovered that Nelson was spending more and more of his nights seeking out the dark excitement and the darker pleasures of London's most dangerous streets.

Joshua was well aware of what Nelson was going through because he had gone through the same restless, reckless stage at that age. It was as if a fire had been burning inside him. In search of a way to channel the fierce energy that threatened to consume him, he had been drawn out into the streets of London's violent underworld.

Victor Hazelton had found him on those streets and forever changed his life. Victor had understood him. The man known as Mr. Smith had shown him how to control the tempestuous energy that seethed in his gut, taught him how to focus and control the wild forces of his nature. Victor had become his mentor, his father in every way save by blood.

Joshua now faced a lifetime of knowing he had failed Victor, the man who had saved him from himself.

"If all goes according to my strategy, this matter will be concluded within a day or two at Alverstoke Hall," he said.

"Nevertheless, it might be useful to have me conveniently at hand," Nelson pointed out, still hopeful.

What the hell, Joshua thought. He had tried to keep Nelson out of the investigation as a favor to Hannah. She did not want him exposed to the world in which Joshua had once moved. But it was Nelson who had first realized that Hannah was being blackmailed. He had a right to assist.

"As it happens," Joshua said, "I have another, very critical task that I would like you to undertake."

Nelson's excitement was palpable. He almost glowed with enthusiasm. "What is that?"

"I want you to look into Fleming's murder. Several months ago it was a sensation in the press because of Fleming's association with the paranormal. I want you to interview everyone you can find who was living or working near the building where the Academy of the Occult had rooms. Shopkeepers, servants, tenants, deliverymen, the local constable, the baked-potato man. Ask them if they noticed any strangers hanging about in the neighborhood in the days before the murder."

Nelson frowned. "I don't understand. I thought you said that the blackmailer was very likely the killer. You are off to Alverstoke's country house to find him."

"I examined the autopsy report this morning. There was information in it that leads me to believe that we may be dealing with a hired killer. It's possible that he is also the blackmailer, but I am now inclined to think that it is more likely the blackmailer employed a professional. And blackmail may not have been the original goal."

"What do you mean?"

"Whoever sent the killer to the Academy intended to have Miss Lockwood abducted."

"Why?" Nelson asked.

"There are those who become obsessed with the paranormal and those who claim to practice that sort of nonsense. It appears that some deranged individual fixed his attention on Miss Lockwood and sent the killer to grab her. Obviously the assassin missed but he evidently found the blackmail material instead and turned that over to his employer, who is now attempting to profit from the affair."

"Why wait nearly a year to blackmail Mother?"

Joshua smiled approvingly. "Excellent question. For all we know the blackmailer has been extorting money from other victims for the past several months and has just now gotten around to threatening Hannah. But there are other possibilities."

"Such as?"

"I don't know," Joshua said. "That is why we refer to our efforts as an investigation. We are looking for answers."

"Right." Nelson was animated and enthusiastic once again. "I was not aware that one could hire a killer the way one does a housekeeper or a gardener."

"It is a good deal more complicated than it sounds, especially if one wishes to employ an expert," Joshua said. "I believe that Fleming's killer was, indeed, an expert. Such men work methodically and cautiously because they do not want to take the risk of being caught. They study the daily habits and routines of their intended victims for some time before they make a plan."

"I understand. You believe that Fleming's killer very likely spent considerable time watching Miranda from various vantage points near the premises of the Academy."

"That's certainly how I would have approached the affair had I been in the assassin's shoes," Joshua said without thinking.

He realized that Nelson was watching him with far too much speculation and curiosity.

"Never mind," Joshua said quickly. "It would be extremely helpful if you were able to obtain a full description of the killer, but after all these months that won't be possible. Even if a few people remember a stranger who spent time in the neighborhood prior to the murder, they won't recall the color of his eyes or hair. The one fact we do have is that the assassin spoke with a heavy Russian accent. That should narrow things down considerably."

"I will get started immediately," Nelson said.

He turned and bounded down the stairs.

"Take good notes," Joshua called after him. "You will find they are useful when it comes to comparing the various descriptions that people will supply. And they will vary greatly, I warn you. No two people remember anything in exactly the same way. Look for the one or two elements all the reports might have in common."

Nelson paused at the foot of the stairs and looked up. "I understand."

"One more thing," Joshua said. "Do not use your real name. Tell the people you interview that you are a writer who is gathering background material to write a penny dreadful about the Fleming murder."

"Right," Nelson said.

He opened the front door and went swiftly out onto the steps. He slammed the door behind him.

Silence fell.

Chadwick chuckled. "I remember the days when you left on your assignments with similar enthusiasm, sir."

Joshua gazed thoughtfully at the front door. "So do I."

For the past several months he had been feeling quite ancient, he reflected; unable to summon up any great interest in the future. But the blackmail investigation had altered his mood. True, his days of loping down staircases were long past. But he was definitely looking forward to seeing Beatrice Lockwood again.

Thirteen

This is the most bizarre house I have ever entered in my entire life." Beatrice looked at the bronze statuette of Bastet that stood on a bedside table. The Egyptian goddess was depicted in her cat-headed woman form. "And I assure you that in the course of my career with the Flint and Marsh Agency, I have been obliged to enter some very unusual households."

The sprawling Alverstoke mansion was crammed with ancient Egyptian antiquities. Some of the items were replicas or outright fakes, but Beatrice was certain that there were a vast number of genuine relics in the house, most of which had come from tombs and temples. She could sense the energy infused into the artifacts.

Many people—not just those who possessed a degree of psychical talent—were sensitive to the chill of the grave and the passion of those who believed in religious mysteries of any sort. That sort of energy was absorbed by the objects the ancients put into their temples and tombs. Walking through the front door of Alverstoke Hall a short time ago had stirred the hair on the back of Beatrice's neck and caused a prickling sensation in her palms.

"It's all these antiquities," Hannah Trafford said. She glanced uneasily at the statue of Bastet. "They are fascinating but I will admit that it is a bit odd to decorate an entire house with objects that should more properly be displayed in a museum."

"Precisely what I was thinking," Beatrice said. "That Bastet gives me chills."

Hannah gave her a knowing look. "It's the paranormal energy in the object that we are sensing, isn't it?"

"I think so, yes."

She and Hannah were standing in her bedroom. The door that connected it to Hannah's room was open. Beatrice could hear Sally, Hannah's lady's maid, moving about inside as she unpacked her employer's trunk. The process involved a great deal of work because, like many wealthy ladies, Hannah brought her own bed linens and towels with her when she traveled.

"Your Bastet is nothing compared to the canopic jar in my bedroom." Hannah shuddered delicately. "I dare not look inside. I should very likely discover the remains of someone's liver."

Beatrice smiled. During the course of the journey from London to the small village of Alverstoke, she and Hannah had become surprisingly comfortable in each other's company. The ease between them was attributable in part to the fact that they had already met as psychical counselor and client over a year earlier. But it was also enhanced by their mutual acceptance of the paranormal as normal. Hannah had explained that she had always been fascinated with psychical matters and had studied the field extensively. She was convinced that she, herself, had experienced premonitions on a number of occasions over the years and she was eager to discuss a range of issues on the subject with Beatrice.

Hannah Trafford was an attractive woman in her late thirties. Her dark hair was arranged in a stylish twist. Her eyes were the same green-gold as Joshua's. She was still dressed in the fashionable maroon traveling gown and high-button boots that she had worn on the train.

"Even if we weren't here to trap a blackmailer, I doubt if either of us would be able to sleep for the next two nights with these artifacts sitting near our beds," Beatrice said. "We have enough on our minds as it is. I suggest that we ask Sally to make arrangements to have the Bastet and canopic jar temporarily stored elsewhere."

"Excellent idea," Hannah said.

She went to the connecting door and spoke briefly to Sally. Beatrice started to unpack her own small trunk. In her guise as a paid companion she had brought only two dresses, one for day, which she had worn on the train, and one for evening.

Hannah turned around just as Beatrice was putting the staid evening gown into the wardrobe.

"Let Sally take care of that for you," Hannah said quickly.

"It's all right," Beatrice said. "I'm almost finished. There's not much to it."

"I can see that." Hannah looked at the unfashionable dress hanging in the wardrobe with dismay. "I assumed that as a Flint and Marsh agent you would be able to afford a more expensive wardrobe."

"I assure you, my employers are very generous," Beatrice said.

"But when I am conducting an investigation, I try to stay in my role as a companion at all times. I learned that lesson in my former career."

Hannah sank down onto a chair and regarded her with a thoughtful expression. "You gave a very fine performance as Miranda the Clairvoyant. I never saw your red hair beneath the black wig and I never realized your eyes were blue. The veil you wore was quite heavy."

"Dr. Fleming believed that Miranda should have a commanding presence onstage." Beatrice carried a folded nightgown to a drawer. "He did not think that I could accomplish that without the costume. But the main reason he insisted I play the part of Miranda at all times was because he worried that there were those who might become obsessed with a woman they believed to be clairvoyant."

"He was right to be cautious." Hannah hesitated. "You have had two very interesting careers, Beatrice."

"I have been fortunate in that regard." Beatrice slipped the nightgown into a drawer. "Both paid well."

"It was not all an act back in the days when you played Miranda, was it? You truly do possess some paranormal talent?" Hannah tensed, as if bracing herself for bad news. "Can you foretell the future?"

"No." Beatrice closed the drawer and sat down on the edge of the bed. "I do not see the future. I do not believe anyone can do that, although it's certainly possible to predict probable outcomes if one has enough information. But that is a function of logic, not fortune-telling. And in my experience it does no good whatsoever to warn people that they are heading down the wrong path."

Hannah smiled wistfully. "Because no one really wants good advice."

"It's the rare individual who is ruled by logic instead of passion."

Hannah sighed. "I know. What is the exact nature of your talent?"

"I see the psychical energy that others leave behind in their footprints and on the things they touch. The colors and patterns of the currents tell me a great deal about the individual who generated them."

"It must be fascinating."

"That is not how I would describe it," Beatrice said. "I won't deny that my talent has its uses. With the exception of a couple of very short stints as a governess that did not end well, I have made my living off my paranormal abilities in one way or another. But there are some disturbing aspects to my other sight."

"How can you say that? It would be such a gift to be able to read other people by viewing their paranormal footprints and fingerprints."

"Psychical energy sticks around for a long time—years, decades, centuries." She looked at the Bastet statuette and heightened her senses. The cat-woman goddess was covered with layer upon layer of hot, seething energy. "I can still see glimpses of the prints of the sculptor who made that figure and those of the priest who put it into the burial chamber. I can see the prints of the tomb thieves who stole it and those of the obsessive collectors who have handled it over the years."

"How can you distinguish the prints of so many different individuals?"

"I can't, at least not with any great precision," Beatrice said. "That's the problem with old objects and old houses like this one. Over the years, the layers of energy set down by people form a dark fog that is . . . unsettling to view for any length of time." She shut down her senses. "I can catch glimpses of the various patterns but not complete prints. My talent is only accurate when I am viewing more recent tracks—those that were laid down in the past several months are usually the sharpest and most distinct. Beyond that things get murky fast."

Hannah rose and crossed the room to close the door to the connecting chamber. She returned to the chair and sat down. She gripped the arm of the chair very tightly with one hand.

"When I booked those private consultations with you at Dr. Fleming's Academy, you saw the truth in my psychical prints," she said. Her voice was surprisingly firm and steady but her underlying tension vibrated in every word. "You said my nerves were badly frayed and that I must find a way to calm my inner agitation. You said my anxiety was based on some underlying fear."

"You knew all those things before you came to see me," Beatrice said gently. "It's why you came to see me."

"Yes, of course. You suggested that I identify the source of the fear and confront it. You indicated that if I did not do so, the anxiety would continue to gnaw at my insides. I tried to do as you said but I could not find any peace. And now this damned blackmail threat has made everything so much worse. My growing dread makes sleep almost impossible."

Beatrice opened her senses again and examined Hannah's prints on the floor. Some of the currents were feverishly hot. "I can see that your nerves are certainly more strained now than they were when you requested the consultations. That is only to be expected, given what you are going through."

Hannah's mouth twisted in a humorless smile. She got to her feet and went to stand at the window. "Nothing like blackmail to bring on a case of shattered nerves."

"I hesitate to inquire," Beatrice said carefully, "but the answer might be important. You have said nothing about the nature of the secret that has left you vulnerable to an extortion attempt. It is certainly none of my business. But do you think there is any possibility that your secret is in any way connected to the anxiety that brought you to me all those months ago?"

"No, at least not that I can see. My secret is linked to the past of a dear friend of mine, not to my own past. She was involved in a dreadful marriage. Her husband abused her terribly. He died— and not a moment too soon, I might add—under what some might call suspicious circumstances."

"Oh, I see," Beatrice said. "In other words, your friend assisted her husband along to the next world."

Hannah turned around. Her eyes were stark. "It was a bit more complicated than that."

Understanding struck.

"You were involved?" Beatrice said.

"In a manner of speaking. I will tell you the whole story. It is only right that you know my secret."

"There is no need—"

But Hannah was already talking. Her voice was clipped and tense. It was as if she needed to get the story out quickly.

"One night my friend appeared at my garden door," she said. "She was bruised and bleeding. Her husband had beaten her unmercifully. Nelson was away at school. My housekeeper and I were alone in the house. Together we got my friend into the kitchen. We were bandaging her wounds when the husband shattered the glass in the back door and burst into the kitchen. He had a carving knife and he was enraged. He made no secret of the fact that he intended to kill my friend and murder my housekeeper and me as well for having tried to help."

"This is a horrible tale," Beatrice whispered. "What did you do?"

"I grabbed a kitchen chair and tried to fend him off. My housekeeper seized an iron skillet. My friend was too badly injured to do anything except crawl under the table. The housekeeper and I were trying to protect her with the chair and the skillet when Josh came through the kitchen doorway." Hannah paused. "He had a knife in his hand."

Hannah stopped speaking altogether.

"You must tell me the rest now," Beatrice said. "You cannot leave me hanging there, for goodness sake."

"Until that night I did not realize that Josh is . . . very skilled with knives," Hannah said without inflection.

"Oh." Beatrice swallowed. "I see. Well, I must say I'm very glad he got there when he did."

"As were we all," Hannah said. She collected herself. "There was a terrible mess, of course. Blood everywhere. But we got it cleaned up and then Josh dealt with the body. It turned up in the river the following day. Everyone assumed that my friend's husband had been the victim of a robber who had murdered him on his way home from a brothel."

"Good riddance, is all I can say."

"Yes, but the bastard moved in Polite Circles," Hannah said. "He was a wealthy man. If it got out that he had been murdered in my kitchen three years ago, the press would go wild. I doubt that there would be a police investigation—not after all this time. Josh has connections at Scotland Yard. I'm sure he could stop an inquiry, in any case. But not even that dreadful man he worked for at the time could silence gossip in the papers. My friend and I would become notorious overnight."

Beatrice drummed her fingers on the quilt. "I just cannot see how Dr. Fleming learned of your secret. I swear to you that he never at any time attempted to hypnotize you on the occasions that you came to the Academy." She paused, frowning. "Unless you booked some private appointment with him?"

"No," Hannah said. "What's more, I am absolutely certain my friend never told anyone. I know for a fact that she never attended any of Fleming's demonstrations. She has no interest in the paranormal. As for my housekeeper, she is very loyal. She has always kept the family secrets. Even if she did confide in someone, I cannot imagine that person found his or her way to Dr. Fleming's Academy of the Occult. It just seems so unlikely. And as for Josh, he never even told that dreadful man who employed him to do his dirty work. And Lord knows, Josh trusted Victor Hazelton like a father."

"I don't understand," Beatrice said. "Who is Victor Hazelton?"

"The real name of that dreadful man who calls himself Mr. Smith."

"I see," Beatrice said. "So the secret was kept, yet somehow it ended up in Dr. Fleming's stash of blackmail materials."

"You can see why Josh's theory that I was hypnotized during

those private sessions made sense. It was the only explanation we could find."

"I honestly cannot see how it could have been done without my knowledge," Beatrice said.

Hannah sighed. "I do believe you."

"But you say it was not the events in your kitchen that night that brought you to me for the private consultations?"

"No," Hannah said quietly.

"We will find the blackmailer and when we do, we will get the answers to all your questions," Beatrice said.

Hannah gave her a misty smile. "I do not doubt it. I have never approved of Josh's career but I will be the first to admit that he has a talent for conducting investigations. He always finds what he sets out to find."

"So I have been told."

Fourteen

The telegram was brief but the message sent a feverish rush of relief and excitement through Clement Lancing. He stood beside the sarcophagus and read it twice to convince himself that the news was real.

He put his hand on the crystal lid and looked down at the woman floating in the Egyptian Water.

"He did it, Emma. That bastard Gage found the practitioner. You will never believe this, but she was working as a paid companion all this time. No wonder she was impossible to locate. We were looking in the wrong places. The strategy is moving forward again. Gage has taken the bait."

The woman in the sarcophagus gave no indication that she heard him. Her sleep was too deep.

He noticed that the level of water had gone down again. Time to prepare some more of the formula. He went to the shelf that held his supply of chemicals. He was almost out of the salts, but then, he would not need them much longer.

Fifteen

The great hall of the Alverstoke mansion was awash in dark energy. The currents swirling around the massed collection of Egyptian artifacts set Beatrice's senses on edge.

Massive stone statues of Egyptian gods, goddesses and demons, many adorned with the heads of animals, gazed down on the crowd with implacable stares. Canopic jars, scarabs and ankhs were arranged on tables. Detailed miniatures depicting everyday life in the ancient land—a fishing boat complete with tiny men casting nets, a house with a walled garden—were set out on shelves. Glass-topped cases held brilliant pieces of jewelry— pectorals, collars and earrings.

Beatrice shivered and wrapped her shawl more tightly around her shoulders. She had positioned herself on a banquette in a corridor just off the great hall. A cluster of potted plants shielded her from the view of passersby. From her vantage point she could watch the elegant guests through a veil of palm fronds. With the exception of Hannah, most of Alverstoke's guests appeared unaware of the heavily charged atmosphere, at least not consciously aware. They chatted with one another and drank their host's expensive champagne while they marveled at the antiquities.

But it seemed to Beatrice that much of the laughter was off-key and the conversations a bit too loud. There was a nervous undercurrent in the room.

She was concentrating intently on trying to keep an eye on Hannah—not an easy task in the crowded chamber—when another kind of awareness feathered her senses.

She turned quickly and saw an elderly, thickly bearded gentleman emerge from a dark passage behind her. He wore gold-framed spectacles. His evening coat and trousers were sadly out of date. He leaned heavily on a familiar ebony-and-steel cane.

"Alverstoke's decorator appears to have gone mad with the Egyptian motif," Joshua said.

"Good heavens, sir, you gave me a start." Beatrice glared at him. "Kindly refrain from sneaking up on me like that. It is very hard on the nerves."

"Something tells me that your nerves are strong enough to withstand the occasional surprise." He peered through the palm fronds at the entrance to the reception hall. "Where is my sister?"

"The last time I saw her she was near the large statue of Osiris talking to a gentleman." Beatrice turned back to search the crowd. "There she is in the blue gown."

"I see her. She is chatting with Ryeford. They are old friends."

Joshua paused to examine a dagger with a gilded hilt that was on display in a nearby glass-topped case. "I assume that there has not been any communication from the extortionist?"

"No, but it's about time you showed up," Beatrice said. "Where have you been? I was starting to wonder if something had happened to you. We have not discussed the method I am to use to contact you if we do receive the villain's instructions."

"When," Joshua said. He spoke in an absent tone, his attention on the dagger.

Beatrice went blank. "What?"

"I said when you receive the villain's instructions, not if. He will make his move here, quite possibly tonight. Tomorrow night at the latest."

"How can you be certain?" she asked, curious. He sounded so sure of himself.

"It's a logical conclusion. The house party lasts only three nights. The blackmailer will want to take advantage of the crowd." Joshua raised the lid of the case. "This is a very interesting blade. I wonder if it is genuine."

He reached into the case.

"Do not touch that," Beatrice snapped before she could stop herself.

He glanced back at her. "Why not?"

"Because it is, indeed, genuine." She regained her composure. "It was used to kill on more than one occasion, and it is stained with some very unpleasant energy."

He studied her intently. "You're telling me that you can detect such details with your paranormal senses?"

"You don't believe me."

"I believe in the powers of a lively imagination," he said politely.

She sniffed. "Why do I bother? You are quite right, sir, go ahead, pick up the dagger. It's no concern of mine."

He gave her a thoughtful look and then, very deliberately, he closed his fingers around the gilded hilt. The false beard and bushy brows concealed his expression but she could have sworn that she saw his eyes heat a little when his fingers came in contact with the ancient blade. She was quite certain he had experienced a small, psychical jolt. She also knew that he would never admit it.

She waited, expecting that he would put the blade down and close the lid of the case. Instead he held the dagger up to the light of a wall sconce to examine it more closely.

"Interesting," he said.

He admired the dagger a moment longer and then put it back into the case with some reluctance. She knew then that he had, indeed, received a paranormal shock of some sort from the relic, but not the kind that sent chills of dread down the spine. Holding the dagger had quite the opposite effect on him. He had experienced a flash of excitement.

Joshua closed the lid of the case and made his way to the banquette. He lowered himself onto the velvet cushions and stacked his hands on the handle of his cane.

"Where are your rooms?" he asked.

"Your sister and I are in the east wing on the floor above. Mrs. Trafford was given the bedroom at the far end. My room is directly adjacent to hers. We both face the gardens."

"Excellent. I can see your windows from the cottage. The simplest methods are usually the best. When Hannah receives instructions from the blackmailer, light a candle and set it on the windowsill. I will send three flashes with a lantern to let you know that I have seen your signal. We will meet in the library."

"How will you get into the house?" she asked. "I'm sure the doors will all be locked after everyone goes to bed."

"I am somewhat of an expert when it comes to that sort of thing," he said.

"Oh, right, you were a professional spy." She kept her own tone just as dry. "Must have slipped my mind. I suppose lock-picking skills were a requirement for the position."

"You don't think much of my former profession, do you?"

"I give it the same degree of regard that you give my former career. Face it, sir, you and I were both in the business of manu-facturing illusions for the purpose of deceiving others. I am still in that line." She gave his beard and unfashionable attire a dismis-sive look. "And evidently so are you."

He absorbed the accusation and then inclined his head. "You are correct, Miss Lockwood. We appear to have a great deal in common."

"Not a *great* deal, merely a talent for deception. I trust your skills have not grown rusty. It would be awkward for your sister and me if you got caught breaking into this house tonight."

"I will try to avoid embarrassing you both." He contemplated the artifacts around them. "I wonder how many of these antiqui-ties are fakes?"

"Some, certainly." She adjusted her shawl again in a futile at-tempt to ward off the chill. "But not all."

Joshua's eyes sharpened behind the lenses of the spectacles. "Do you have some expertise in Egyptian antiquities?"

"None whatsoever, Mr. Gage. But I do not need any to sense the dark energy that is infused into several of these pieces. I suspect you feel it, yourself, but you no doubt choose to explain away the sensation with some forced bit of logic."

He was amused and also, she thought, curious.

"Exactly how would I do that?" he asked.

She moved one hand in a small gesture. "Perhaps you tell yourself that you are on edge simply because you are in the middle of an investigation. You are, therefore, in a state of acute awareness. That generates a certain level of excitement which, in turn, explains any odd sensations you are feeling."

"A reasonable chain of logic if not for the fact that it's founded on a false premise."

"In addition, that there is a personal aspect to this case neatly explains some of your reaction. You are here to save your sister from a blackmailer. To do that you are obliged to work with a woman you do not entirely trust. That is bound to affect your nerves. You prefer to be in complete control of a situation. I am supposed to be a pawn in your game but you cannot be sure that I will prove reliable."

"Ah, now there you are wrong, Miss Lockwood."

"Really?" She did not bother to conceal her disbelief.

"You are most certainly an unpredictable element but I do not consider you to be a pawn," he said.

"Is that so?" She tipped her head slightly to one side. "How do you see me?"

"I'm not sure yet." He hesitated, as though struggling with the answer. "I am still evaluating your role in this affair."

He sounded so serious she almost laughed aloud.

"As it happens, I still have a great many questions about you, as well, sir," she said smoothly. "Nevertheless, you make my point. You can explain away your unease without resorting to the paranormal."

"In other words, you cannot prove that there are currents of paranormal energy emanating from some of the genuine artifacts in this room."

"No," she said. "Furthermore, I see no reason to try to prove the existence of the paranormal to you. Your low opinion of me is, of course, quite crushing, but in the long run it does not matter."

The corner of his mouth edged upward. "I merely said that you possess a lively imagination. That does not mean that I hold a low opinion of you. I am crushed, in turn, to hear that my opinion of you is of no particular significance."

"How could it possibly matter, sir?" she said politely. "After all, when this case is over we will each go our own way and never meet again."

"You sound as if you are looking forward to the end of our short acquaintance."

"I'm sure you are, as well," she said.

"No, as a matter of fact, I'm not looking forward to a parting of the ways."

He sounded vaguely surprised by his own words.

"I find that hard to believe, Mr. Gage."

"Unlike you, I have found our brief association to be . . . stimulating."

Startled, she eyed him with growing suspicion. "Rubbish."

"I'm very serious." He massaged his thigh in an absent manner and concentrated his attention on the crowd. "You are a very re-freshing female, Miss Lockwood."

"Refreshing?"

"I am not sure how to explain myself."

"No need to explain, sir," she said. "I quite understand."

His false brows rose. "You do?"

"Your problem is simply that you have been living a rather boring life for the past year. You had no business retiring to the country while still in your prime in the first place. Really, what were you thinking?"

His amused, teasing manner vanished in a heartbeat. The ice was back in his eyes.

"Who the devil do you think you are, Miss Lockwood, to be handing out advice and asking personal questions?"

She was startled by the uncharacteristic edge in his voice. True, it was barely discernible, but it was there, like a shark under the waves. In the course of her short acquaintance with Joshua the one thing she had learned was that he was a master of self-control. This was the first time she had seen any indication that he might occasionally allow himself to reveal a flash of anger or impatience.

Then again, she reminded herself, he had acquired all that ironclad self-mastery for a reason. A man of strong passions needed to be able to control those passions.

Perhaps the more intriguing question was why she was relishing the knowledge that she could draw him out of the shadows, even for a moment. Baiting a tiger that lived inside a self-imposed cage was a risky game. It was the tiger, after all, who possessed the keys.

"I happen to be your associate in an investigation, Mr. Gage," she said. "And do not forget that this partnership of ours was formed at your suggestion."

"That does not entitle you to pry into my private affairs."

"I wasn't prying, I was making an observation."

"And giving advice."

"I'm sorry to say that the urge to do so is an unfortunate side effect of my talent," she said. "I realize that you required some time to recover from the metaphysical as well as the physical aspects of your injuries. However, today in the course of our journey from London, your sister told me that you became almost a complete recluse this past year. It is high time you emerged from your isolation and returned to normal life."

"I have not lived a normal life for a very long time."

She waved that off. "You know very well what I mean, sir."

"Did Hannah tell you why she is being blackmailed?"

Beatrice hesitated and then concluded there was no reason to conceal the truth.

"Yes," she said.

He nodded. "I thought so."

"I would remind you that this is not the first time Hannah and I have met. We get along quite well. Mutual interests and all that."

"A mutual interest in the paranormal."

"Indeed. But I think Hannah entrusted me with her secret because she felt that, given my own involvement in this affair, I had a right to know."

Joshua was silent for a moment. "I assume she told you about my part in the business?"

"Yes. I can't say I was surprised by your role in the affair. You are a professional, after all. I'm just very glad to know that you were there to deal with that terrible man that night."

"Hannah and her housekeeper were doing very well when I got there, but it is difficult to stand against an enraged man armed with a knife who is bent on murder."

Memories of the iridescent prints around the dying Roland Fleming sent a ghostly shiver through Beatrice.

"That is what Roland told me that night when he lay dying on the floor of his office," she whispered. "He said my stocking gun would be of little use against a determined killer."

"That is especially true when that killer is experienced in his craft," Joshua said. "You would have gotten only one chance to fire the gun—if that. And if you had missed or if you had not hit a vital spot, which is unlikely with that small weapon—"

"I know."

"Hannah was right," he said. "You do deserve to know the truth. But the more people who share a secret, the more risk there is that sooner or later that secret will no longer be a secret."

"I give you my word I will not tell a soul."

He did not respond to that. When she looked at him she saw that he appeared lost in thought.

She frowned. "I am well aware that you do not trust me, Mr. Gage. There is no need to be rude about it. I would remind you, however, that I, too, am a professional. Over the years I have kept a great many secrets for my clients both in my role as Miranda and now as an agent for Flint and Marsh. I will hold your secrets close as well."

"Oddly enough, I do trust you, Miss Lockwood." He smiled. "Damned if I know why."

"Do you find me amusing, sir?"

"No. It is myself I am laughing at."

"Because you have decided to trust me?"

"Something like that, yes."

"If it makes you feel any better," she said, "I have concluded that I trust you, as well, Mr. Gage, and there is no logical reason for it."

He stopped smiling. "I have a certain reputation in that regard."

"Perhaps, but that is not what persuades me to trust you."

He frowned. "Why do you trust me, then?"

She gave him her coolest smile. "Because I can read your energy prints and I am reassured by what I see. But I know you do not accept paranormal explanations so why bother to explain my reasoning?"

"What do you think you see in my prints?"

She widened her eyes. "Are you sure you want a psychical reading from a fraudulent practitioner?"

"I think of you as an accomplished actress, not a fraud."

She laughed. "A very smooth response. I'm impressed."

"It's the truth." He went back to studying the crowd. "What do you see in my prints?"

"Why do you want an answer from an accomplished actress?"

"I have no idea. Call it professional curiosity."

She debated the wisdom of giving him the information he sought and then decided there was no harm in satisfying his curiosity. He was no different from any of her clients in her days at the Academy. People—even those who did not believe in her talent—always wanted to know what she perceived in their prints.

In this case Joshua would no doubt attribute the results to her lively imagination.

Mildly annoyed, she opened her other senses and studied the fierce energy in the prints Joshua had left on the floor. There were more of his prints on the glass case and the dagger.

Currents of dark, iridescent light in a spectrum of colors that had no names radiated in strong, stable patterns from the residue of energy that glowed on everything he had touched.

"Very well, Mr. Gage," she said, "I see power, control and underlying psychical stability."

"What the devil is psychical stability?"

"In my experience, weak or unstable currents in prints usually indicate some degree of mental or emotional strain. We all experience occasional shocks to the nerves. We all go through periods of depression, grief and anxiety, just as we all suffer bouts of physical illness. But certain highly erratic waves that appear to be permanent or very weak are marks of an underlying lack of stability. They are the hallmarks of madness or a total absence of conscience." She paused. "It is the latter sort I find most frightening."

"How often do you encounter such prints?"

"They are more common than one might think." She shuddered. "Believe me when I tell you that I do not go out of my way to look for them."

"What did you see in the prints of the assassin who murdered Fleming?"

"The cold energy of a man who has no conscience. He not only kills without remorse, he takes satisfaction and pride in the act, perhaps even a perverse pleasure."

Joshua clamped both hands around the hilt of the cane and looked thoughtful. "Definitely a professional."

"You never answered my question, Mr. Gage," she said quietly.

"What question?"

"What in heaven's name were you thinking when you elected to retire to the country a year ago?"

"I was thinking that I no longer possessed the attributes and abilities that had once made me a good spy."

"Because of the nature of your injuries?" She glanced at the cane. "Nonsense. I understand that you now face certain physical limitations that would necessitate a different approach to your work, but you still have your analytical abilities." She surveyed the beard that concealed the scar. "And obviously you still possess a talent for concealing your identity."

Joshua did not take his eyes off the crowd. "There was more to my decision to retire than my injuries, although they were a factor."

"I see."

He did not volunteer any more information. He just sat very quietly, watching the elegant guests mill around the hot artifacts.

And that was as much as he was going to tell her, she thought. Whatever had occurred in the course of his last assignment had left psychical wounds as well as his physical injuries.

"Allow me to tell you, Mr. Gage, that the reason you are feeling invigorated isn't because of me," Beatrice said. "It's because you have been summoned to consult on a case of great personal importance. It has given you an objective. You needed a suitable goal to bring you out of retirement, a reason to use your talents once again."

"Invigorated," he repeated, as if speaking to himself. "You may be on to something. I have been feeling more . . . vigorous lately."

There was a little heat in his eyes. The woman in her recognized it at once. She was annoyed by the realization that she was blushing.

"I'm not surprised to hear that, sir," she said, keeping her tone brisk. "It is obvious that, your need for a cane aside, you are possessed of a sound physical constitution and an agile mind. Rusticating in the country for an extended period of time was bound to prove depressing to a man of your nature."

"An interesting theory," he said. He paused a beat before adding, "I will admit it was a very long year. In fact, sitting here with you now, I am acutely aware of just how long this past year has been."

Something in his voice, a hint of sexual innuendo, jolted her senses.

"Yes, well, one way or another, I'm certain we can contrive to muddle through with our partnership because, for now at least, our goals are aligned," she said quickly.

"As long as that is the case we can work together, is that what you are saying?" he asked.

"Precisely. I do understand that your first priority is to catch the person who is blackmailing your sister. If that person proves to be the same individual who hired an assassin to murder Dr. Fleming and kidnap me for unknown reasons, I will be exceedingly grateful to you."

"I do not want your gratitude, Miss Lockwood."

Each word was delivered in ice. Before she could respond, Joshua gripped his cane and pushed himself to his feet.

"Leaving already, Mr. Gage?" she asked. "I do hope it's not on my account."

"This conversation has been quite . . . stimulating, but I think we have exchanged enough pleasantries for one evening, don't you? If we continue along these lines, I fear we will soon be at each other's throats. And while that might be entertaining in some ways, it would no doubt cause a scene that would interfere with the investigation. Good evening, Miss Lockwood."

"Good evening, Mr. Gage."

She could make deliveries in ice, too.

"I will watch for the candle in your window," he said.

He disappeared back into the shadows of the passage from which he had appeared a short time earlier. For a moment longer she thought she could hear the faint tapping of his cane echoing down the hallway. The sound faded into silence.

When she was certain that he was gone she rose and crossed to the display case that he had opened.

Steeling herself, she raised the glass lid and heightened her senses. The hilt of the blade blazed with the intense energy of Joshua's prints.

Gingerly she reached inside to touch the gilded handle.

Small shocks of lightning sparked across her senses.

"Damn," she whispered. "That hurt."

Hastily she withdrew her hand and lowered the lid.

She had known that the ancient blade was saturated with the dark, seething energy of old violence. But the invisible lightning that danced through her just now was not ancient. It had been laid down by Joshua. Her senses found it very stimulating, very masculine and, yes, quite vigorous.

s long as I have told you the reason I am being blackmailed, I may as well tell you what brought me to see
you at the Academy," Hannah said.

The reception in the great hall had ended. The guests were
drifting upstairs to their rooms. Beatrice and Hannah were in Beatrice's bedroom waiting for Sally to finish turning down Hannah's bed.

"Please do not feel compelled to tell me anything that makes
you uncomfortable," Beatrice said. "The source of your anxiety is
none of my affair."

"That may have been the case at the time, but things have
changed," Hannah said. "You are now involved with Josh and it is
plain to see that your relationship with him is not a simple matter
of business."

"That's not true," Beatrice said quickly.

"I know Josh," Hannah said. Her brows rose. "It is clear to me that he is fascinated by you. Now that I have met you, I understand why."

"No, really, you are mistaken."

"I told you, I know my brother," Hannah said. "I love him, but he is part of the reason why I cannot find any peace of mind these days."

"There is no need to confide in me."

"I must talk to someone. You now know more of my family's secrets than anyone else outside the family. I did everything I could to protect Josh when he was young. In the end I failed. I lost him to the wildness that runs in the men of my side of the family. It was that streak of recklessness that made it so easy for that dreadful man to turn Josh into his own personal weapon."

"What, exactly, did Victor Hazelton do to your brother?" Beatrice asked.

Hannah went to the window and stood looking out over the night-darkened gardens. "When Josh was in his late teens it became clear that he had inherited the wild blood that runs through the male line of our family."

"Wild blood?"

"I swear, it's like a curse," Hannah said. She took a hankie out of her pocket and dabbed at her eyes. "It draws them to danger and risk. The wild streak killed my father. A year ago it nearly got Josh killed. And now my son, Nelson, is showing every indication that he has inherited the same taste for violent excitement."

"I understand. You fear this wild blood will be the death of your only child." Beatrice went to stand with Hannah at the window. "No wonder you were in such a state of anxiety when you consulted with me."

"Nelson tries to protect me from the truth." Hannah sniffed into the hankie. "He moved out of the house and into his own lodgings a few months ago."

"Many young men do that."

"I know. He never tells me what he is doing and he visits me faithfully. But I recognize the same pattern in him that I saw in Josh when he was the same age."

"Men that age yearn to experience the world."

"Trust me, I am well aware that Nelson does not want his mother hovering. I've tried not to fuss." Hannah blinked away a few tears. "But my intuition tells me that he is doing what Josh did at that age. At night he is going out into the worst neighborhoods looking for excitement. He is risking his neck in the gaming halls. Hanging out with a bad crowd."

"In other words, he is looking for trouble."

"And sooner or later, he will find it, just as Josh did. In his case, trouble came in the shape of Victor Hazelton."

"Mr. Smith."

"Yes," Hannah said.

"I see." Beatrice hesitated. "Perhaps you could ask Josh to speak with Nelson? It might be easier for a mature man to nudge a younger man in the right direction."

Hannah's fingers clenched around the hankie. "The last thing I want is for Josh to lead Nelson down the same dark path that Hazelton set my brother on all those years ago."

"I understand," Beatrice said. "But in this situation—"

She broke off because Sally had opened the connecting door.

"I apologize for interrupting, ma'am," she said to Hannah. "But I found this envelope on your pillow when I turned down the bed. It's addressed to you."

Hannah went very still. She looked at Beatrice.

"I'll turn down the lamps and light a candle," Beatrice said.

Seventeen

Beatrice left a worried Hannah in her bedroom and descended the main staircase. She wore her plain day dress and a pair of soft-soled leather slippers in an attempt to make as little noise as possible. The big house had finally fallen silent a short time ago. Lord Alverstoke kept early hours in the country and his guests were obliged to do the same. Not that the elegant, bored people who had accepted his invitation were bothered. They had other plans for the evening.

Beatrice was well aware that the hush was deceptive. In her role as a paid companion she had attended enough house parties to know that the main attraction of such affairs was not the fresh air and scenic landscapes of the countryside. Nor were many of Alverstoke's guests truly interested in his collection of Egyptian antiquities. They could view any number of relics at the British Museum were they so inclined.

Country-house parties were popular for one reason and one

reason only: They provided ideal opportunities to conduct illicit trysts. Sprawling Alverstoke Hall, with its many bedrooms, ante-chambers, storage rooms, gardens and other secluded locations, was perfect for discreet liaisons. She had no doubt but that the many staircases scattered throughout the mansion were already seeing a steady stream of traffic as lovers and seducers made their way between floors.

The house was not completely dark. The servants, obviously aware that many of the guests were interested in matters other than antiquities, had thoughtfully left several wall sconces burn-ing. But with the lamps turned down and the mansion draped in relative silence, she was more aware of the eerie energy of the artifacts seething in the atmosphere. Paranormal currents always seemed stronger and more easily detectable at night.

She reached the ground floor and paused briefly to get her bearings. The surroundings appeared different—more mysterious and somehow more ominous—now that they were cloaked in shadows.

The hot energy of the artifacts was disorienting but there was another problem as well. The original core structure of the man-sion was very old. Over time various occupants had remodeled sec-tions, built entire new wings, and added floors. In addition structural modifications had been made to the existing house in order to install modern amenities such as gas lighting and proper plumbing. The result was that Alverstoke Hall was a maze of oddly connected passages, hallways and staircases.

Earlier she had taken care to note the route to the library, but she was alarmed to realize that things looked so different now that the lamps had been turned down.

After a moment's close reflection she started forward. She shuddered when she passed the massive, vault-like doors that guarded the great hall. The chamber that held Alverstoke's most valuable antiquities had been locked for the night following the grand reception. Rumor had it Alverstoke was very proud of his security measures. But no locks could stop the dark energy that seeped out from under the lower edges of the heavy doors.

She breathed a sigh of relief when she located the long, moon-lit gallery where she had been sitting earlier when Joshua had found her. Now she had her bearings. The library was at the far end of the passage.

The gallery was cloaked in shadows but she saw the wobbly flame of a candle in the distance. As she watched, it moved toward her in an unsteady manner, as though the person carrying the candlestick walked with a limp.

Relieved, she hurried toward him.

A solid thud, followed by a sharp gasp, warned her that she had made a mistake. The light of the flame flared wildly on the stone walls.

"Bloody hell," a man rasped, his voice slurred by drink. "Damned artifacts."

Definitely not Joshua, Beatrice thought.

She halted and looked around, searching for a convenient staircase or room she could dart into. But there was no time. The man who had just run afoul of one of the relics was almost upon her. In the glow of the fluttering candle his face was cast in de-monic chiaroscuro.

When he spotted her his anger immediately transmuted into lecherous anticipation.

"Well, well, now what have we here?" he said. "You must be one of the maids. Off to meet a lover, eh?"

"You have made a very grave mistake, sir," she said coldly. "I'll thank you to step aside."

"You're no maid, not with that accent. Not a governess, either. There aren't any children here at Alverstoke Hall. You must be some lady's companion."

"You are correct, sir, and as it happens I am on a very important errand for my employer. She will not be pleased if I am delayed."

"Carrying a note to her paramour, are you?" He chuckled. "You have my deepest sympathies. Yours is a hard lot, is it not? You are doomed to convey messages between lovers but never to have one of your own."

"I will ask you once again to step aside, sir."

He held the candle higher and examined her with a critical air.

"You are no beauty," he announced. "No figure to speak of and red hair is always off-putting. But I've tumbled worse in Covent Gardens." He grinned. "Fortune has smiled upon you tonight. My plans for the evening have changed. The bitch I was to meet opened her door to another man. So, as you are convenient and I am not feeling overly selective at the moment, let's get on with the business."

"Sorry, not interested."

Aware that flight would likely invite pursuit, she moved forward decisively, meaning to step around him. The bold tactic failed. He reached out and grabbed her arm.

"You bloody well will be interested by the time I've finished with you," he snarled. "Who do you think you are to refuse your betters? A woman like you ought to be down on her knees thanking me for sparing a few minutes of my time for you. Now that I consider the matter, on your knees is where we'll start. If you show any talent with your mouth I might be persuaded to give you a few other lessons in the art."

He set the candle on a nearby table and used his grip on her arm to force her to her knees. With his other hand, he opened his trousers.

She reached for the vial attached to her chatelaine. "Let me go."

"What's that? Your smelling salts? I trust you're not about to faint on me. I'm going to give you a taste of the finest cock in London. You'll remember this night for the rest of your life, I promise you."

"So will you the next time you accost another woman," she said.

She twitched out from under his restraining hand, leaped to her feet and removed the stopper of the vial of smelling salts. She splashed some of the liquid contents straight into his face.

The shock of the pepper-based brew caused her assailant to stop breathing for a moment. He stared at her in horror. And then he squeezed his eyes shut against the burning sensation.

Gasping for air, he released her to claw at his throat.

"What have you done, you crazy whore?" he wheezed.

"Nothing permanent." She moved back another few steps. "I trust you will spend the next few minutes contemplating the fact that not every woman you meet is helpless to resist your charms."

"You don't know who you're dealing with, you damned witch." He was trying to shout but the pepper concoction still had a grip on his throat. The words were scratchy and barely audible. "I'm Covington. I'll see that you're arrested."

"For tossing smelling salts into your face? I doubt that will be enough to get me arrested."

"These aren't smelling salts."

"No one will ever know otherwise," she assured him. "The damage is not permanent."

"I'll see that your employer turns you off without a character." He sank to his knees. "You're too old to make your living on the streets. You'll end your days in the workhouse, damn you."

A faint, steady tapping sound came from the entrance of a doorway at the end of the hall. A dark shadow emerged. In the moonlight Beatrice could see that Joshua was no longer wearing his disguise. He paused to extinguish the candle.

"There you are, my dear," Joshua said. "I wondered what had delayed you. I would offer to be of assistance but, as usual, you seem to have the situation well in hand."

"Who is that? Who's there?" Covington turned toward the sound of Joshua's voice but tears were streaming down his face. It was obvious that he could not make out Joshua clearly. "You must help me, sir. I have been attacked by this woman, poisoned, I think."

"He'll live," Beatrice assured Joshua. "But it will take a while before the effects of my smelling salts wear off."

"Then there's no point wasting any more time standing around out here," Joshua said. "You and I have other things to discuss."

"Quite right," Beatrice said.

She moved quickly around Covington and joined Joshua.

"Help," Covington squeaked. "This creature has murdered me. *Help.*"

"You heard the lady," Joshua said. "You will live. I'm not convinced that is the most desirable outcome, but it will probably cause less fuss than the alternative. Rest assured, however, that if you offend her again in any manner whatsoever, you will find yourself dealing with the other possible ending."

"Who the devil are you and why are you bothering with this little whore? She's just someone's paid companion."

"Enough," Joshua said, his voice lethally soft. "You were warned."

Bracing himself on his cane, he leaned down and gripped the back of Covington's neck with one powerful hand. Covington went limp and collapsed, unconscious, to the floor.

"Oh, dear," Beatrice said. "I do hope you didn't kill him. As much as I appreciate the gesture, it would create no end of trouble."

"Give me some credit, Miss Lockwood. I'm never sloppy when it comes to my work. Rest assured he'll wake up in a few minutes. With luck he won't remember you, but if he does and if he becomes a problem, I will find a more permanent solution."

"Very well, then."

"Come, let's not waste any more time. You are here because you have news for me. We have the library to ourselves."

When his powerful hand wrapped around her arm she got the small, thrilling shock across all of her senses. She would always know his touch. No matter what the future held, she would remember these whispers of deep, stirring awareness for the rest of her life. *I will never forget this man.*

Joshua's fingers tightened for an instant. She sensed that he, too, experienced some sensation when they were in direct physical contact. She wondered how he interpreted the flashes of connection. He would have some logical explanation, she thought, amused, possibly something involving static electricity.

He guided her along the gallery and through a doorway. She moved ahead of him into a room lit by moonlight. She inhaled the smell of leather-bound books and old, frequently polished furniture.

Joshua released her arm with, it seemed to her, reluctance. He closed and locked the door. When he turned back to face her she sensed the energy in the atmosphere. For the first time she realized that he was coldly furious.

"Did that bastard hurt you in any way?" he asked.

"No, really, I'm fine. It certainly is not the first time I've had to deal with a drunk, lecherous man. Encounters like tonight are one of the hazards of my work. That is why all of the Flint and Marsh agents now carry Mrs. Marsh's new special smelling salts."

"I don't like the idea that you are forced to come into contact with men like Covington on a frequent basis."

"Generally speaking, the Covingtons of this world can be avoided," she assured him.

"That's not the point."

"What is the point?" she asked, going rather blank.

"You should not be placed in situations that require you to defend yourself."

She raised her chin. "It's how I make my living, Mr. Gage.

And given what you used to do for a living, I do not think that you are in a position to criticize."

"Damn it to hell." He spoke with great depth of feeling. Then he exhaled heavily. "I will allow you that point. What the devil is in your vinaigrette bottle? It appeared to be quite effective."

"Mrs. Marsh recently created the concoction in her laboratory. She gave each of the agents a vial filled with the stuff. I believe the formula is based on a distillation of some extraordinarily hot peppers."

"I have long admired Mrs. Marsh's talent as a chemist," Joshua said.

"She was inspired to brew the pepper vinaigrette after another employee of the firm, a close friend of mine named Evangeline Ames, was very nearly murdered. Following the Crystal Gardens affair, Mrs. Flint and Mrs. Marsh concluded that all of their agents should carry some means of self-defense that was a bit more discreet than a gun."

"Firearms have their uses but they frequently cause far more problems than they solve," Joshua said. "And they are not what anyone would call discreet. The police tend to take notice when someone gets shot."

"Discretion is the primary reason our clients come to us," Beatrice said, not bothering to conceal her pride. "Flint and Marsh agents go into some of the wealthiest and most exclusive homes. Our goal is to be as inconspicuous as possible."

"That is the goal of any good investigator," Joshua said.

"Since we're on the subject of self-defense, I would be very interested to learn that little trick that you used on Euston and Covington."

"Please do not take this as an insult, but it is not a very useful technique for a lady. It requires considerable strength, not to mention a great deal of training and practice."

"Oh, I see."

"You need not sound so disappointed," he said. He was amused. "You are very well armed as it is. Let us get on with the matter at hand. I assume you signaled me with the candle because you have had word from the blackmailer?"

"Yes." Beatrice took the note out of her pocket and handed it to him. "When your sister and I went upstairs to retire for the evening we found this note. It was on Hannah's pillow in an envelope that was addressed to her. A man's handwriting, I'm sure of it."

Joshua turned up a lamp and read the note aloud.

The great hall. Three o'clock, precisely. The doors will be unlocked. Send the paid companion with the money. If she is seen, no one will take any notice. You, however, might attract unwanted attention. Tell the companion to leave the offering inside the stone box at the foot of the sarcophagus. If these instructions are not followed exactly, the first of many revelations concerning the events of the night of January 9 three years ago will be sent to the press.

Joshua looked up from the note. In the glare of the lamp Beatrice could see that he was very focused. "He specifies that you must deliver the blackmail payment."

"His logic is clear. If I am seen coming and going in the halls tonight no one will ask questions. But if Hannah is spotted outside her bedroom there will be gossip. The blackmailer does not want anyone to ask questions."

"The great hall holds the most valuable artifacts in Alverstoke's collection. It's well secured at night with the most modern of locks," Joshua noted.

"How do you know that the lock is modern?" she asked.

"I watched Alverstoke and his butler secure the chamber for the night."

"Have you been prowling through the house tonight, sir?"

"As my former employer used to say, *Know the terrain and you will be able to predict your opponent's strategy.*"

"Ah, yes, the mysterious Mr. Smith, otherwise known as Victor Hazelton?"

Josh's brows rose. "Hannah certainly did confide in you."

"Your Mr. Smith may have a few things in common with my former employer. Roland was fond of saying, *Know your audience but make sure your audience does not know you. Mystery is everything onstage.*"

"Excellent advice," Joshua said gravely.

"Yes, well, obviously whoever sent that note to Hannah has access to the key to that great hall." A jolting thought made Beatrice catch her breath. "Do you think that Lord Alverstoke is a party to this extortion business?"

"No," Joshua said. He spoke with cool confidence. "I thought I made it clear, Alverstoke's temperament and his eccentricities are such that it is impossible to imagine him as a blackmailer. In any event, he commands a fortune. He has no need to take the risk of extorting money from others. I'm quite certain that he is an unwitting pawn in this affair."

"How difficult would it be for someone to steal the key to the great hall?" Beatrice asked.

"Based on what I observed tonight, it would be a relatively simple business. But the thief would have to have some knowledge of the household and its routines." Joshua paused in thought. "There is an alternative, of course. He could try to bribe one of the servants. Either way, the theft of the key is the most easily explained aspect of this case."

"The thing is, why go to the trouble of using the great hall as the location for the blackmail payment in the first place?" Beatrice tapped one finger on a table, thinking. "There are a thousand nooks and crannies here at Alverstoke Hall, not to mention all sorts of hidden places in the gardens. Why not arrange for the payment to be left in a less conspicuous, more accessible location, one that does not necessitate taking the risk of stealing a key?"

"A very good question, Miss Lockwood. The answer is obvious."

She frowned. "It is?"

"The great hall is a room that the blackmailer feels he can control. It is certainly the one place where no one is likely to intrude this evening because it has been secured for the night."

"Yes, of course," Beatrice said. Admiration flashed through her. "Guests are even now skulking about the mansion searching for discreet locations for romantic trysts. But no one will bother to try the antiquities chamber because everyone is aware that it is always locked. That is a brilliant observation, sir. You really are quite good at this sort of thing."

"I try."

She ignored the dry humor in his tone. "Besides, what woman

could possibly feel romantically inclined when she was surrounded by so much dark tomb and temple energy?"

"Some might find the surroundings . . . exotic." Joshua spoke as if he was giving the issue close consideration. "An inspiration to the imagination."

She wrinkled her nose. "Now you are teasing me, sir."

"My apologies. Couldn't resist."

"You have made your disdain for the paranormal plain," she said. "Tell me, have you never experienced anything that was beyond explanation, Mr. Gage?"

"Frequently. But the fact that I could not explain things at the time does not mean that the events were of a paranormal nature. Merely that science does not yet have all the answers."

"Yet you survived in a very dangerous business for several years," she said. "That leads me to conclude that your intuition is quite acute, perhaps even psychical in nature."

"Trusting my so-called intuition is why I am now forced to walk with a cane and why small children stare at my face on the street," Joshua said.

"Forgive me," she said, mortified. "I did not mean to bring up the subject of your past, not tonight."

"I would appreciate it if you did not bring up the subject on any other night, as well," he said.

"I understand, it is a very difficult topic for you." She was feeling more miserable by the moment. "About our plan tonight. I assume you will be watching the great hall after I leave to see who enters the chamber to collect the payment?"

Joshua smiled. "You sound as if you have had some experience with extortion investigations."

"As a matter of fact, yes, I have. In the course of my work with Flint and Marsh, I have had some clients who were being blackmailed. It is actually a rather common problem in the circles in which I operate. Everyone has secrets. Wealthy people with secrets are always vulnerable to extortionists."

"I never considered that you might have investigated something as serious as a case of blackmail."

"For pity's sake, sir, what do you think I *do* as a Flint and Marsh agent?"

"I meant no offense."

"Yet you offend so well."

"My apologies." He glanced at the tall clock in the corner. "In answer to your question, yes, I will be watching the entrance to the great hall tonight. I will be there when you go inside. After you leave, I will wait for the blackmailer to arrive."

She cleared her throat. "May I ask what, exactly, you plan to do with him when you catch him?"

"I intend to have an informative conversation."

And that was all she was going to get on that subject, she decided.

"I see," she said.

"I will escort you back to the floor where your room is located."

"I came down the main staircase because I thought the servants' stairs would be rather crowded tonight."

"A good plan, but the main staircase is a bit too public for my liking," Joshua said. "It would not do for us to be seen together going up to the bedroom floor. We will use another set of steps that I discovered earlier when I explored the house. This mansion is riddled with old stairwells. The one I found appears to have been closed up for years."

He turned down the lamp, opened the door and surveyed the shadowy gallery. Satisfied, he stood back to allow her to move past him into the hall.

"Don't dawdle, Miss Lockwood," he said behind her.

"Wouldn't think of it, Mr. Gage."

She caught up the folds of her skirts and went briskly along the gallery pretending not to hear the muffled thud of his cane on the carpet behind her.

She walked more quickly, almost trotting now. He had ordered her not to tarry. If he chose to follow her and could not keep up, that was his problem, she thought. Really, the man was insufferable.

She was relieved to see that Covington was no longer lying unconscious on the floor of the gallery.

"I told you he would wake up in a few minutes," Joshua said in low tones. "Don't worry, I doubt he will remember anything of what happened here."

"I hope not."

"If he tries to make trouble I will ensure that he does, indeed, forget everything that occurred between the two of you."

The steel in the words made Beatrice swallow hard.

"Oh," she said. "Thank you."

"You're welcome. By the way, the door to the staircase I mentioned a moment ago is ahead on the right, just inside that intersecting hallway."

She stopped and peered into the deeper shadows of the adjoining hallway.

"I don't see the entrance to the hallway," she said.

He caught up with her and took her arm. She took a sharp breath.

"I'll show you," he said.

"Really, there is no need to escort me all the way to my room," she said.

"I will not go that far. I want to make sure you are not accosted again."

"This is ridiculous," she said. "I can take care of myself, Mr. Gage."

She was about to continue with a stern lecture but abruptly there was a shift in the atmosphere. She glanced at him and saw that he was looking past her toward the far end of the gallery.

"What is it?" she asked.

Then she saw the couple coming toward them along the gallery. A woman's seductive laugh was followed by a masculine voice that was blurred with drink.

"Come, my dear. Earlier this evening I noticed a number of empty rooms in the old wing of the house. I think we can find the privacy we seek there."

"I insist upon a bed," the woman declared, giggling. "I am not about to let you have your wicked way with me out in the gardens as you did last time. It was most uncomfortable to say nothing of my ruined gown."

"I'm sure we will find suitable accommodations."

The couple was closer now. Beatrice suppressed a frustrated groan. It was only a matter of time before the two people noticed that they were not alone in the gallery.

"There is no help for it," she whispered. "We shall have to brazen it out. We must pretend to be another couple seeking a private location for a tryst."

"An excellent plan," Joshua said. "Why didn't I think of that?"

The dryness of the words made her realize that he had already conceived a similar strategy. Before she could inform him that she found his attitude quite arrogant, he drew her into the dense shadows of a nearby alcove. A pedestal displaying a small quartz sphinx occupied the center of the space.

Her senses heightened intuitively. She had time enough to register the faint, ultralight shadows emanating from the sphinx and then she was in Joshua's arms. He propped his cane against the pedestal and positioned himself so that his broad shoulders were turned toward the oncoming couple, thereby concealing her face.

He covered her mouth with his own.

Lightning danced across her senses. In that moment she knew that nothing would ever be the same.

Eighteen

The blackmailer unlocked the door of the great hall. The key rattled in the lock. He did not understand why his hand was shaking but there was no getting around it, he was very nervous tonight; far more anxious than he had anticipated. Then again, a large amount of money was at stake, more money than he had ever seen in his entire life.

He had come a long way, he thought proudly. From his early days as a footman stealing small valuables from his wealthy employers and a career as a small-time con artist, he had always managed to scrape by making a modest living. But now he was about to vault into the highest ranks of successful businessmen. Tonight was only the beginning. From now on he would live a very different life—a life of luxury—and all of it financed by those in the upper classes, who would pay any price to keep their secrets.

He finally got the door open and slipped into the thick darkness that cloaked the chamber full of artifacts. The uneasy feeling that had been rattling his nerves all evening intensified into a far more ominous sensation. For a few beats of his heart he had trouble catching his breath.

It was the atmosphere of the place, he told himself. Some of the relics around him had been removed from tombs, after all—ancient tombs, but tombs nonetheless. The dread that gripped him was not unlike the crawling anxiety that he got when he walked through a cemetery late at night.

A man had to guard against the effects of his own imagination.

He got the door closed and fumbled around in the absolute night until he managed to light the shielded lantern. He breathed a little easier when the yellow glare consumed some of the darkness in the immediate vicinity. Then he saw the hellish shadows that moved among the artifacts and a shudder went through him all the way to his bones. It was frighteningly easy to imagine that he was surrounded by the gods and demons of the Egyptian underworld.

He found himself standing next to a granite statue that had the body of a man and the head of a falcon. In the lantern light the eyes of the god seemed to glitter with life.

He moved hastily away from the falcon-headed figure and hurried toward the large stone platform that held the massive sarcophagus and the stone box. The lantern wobbled in his hand. He was shaking harder than ever. The faint scent of incense drifted in the chamber.

Get ahold of yourself, man. Nothing to be alarmed about in this room. Just a collection of old relics that belong in a proper museum.

But his fear grew with each step. The monstrous figures around him seemed to shift in the shadows. Earlier in the evening he had heard talk of curses. Some of the guests had laughed at the notion. So had he at the time. But now he wondered.

Don't think about curses and tombs. Think about the money.

The plan was simple. He would conceal himself among the clutter of artifacts and wait for Hannah Trafford's companion to deliver the payment. She had been instructed to leave it inside the stone box that sat at the foot of the sarcophagus. As soon as she left the chamber he would take the money and disappear.

He saw the box at the foot of the sarcophagus. The flaring light of the lamp illuminated the figure of a cat surrounded by a hunting scene carved into the quartz. He'd overheard someone say that the box was actually a miniature sarcophagus designed to hold the mummified body of a cat, but he did not believe that. He could not imagine anyone going to all that trouble just to bury a cat.

Not that he cared about the original purpose of the box. All that mattered tonight was the money that would be placed inside.

As soon as he had collected the payment he would return to his room downstairs. Tomorrow he would disappear. No one would take any notice of him. No one ever did. His disguise was perfect. He was just one more servant among the many who had accompanied their employers to the country-house party for the weekend.

The lantern light splashed across the great sarcophagus as he went past. He averted his eyes and tried not to think about the nonsensical legends and stories with which Lord Alverstoke had regaled his guests that evening. But it was difficult to put aside the fantastical images that his lordship had conjured when he had enthusiastically described the embalming practices of the ancient Egyptians. *". . . Brain and other vital organs removed with special tools, bodies packed in natron to dry, magical spells chanted . . ."*

He must stop thinking about death and focus on his future as a wealthy man.

He saw a massive stone altar. It would make an ideal hiding place. From that vantage point he could watch Trafford's companion deliver the blackmail money without being seen.

The scent of incense was growing stronger now. The faint smoke was making him dizzy. For the first time he wondered about the source. One of the servants must have indulged in a cigarette before locking up for the night.

But if that was the case, why was the incense growing stronger?

It dawned on him that he might not be alone in the chamber. A cold chill slithered through him. He held the lantern aloft, searching the shadows.

"Who's there?" he said, trying to sound authoritative, like the valet he was impersonating. "Come out, whoever you are. No one is allowed in this room at this time of night."

Someone or something stirred in the deep shadows between two of the tall statues. A figure moved toward him. In the yellow glare of the lantern he saw with horror that one of the gods had come to life. It had the body of a man and the head of a jackal.

The blackmailer remembered Alverstoke's description of the god associated with death and embalming. *Anubis.*

"No." The blackmailer struggled for breath. The single word came out as a hoarse whisper.

Anubis raised a dagger.

"Put the lantern on the altar," Anubis ordered.

The god spoke with a thick Russian accent.

"You," the blackmailer whispered.

"The lantern."

Brass clanged on granite when the blackmailer set the lantern on top of the altar.

"What's this all about?" he demanded. "Why are you wearing that ridiculous mask?"

"That is none of your concern."

"See here, we had an arrangement."

"Your services are no longer required."

The blackmailer floundered backward and came up hard against the granite altar. He tried to scream but fear tightened a fist around his lungs.

He saw the dagger flash in the hellish glare, felt the cold shock when it struck, and then he knew no more.

Nineteen

The electrifying shock of the embrace made Beatrice go very still. She thought she had grown accustomed to the little jolts of intimate awareness that sparked through her every time Joshua touched her. But she was wholly unprepared for the breathtaking thrill of his kiss.

Frantically she reminded herself that this was not the first time she had been kissed. Furthermore, this was a staged kiss, done for the sake of deceiving the couple in the hall. It was not a real kiss.

But it felt far more real than the kisses she had enjoyed with Gerald before he had run off with the séance practitioner. At the time she had been rather disappointed with kissing in general and had wondered if perhaps passion was highly overrated. Now, tonight, she understood that what she had known with Gerald did not amount to anything more than a mild flirtation.

Joshua's kiss, on the other hand, was the gateway to the fiery passion one read about in the sensation novels that her friend Evangeline wrote. This was the kind of searing excitement that could overwhelm the senses and common sense. A passion like this could tempt a woman to take risks.

Joshua's mouth was hot and hungry on hers, as if he was demanding—*needing*—a response. His embrace was fierce and devastatingly powerful and yet she did not feel threatened. Instead she reveled in his strength. She was crushed against him—she could scarcely catch her breath—but the sensation was intoxicating. There was an unfamiliar heat in the atmosphere. Her senses were stirring in ways that she had never known.

She forgot about the approaching couple and threw her arms around Joshua's neck, allowing herself to sink into him. He groaned and wrenched his mouth away from hers with an effort.

"You smell so good," he rasped against the skin of her throat. "I could get drunk on your scent. I want to get drunk on it."

Her pulse was racing and not because of the danger of discovery. She was certain that Joshua was no longer faking the kiss.

"Joshua," she whispered.

And then the couple was upon them. Beatrice heard the woman's muffled laughter. The man snorted lewdly.

"Looks like those two couldn't wait long enough to find a bed," he said.

"Don't get any ideas," the woman warned sharply. "I'm certainly not going to do it in a doorway like a common whore."

Joshua went abruptly still, every muscle rigid. An icy-cold sensation permeated the atmosphere. Beatrice knew that he was on the verge of turning to confront the couple. She clamped her fingers around his shoulders.

"Darling," she said, speaking in what she hoped were sultry tones. *"Don't stop."*

She could feel Joshua fighting to rein in the wave of icy anger.

"Please," she said.

The man laughed. The woman snickered. They both hurried off down the gallery.

Beatrice was once again alone with Joshua.

"My apologies," he said stiffly. "I did not mean to subject you to such insults."

She realized that the roughness of the embrace had dislodged a few tendrils of her hair. She took a deep, steadying breath and started to put herself to rights.

"I make my living as a private inquiry agent who poses as a paid companion," she said, trying to catch her breath. "Before that, I pursued a career as a paranormal practitioner for a certain individual who was evidently engaged in blackmail. I assure you, it takes more than a few snide comments from my betters to insult me."

"They aren't your betters."

She paused in the act of adjusting her hair. "What?"

"You are so much better than they are," he said. He touched her cheek. "Better in spirit, better in character, better in every way imaginable. You are . . . amazing, Beatrice."

Stunned, she could only stare at him, aware that her mouth was open.

"Uh," she said. And stopped. She could not think of anything else to say.

He used the edge of his hand to gently close her mouth. And then he kissed her again, a light, glancing kiss that was at once affectionate, proprietary and somehow filled with the promise of more to come.

But before she could collect her scattered senses he broke off the embrace, wrapped a hand around her arm and drew her into the adjoining corridor.

He opened a door. The dim light from the gallery sconces splashed over the worn stone steps of an old spiral staircase.

"It leads to the floor where your bedroom is located," Joshua said. "Stay close to the wall. The steps are quite narrow at the outer edge and there is no railing."

She surveyed the staircase, her heart sinking. Once the hall door was closed they would be locked in darkness. Out of nowhere, memories of her terrifying escape from Fleming's office slammed through her. But at least on that occasion she'd had the benefit of a lantern. She tried to steel herself but she knew she could not face the absolute darkness of the stairwell, even knowing that Joshua was with her.

"I'm sorry, I cannot climb that staircase without a light," she said.

"That did occur to me."

He closed the hall door, cutting off the faint illumination from the gas lamps. When complete night descended, Beatrice felt the panic start to well up inside her. She shivered. Her breath caught in her throat. Tentacles of fear unfurled. She knew her reaction was illogical. She was in no immediate danger. But that awareness did nothing to calm her nerves.

"Joshua, I regret to say that I cannot stay in this place much longer," she whispered. "I appreciate your high opinion of my spirit but the truth is I have a certain weakness of the nerves when it comes to dark, enclosed places."

"That's not a weakness, it's common sense. Dark, enclosed places can be dangerous."

She heard a rasping noise. A bright spark flashed and burned steadily, driving back the tide of night. Joshua had struck a light.

"Will this do?" he asked quietly. "It will last for a couple of minutes, long enough for us to get upstairs."

She took a deep breath. "Thank you."

She grabbed fistfuls of her skirts and started up the steps, careful to keep to the widest section of each stone tread. She put one hand on the wall to steady herself. Joshua followed, his cane thudding heavily on each step.

When they reached the upper floor Beatrice was relieved to see a small landing and a thin, pale line of light beneath a door.

"It opens into a storage room that, in turn, opens onto the hall," Joshua said.

He put out the light and opened the door. Beatrice moved into a small space. At the far end of the room she saw another, brighter, strip of light beneath the hall door. Her nerves steadied. The small ordeal was over.

Joshua listened at the hall door for a few seconds. "There is no one nearby. You should be able to make it to your room without being seen. But if anyone does appear, make it plain that you were on an errand for your employer. No one will question that story."

"I assure you, I am quite capable of inventing my own cover stories," she said coolly.

"Right. Sorry. I have been out of the field for some time now.

I am not accustomed to working with other professional investigators."

She suspected he was smiling but as it was too dark to be certain, she decided to ignore him.

He opened the door partway and surveyed the hall.

"All clear," he said.

She started past him and then paused, remembering. "I almost forgot. I brought this for you."

She removed the small bottle from her pocket and handed it to him. When he took it from her his fingers brushed hers and she got another tingle of awareness. The little jolts of intimacy were getting stronger, she thought.

"What is it?" he asked.

"A pain tonic. Mrs. Marsh brews it in her laboratory. I always travel with a bottle of the stuff. I thought you might want to try some. I believe you will find it helpful for your leg pain."

"Thank you," he said, excruciatingly polite but not the least appreciative. He pressed the small vial back into her hand. "Given what I know of Mrs. Marsh's talent for chemistry, I suspect it works well. But I never use medications derived from the poppy. They interfere with my thinking."

Beatrice smiled in the shadows. "I'm not the least bit surprised that you would refuse a tonic based on an opiate."

"You know me so well after our short acquaintance?"

"Naturally you would not want to take anything that might cloud your judgment or your talent."

"My talent?" The edge was back in his tone.

"Forgive me," she said smoothly. "I do not refer to a paranormal talent, of course. I meant your acute powers of observation and logic. Trust me, I understand your fear of the opiates. Rest assured there is nothing of the poppy in this tonic. Mrs. Marsh concocts it using salicylic derived from the willow and other plants. It's her own special formula. Very good for fever and certain kinds of pain. She regularly treats her own rheumatism with the stuff. My friends and I have all taken a dose or two from time to time for the headache."

"I do not like to take any kind of medicine."

"Is that so? Are you going to stand there and tell me that you have never downed a quantity of brandy or whiskey late at night when the pain in your leg flares up?"

There was a short pause.

"I will allow you that point," he said. "But that is different."

"Are you always so stubborn and hardheaded, Mr. Gage? Or is it something about dealing with me that brings out your illogical side?"

"Something about dealing with you, I believe."

In the darkness she could not tell if he was teasing her again. She decided she was not in the mood to find out.

"Never mind," she said. "You may dose yourself with Mrs. Marsh's formula or not, as you please. I am not going to waste any more time arguing with you. If you will step aside, I shall return to my room."

"Before you go," he said very softly, "there is one thing I would like you to know."

"What is that?"

"Downstairs in the hall when we kissed a few minutes ago, I was not aware of any pain at all. In fact, I found our embrace to be remarkably therapeutic."

"If that comment was meant to be humorous, it fails the test."

"I am serious."

He sounded serious, she thought. She got the impression that he was trying to work out the logic behind the observation and not making much progress.

"Yes, well, we were at risk of discovery," she said stiffly. "Excitement of that sort can cause one to temporarily ignore an otherwise nagging pain. I'm sure you're aware of that, given your former career."

"I know all about the numbing effect that violent excitement has on the body," he shot back impatiently. "But that couple in the hall hardly posed a serious risk. No, Miss Lockwood, I am convinced that it was your kiss that made me forget the discomfort in my leg."

She cleared her throat. "As you said, you recently spent a very long year in the country. I must go now. We are in the middle of an investigation, if you will recall, and I have a blackmail payment to deliver."

He opened the door wider and stood aside. She swept past him and hurried down the hall to her room. She knew that he watched her until she was safely inside.

Twenty

Joshua waited until the door of Beatrice's bedroom closed and then he made his way back down the old staircase to the ground floor. He winced at every step. Going down a flight of stairs was always more painful than climbing them in the first place. Worse yet, he did not have Beatrice to distract him now.

At the bottom of the staircase he stopped and opened the door. There was no one about in the hall. The house was quieter now. Traffic would pick up again just before dawn. There was nothing more predictable than the nightly routine of a country-house party.

A short time later he let himself into a small chamber that looked as if it had once been a monk's cell. The little room was empty save for two old steamer trunks that someone had stored there years ago and evidently forgotten. With the door partially cracked he had a clear view of the heavy doors that guarded the great hall at the far end of the gallery.

He sat down on one of the trunks and took the small medicine bottle out of his pocket. For a moment he examined it in the narrow band of light that seeped through the doorway.

He was not sure how he felt about the tonic or the fact that Beatrice had given it to him. Certainly part of him was irritated. He did not like it that Beatrice was aware of his pain. Another part of him was oddly touched by the gift.

But it meant that even though she had been acquainted with him for only a few days, she knew him well enough to be able to discern those times when the leg plagued him. That alone was sufficient evidence that he was not doing a proper job of concealing his emotions.

It was the heated embrace in the hallway, however, that ought to alarm him the most. He had not intended for the kiss to get out of hand. It was to have been a charade, nothing more. But the instant he had crushed her against him, inhaled her scent and felt the sweet, soft, gently rounded form of her body beneath the fabric of the gown, something inside him had threatened to break free.

He had spent much of his life learning to control the powerful tides that threatened to wreak havoc on his carefully ordered world. The rigorous physical and mental training he had practiced for years had taught him to channel the fire inside. He had learned the hard way that when he violated his own rules, bad things happened.

A year ago he had slipped the bonds of logic in the course of an investigation and he was still paying for it. He still woke up in a cold sweat, wondering how he could have been so wrong about Clement Lancing.

The answer was always waiting for him. He had allowed himself to be ruled by his emotions, not logic.

Tonight, downstairs in the shadowed hallway, he should have been concentrating on the investigation. Instead he had been pulled into the sensual fire of Beatrice's kiss.

In that moment he would have been willing to consign his powers of self-mastery to hell if it meant that he could have Beatrice for even an hour in exchange.

After all, what good had all of his training and focused meditation done? In the end, when it had mattered most, he had made the biggest mistake of his life. He had trusted the one person he should never have trusted.

Now a redheaded woman with incredible eyes, and a shady past—a woman who had a talent for deception—was asking him to trust her. She wanted him to drink some mysterious potion she just happened to have in her pocket tonight. This would be the same amazing female who carried a stocking gun and a vinaigrette filled with some vile concoction that was capable of bringing a man, sobbing, to his knees.

He would have to be a fool to risk even a single swallow of the tonic. The leg was uncomfortable tonight but it was not intolerable. He had known far worse nights.

Trust me, Mr. Gage.

He opened the bottle and swallowed some of the tonic. It tasted slightly acidic but it went down easily enough.

He put the cap back on the bottle and thought about how he had just broken the most important rule in an investigation. He had trusted someone connected to the case, a lady who no doubt had any number of secrets to conceal.

He had a feeling he would be breaking a few more rules for Beatrice Lockwood. He wondered why he did not find that prospect alarming; why he was filled with anticipation instead of deep concern.

Twenty-One

"A re you certain this is safe?" Hannah asked.

"There is no reason to worry about me," Beatrice said. "The blackmailer is only interested in obtaining his payment. He has no reason to harm the person who delivers it. Quite the opposite, in fact. After all, he will want more extortion payments in the future."

"Bastard," Hannah said grimly.

"The one who will be taking a risk is your brother," Beatrice said. "There will no doubt be some danger involved when Mr. Gage grabs the villain in the act of retrieving the blackmail."

Hannah made a face. "Yes, well, one does not worry overmuch about Josh. Heaven knows he can take care of himself. After all that he has been through, I'm sure a simple blackmailer will not cause him any serious problems."

Beatrice smiled. "Nevertheless, you do worry about him, don't you?"

Hannah sighed. "He has been lost to us this past year. It was as if the shadows had finally claimed him utterly. True, he traveled to London on a couple of occasions to take care of some business and he wrote dutifully every month. But the letters were dreary, filled with news of the weather and the state of the crops and plans for repairs that he was carrying out on his country house. Nelson went to see him a few times and reported that Josh seemed strangely withdrawn. I had begun to fear—"

"I know what you feared," Beatrice said. "But I do not think you need to worry about that. Mr. Gage required some time to recover from his injuries but, as I told him, he stayed too long in the country. It was past time for him to return to the world."

Hannah's brows rose. "Did you actually tell him that?"

"Yes, I did. Tonight, as a matter of fact."

"How did he take your advice?"

Beatrice wrinkled her nose. "Like everyone else, he did not seem to appreciate it."

"I'm not surprised."

"But I do believe that coming to your aid has accomplished what all the good advice in the world never could. I think you will find that this blackmail affair has given him a new purpose and reinvigorated his spirits."

"Something certainly has brought about a change in him recently," Hannah said. She watched Beatrice with a knowing look. "I noticed the difference in him shortly before we left London. I think you are the tonic he has been needing."

Beatrice felt the heat in her cheeks. She cleared her throat and glanced at the clock. "It's time. I will take the payment to the great hall and return in a few minutes."

"Do be careful, dear. I have a most uneasy feeling about this affair."

"It will all be over soon," Beatrice said.

She decided that she would not tell Hannah that she, too, was experiencing a sense of dread. Hannah was the client. Mrs. Flint and Mrs. Marsh maintained that it was important to keep those who paid the hefty Flint and Marsh fees as calm as possible as they were often the ones who created the most problems in the course of an investigation. Clients were forever being swayed by their emotional connections to the case.

She picked up the envelope that contained the money and an unlit candle and opened the door. The corridor was empty.

She raised a hand in a reassuring gesture to Hannah and slipped out into the hall.

The big house was almost silent now. There were no low voices behind bedroom doors, no muffled footsteps on the servants' stairs. The secretive comings and goings had ceased until dawn.

The wall sconces still glowed dimly on the ground floor. When she reached the bottom of the staircase she started toward the passage that led to the great hall. She glanced around but saw no sign of Joshua. She knew that he was somewhere nearby, watching from the shadows.

The darkness deepened as she went closer to the big doors. She wondered what she would do if they were locked. That would mean that for some reason the blackmailer's plans had gone awry, she thought. But there was another possibility. If the antiquities chamber was still secured it might indicate that the villain suspected the trap that Joshua had set.

That thought heightened her alarm and her senses. Her pulse

was beating rapidly by the time she reached the massive doors. She glanced down and saw several decades' worth of seething energy on the floor. Everyone who had entered the room that evening had left a bit of paranormal residue behind, but one set of prints in particular glowed with the heat of a man who was in a state of nervous excitement. The only thing she could be certain of was that she did not recognize the hot tracks.

She took a breath and wrapped one hand around a big brass handle. Cautiously she tried the door.

Nothing happened. Something had gone wrong. No wonder her nerves were so on edge.

She tugged harder, putting her full weight into the task. This time the heavy door opened slowly, ponderously, but with surprisingly little noise.

A heavy darkness freighted with the disturbing energy of the massed artifacts inside the room flowed out of the narrow opening. She should be experiencing a surge of relief, she thought. All signs indicated that Joshua's plan was going forward. The blackmailer had taken the bait.

Yet she felt more rattled than ever. Her senses were crackling and sparking like an electricity machine. Her intuition was screaming at her.

It was the combined effects of the relics, she thought. The currents of power inside the space had been unpleasant earlier in the evening when the chamber had been illuminated. They were much stronger and far more ominous now that the room was steeped in darkness.

Steeling herself against the energy that whispered and howled silently in the chamber, she slipped across the threshold. The heavy door immediately started to close behind her. Hastily she lit the candle.

The small flame flared quickly but it did not reach far into the darkness. The artifacts and the gods and goddesses loomed around her, menacing and eerie. The atmosphere was oppressive.

Until now she had only viewed the relics from the hallway outside. That was as close as she had wanted to get. But now she was standing in the midst of the energy-infused artifacts. The intensity of the dark paranormal currents in the atmosphere was startling. The energy laid down in objects that had come from tombs and temples of any sort was always strong, but tonight the essence of death felt horribly fresh.

So fresh that she could have sworn she caught the scent of recently spilled blood.

Blood and smoky incense.

Impossible.

She steadied herself and lowered her talent before her feverish imagination started to conjure ghosts and demons.

The rational side of her nature assured her that there was nothing to fear from the antiquities. It was a very human blackmailer who was the threat tonight. Joshua was quite capable of dealing with him.

She went forward cautiously, mindful of the myriad pedestals, statues and vases arrayed inside the chamber. It would be all too easy to stumble over one of the smaller relics. An accident of that sort would not be helpful.

She made her way down an aisle framed by animal-headed

gods and goddesses to the stone platform that held the two sarcophagi. The candle flickered on the small quartz box. In the dancing shadows she could make out the image of a cat and a hunting scene. It was oddly touching to know that someone had valued a pet cat so highly.

The lid of the cat sarcophagus had been partially shoved aside. She started to drop the envelope inside. Her hand stilled in mid-air. The scent of blood was stronger now. So was the incense.

She turned away from the cat sarcophagus and raised the candle higher. In the flickering light she saw a massive granite altar. The figures and symbols carved into the stone were not as compelling as those on the sarcophagus. The craftsman who had created the images had not possessed the kind of talent that could be sensed over the centuries. But there were other currents emanating from the stone, layers upon layers of dark, disturbing forces swirled in the atmosphere.

It was not the ancient energy that sent slivers of horror through her. It was the sight of the waterfall of fresh blood dripping over the edge of the altar that tightened her throat so that she could not breathe.

She stumbled back a step and raised the candle higher. That was when she saw the motionless form on top of the altar. The man was sprawled on his back, his head turned slightly to the side so that she could not see his face.

Her first panicky thought was that the dead man was Joshua.

"No," she managed.

She moved closer and forced herself to look at the face of the victim. Death had crafted a rictus mask but a thunderbolt of relief snapped through her when she saw that it was not Joshua who lay stretched out on the altar.

The shock of the realization left her feeling weak and light-headed. *Not Joshua.* That was the important thing. The black-mailer, perhaps. It was certainly not beyond the realm of possibility that the extortionist had been murdered by one of his victims.

Joshua would not be pleased. She knew that he wanted to question the blackmailer.

One thing was evident. She had to get out of the chamber immediately. She could not afford to be found at the scene of a murder. She was a paid companion. Everyone would assume the worst—that she had murdered a lover or, heaven forbid, conspired with a partner in crime to steal some of the valuable artifacts. The police would likely leap to the obvious conclusion—that there had been a falling-out among thieves.

She tried to think but it was not easy. She was shivering violently now and the dazed sensation was growing worse. She could not believe that she was on the verge of fainting. Flint & Marsh agents never fainted.

But a strange fog was starting to rise around her. Within the depths of the mist she could see the gods and demons stirring.

"It's a dream," she whispered. Desperately she tried to collect her senses. "It's not real. *None of this is real.*"

And then she saw the seething footsteps on the floor near the altar.

"Did you think you could escape me again, little whore? I never fail."

The heavy Russian accent came out of the darkness to her left.

She tried to turn toward the sound but another wave of dizziness nearly overwhelmed her. Terrified that she might drop the candle and start a fire, she set the candlestick on the altar with a trembling hand.

Her senses were flaring but the incense was affecting her other sight, causing her to see things that her mind told her could not exist. The eyes of a falcon-headed statue glittered. A jeweled cobra hissed and swayed. An image of the goddess Nut stretched out vast wings. The gods of the Egyptian underworld—said to have skins of pure gold and hair like lapis lazuli—were coming to life around her.

The scented smoke was growing heavier. She fumbled with her skirts, trying to find the stocking gun but it was hopeless. She knew that she was losing consciousness.

The weak candle flared on a figure coming toward her. She recognized the jackal-headed god.

"Anubis," she said. "This cannot be happening. I am dreaming."

"I never fail."

A lantern blazed in the distance. It drew closer rapidly. She heard the thud of a cane on the floor.

"Joshua," she breathed. Hope and fear gave her strength. She pulled hard on her talent and raised her voice. "There is a killer in this chamber."

"I have a gun," Joshua said.

But the Anubis figure was already fleeing toward a wall on the far side of the chamber.

And then Joshua was upon her. She realized that he had a handkerchief tied like a mask around the lower half of his face. He scooped her up and tossed her over his shoulder.

"I should have known that things would not go according to plan tonight," Joshua said. "They never do when you're involved."

She was safe.

She abandoned the effort to stay awake and gave herself up to the sea of darkness.

Her last conscious memory was that of the familiar psychical prints she had seen near the altar. *Impossible,* she thought. She was hallucinating.

HE GOT HER UPSTAIRS without encountering any of the guests or servants. He could not be certain that no one saw them but he consoled himself with the thought that if that were the case it would be assumed that Hannah's paid companion had imbibed too much gin.

Hannah was waiting in the room. She stared at him and his burden, shocked.

"Dear Lord, is she—?"

"Unconscious," he said. "But her pulse and breathing appear to be normal." He eased Beatrice's limp form down onto the bed. "I think she was drugged. Do you have some smelling salts?"

"Yes, of course. Sally always packs some for emergencies. But I have noticed that Beatrice carries her own." Hannah reached for the vial that dangled from the chatelaine around Beatrice's waist.

"Not a good idea," Joshua said. "Believe me when I tell you that you do not want to use those particular salts. The formula is a very special one concocted by her employers. The stuff is designed to ward off mad dogs and would-be assailants."

"I see. How unusual. Josh, what happened tonight?"

"I'm not sure yet but I intend to find out. I must leave Beatrice to you and Sally for now. It would not be good for me to be seen in this room. In any event, I must deal with the murder."

"*What* murder? What are you talking about?"

"I suspect that the man who was attempting to blackmail you is the victim. The question is, who killed him?"

Twenty-Two

He used the old spiral staircase in the storage room to go back downstairs. When he reached the ground floor he made his way along the long, dark corridor that led to the antiquities chamber. He was aware that he was in a strange state of mind. A volatile storm of emotions seethed inside him. Among those highly charged sensations was a cold fury, a good deal of which was aimed at himself. He had put Beatrice in grave danger tonight.

Everything had gone wrong. Again. *Just as they had a year ago,* he thought. At least this time an innocent woman had not died, but it had been a very near thing.

The massive doors were still closed, just as he had left them a few minutes ago, and still unlocked. Assuming the killer had fled, it was unlikely he would have taken the time to lock the doors on his way out. Still, one never knew. The criminal mind was often predictable but not always.

He pulled out the handkerchief he had used earlier when he had realized that there were dangerous fumes in the room. He held the large square of linen across his nose and mouth.

He entered the cavernous space, struck a light and pulled the door closed behind him.

The scented smoke had largely dissipated but he could still feel some of the disorienting effects. The arm of a nearby statue appeared to move. He ignored the hallucinations and focused on his objective.

He turned up two of the wall sconces. The glare fell across the body on the altar. An unlit lantern sat near one of the dead man's hands.

He moved forward, listening intently for another presence in the room. He was certain that he had the chamber to himself now. The killer was gone.

The victim was not one of the guests. He was dressed like a high-ranking servant, a valet, perhaps. Joshua doubted that anyone would claim him in the morning.

It was the sight of the wound that sent a flash of knowing through him. The fraudulent valet had been killed with a single, expert thrust to the heart. It was possible there were two highly skilled assassins involved in the affair, but the probability was very low. In any event, professionals killed in unique ways. No two did it in exactly the same manner. There was little doubt but that the man who had murdered Roland Fleming months ago had killed the valet tonight.

What in bloody hell is going on? Joshua thought.

The valet's pockets produced a train ticket, some money and a watch but little else. The watch was far too expensive for a valet.

The inside of the lid was engraved with a set of flowing initials—
E.R.B. Joshua doubted that the dead man's initials, whatever they
might be, were the same. The watch had been stolen at some
point.

"You were a petty criminal who turned to blackmail," Joshua
said to the dead man. "How did that come about?"

He took a step back from the altar. His boot brushed against
an object on the floor. He looked down and saw the envelope
filled with money that Beatrice had brought with her earlier.

He picked up the envelope and started a methodical search of
the room, gradually expanding the circle around the altar until he
found what he was looking for. The killer had not had time to
retrieve the remains of the pot of burning incense that he had
placed in an alabaster bowl.

Joshua looked at the device for a long time, constructing a
variety of possible explanations and conclusions. But in the end
he knew he could not escape the truth.

The past was not dead, after all. And now, somehow, it was
linked to Beatrice.

Twenty-Three

The smelling salts exploded through her senses.

Beatrice came awake in a rush, mildly amazed to discover that she was alive. She opened her eyes and saw Hannah and Sally bending over her.

"Thank goodness," Hannah said. "You had us worried there for a bit. How do you feel?"

"Like my brain is on fire," Beatrice said.

"It's the salts," Sally explained with satisfaction. "Nothing like spirits of ammonia to clear the head, I say."

"Do you still feel faint, Beatrice?" Hannah asked anxiously.

Beatrice sat up against the pillows and contemplated the question. She took a cautious breath and was relieved to discover that the painful sensation was fading.

"No," she said. "I am definitely not going to faint. I don't think I would survive another dose of those salts." She looked around, trying to pull her memories together. "What is going on? Where is Mr. Gage?"

"He went back downstairs after he brought you up here," Hannah explained. "Something about a body."

"Oh, Lord, yes, the body on the altar," Beatrice said. She sank back against the pillows. "I'm afraid that there is going to be a great scene. Nothing like a murder to bring a quick end to a country-house party."

HALF AN HOUR LATER, Joshua knocked quietly on the door of the bedroom. Hannah let him in and shut the door behind him.

Joshua looked at Beatrice, who was sitting in a chair.

"Are you all right?" he asked.

"I'm fine," she assured him, "thanks to you and Sally's smelling salts. What is happening?"

"Alverstoke has been awakened and informed that there is a body in his antiquities chamber. He is in shock, I believe, but he managed to send for the local authorities. They will arrive at any moment."

"I am curious, sir," she said. "Did you really have a gun with you tonight?"

"No, I dislike guns. They are noisy and not particularly accurate. Nor are they a good choice of weapon for someone who favors discretion, as I do. There is always a great uproar when a gun is employed. But I will admit that firearms can make for an effective threat. In the darkness the killer could not see if I was armed with one."

"I see," she said. She remembered what Hannah had said earlier. *Josh is very skilled with knives.*

———

"THERE IS SOMETHING I want you to know before the authorities get here," Joshua continued.

"What is it?" she asked.

"I do not pretend to know what happened tonight but I am almost certain of one thing. Whoever murdered the man downstairs is the same person who killed Roland Fleming."

The cold shock of memory lanced through her. "Dear heaven. I thought I saw his footprints but I told myself that I was hallucinating. What is this all about?"

"Among other things, it means that what happened here is connected to what happened on the night of Fleming's death."

"I don't understand," Hannah said. "What about the blackmail threat that I received?"

"I think," Joshua said, "that it was bait in a trap. And I took the bait."

"Why would someone need to set a trap for you?" Hannah said. "You have been a recluse this past year but you have certainly not been in hiding."

"No," Joshua said. "But someone else was."

Beatrice swallowed. "Me."

"I cannot be sure yet, but I am starting to think that someone required my services to do what I do best."

"Find people," Hannah whispered. "Good grief. Someone sent you to find Beatrice?"

"Not Beatrice," Joshua said. "Miranda the Clairvoyant. The woman who disappeared the night of Fleming's murder."

Twenty-Four

Murder." Lord Alverstoke blotted the sweat from his brow with a handkerchief. "Astonishing. Utterly astonishing. Murder here at Alverstoke Hall and in the room where I display the finest artifacts in my collections. It's intolerable. And it will revive all of that silly chatter about a curse."

"The quickest way to put the talk of a curse to rest is to find the killer," Joshua said.

Beatrice glanced at him. He had not bothered with a disguise today. The false beard and glasses were gone. When he had awakened Alverstoke's butler with the news of the murder he had explained his presence in the household with something very close to the truth. He told Alverstoke that he was Hannah's brother and that he had been staying nearby so as to be available to escort her and her companion back to London at the end of the visit. He had noticed some "odd lights" in the household tonight and, fearing burglars, he had come to investigate.

Alverstoke was still too unnerved by the discovery of the attempted theft and the murder to question the story.

Joshua was growing increasingly impatient with Alverstoke's dithering. There was an edgy energy about him that spoke louder than words. Beatrice knew he wanted to get on with his investigation but he needed Alverstoke's cooperation. His lordship, however, appeared oblivious. He was still consumed with outrage and disbelief.

Alverstoke Hall was nearly empty. Word of the murder had ignited a firestorm of bustling servants and hastily summoned carriages. It was amazing, Beatrice thought, how quickly the upper classes could move when threatened with possible involvement in a police investigation. Joshua, Hannah, Sally and herself were the only guests remaining at the castle.

Now all of them with the exception of Sally, who was upstairs packing Hannah's things, were gathered in the library with their distraught host. Beatrice and Hannah were seated on a sofa. Alverstoke was slumped in the chair behind his vast mahogany desk. Joshua was at the cold hearth. He had one arm braced along the mantel. He gripped the handle of his cane very tightly with his other hand.

The investigation conducted by the local authorities had been perfunctory, to say the least, Beatrice thought. It had seemed obvious to one and all that two thieves had conspired to steal one or more of the artifacts. There had been some sort of quarrel—presumably an argument about which of the villains got the most valuable relics—and murder had ensued.

Lord Alverstoke had been assured that the affair was concluded because it appeared obvious that the murderer was already on his way back to London, where he would disappear into the dark streets of the criminal underworld. There was no reason for the authorities to trouble his lordship with further inquiries.

Joshua, however, was determined to do precisely that.

"I say, I have no interest in finding out who murdered that man," Alverstoke announced. "My only concern at the moment is locating a good locksmith, one who can protect my collection properly. I shall demand that the old locksmith refund the small fortune I paid him for what he claimed was an unbreakable lock. It's a miracle that nothing appears to have been stolen last night."

Beatrice noticed a subtle tightening in Joshua's jaw. His eyes narrowed in what she suspected was a rather dangerous fashion. She knew that he was on the edge of losing his temper. No good would come of pushing Alverstoke too hard, she thought. Pressure of the sort would only alarm his lordship and make him more difficult to handle. She decided it was time she got involved.

"Sir, you must not blame your old locksmith," she said smoothly. "It was not his fault that those intruders were able to gain entry into the chamber. The finest lock in the world will not keep out a thief who possesses the key. What Mr. Gage proposes to do is discover how the key was stolen in the first place." She looked pointedly at Joshua. "Isn't that right, Mr. Gage?"

Joshua drummed his fingers on the mantel once in a staccato fashion and then instantly stilled his hand. He looked annoyed, this time with himself.

"I told you," he said, "stealing the key would not have been dif—"

"*Possible* under most circumstances," she said, interrupting him before he could finish the word *difficult*. Alverstoke would not appreciate hearing that his security arrangements were inadequate. "Precisely. It's obvious that Lord Alverstoke has taken great care to secure his spectacular collection."

"Spent a bloody fortune on security," Alverstoke muttered.

"Yet tonight, two intruders managed to gain access," Beatrice pointed out gently. "And that is why you might want to consider Mr. Gage's offer of a very discreet investigation."

Joshua's expression darkened further. He had not so much offered his services as he had tried to bludgeon Alverstoke into letting him conduct an inquiry.

Beatrice looked at Hannah, who caught on immediately.

"Miss Lockwood makes an excellent point, sir," she said to Alverstoke. "How can you protect your valuables in the future if you don't discover what went wrong this time?"

Alverstoke scowled. "Huh."

He pondered the question for what seemed a very long time.

"As it happens," Beatrice said coolly, "Mr. Gage does have some expertise in matters of this sort of thing."

Joshua slanted her a grim look. She ignored him.

Alverstoke, bushy brows bunched together, peered at Joshua with obvious suspicion.

"Here now, what do you know about conducting a criminal investigation, sir?"

"Done a bit of consulting work for Scotland Yard," Joshua said in a deliberately vague, confidential tone that implied the consulting work was of a very delicate nature. "Let's just say that I was able to assist in certain matters where discretion was required. Sorry, can't divulge the details. I'm sure you understand."

"Yes, yes, of course, discretion." Alverstoke was visibly relieved by that news. "Perhaps Miss Lockwood is right. It would be a good idea to discover how the damned thieves got into the great hall in the first place so that I can prevent that sort of thing from happening again."

"What a good idea," Hannah agreed.

"Indeed," Joshua said. He fixed his attention on Beatrice. "Excellent plan, Miss Lockwood," he said, his tone very dry.

She gave him a demure smile. "Thank you, sir."

"Very well then," Alverstoke said. "In that case, sir, I would appreciate it if you would look into the matter of the stolen key for me."

"I'll be happy to conduct the investigation for you," Joshua said. He took his arm off the mantel and gripped his cane with both hands. "There is one more thing I would suggest."

Alverstoke looked wary. "Yes?"

"I assume you have a catalog of the antiquities on display in the great hall?"

"Certainly." Alverstoke was clearly offended by the suggestion that he did not have a complete list of the items in his collection. "I keep excellent records of all my acquisitions."

"I think it would be wise to conduct a thorough inventory as soon as I have finished my examination of the crime scene," Joshua said.

Panic flashed across Alverstoke's face. "Good Lord, man, do you think that the killer might have succeeded in making off with one of my artifacts?"

"We won't know for certain unless you conduct the inventory," Joshua said.

He was letting his impatience show again, Beatrice thought.

She gave him a quelling look. He was irritated but he did not add anything else.

"That will take a considerable amount of time," Alverstoke said.

"I understand," Joshua said. "But it would be extremely helpful to know exactly what, if anything, is missing."

"Yes, of course." Alverstoke was starting to become agitated again. "Hadn't considered the possibility that the thief actually got away with one of my relics." He rose to his feet and went to the door. "If you will excuse me, I will ask my butler to make arrangements to start the inventory as soon as you have concluded your investigation, Gage."

Joshua waited until the door closed behind Alverstoke. Then he looked at Beatrice. She gave him a cool smile.

"You're welcome," she said.

"I could have convinced him to allow me to investigate," Joshua said.

"Hah. At the rate you were going it was only a matter of time before he chucked all of us out of the house," Beatrice said. "Admit it."

Amused, Hannah raised her brows. "Beatrice is right, Josh, and you know it. You are in her debt."

"In the old days I did not have to request permission to conduct an investigation," Joshua grumbled.

"No, you used other methods," Hannah said briskly. "Namely the calling card of that dreadful Victor Hazelton. But your days of unraveling conspiracies for the Crown are over, thank heavens."

"Perhaps not quite yet," Joshua said. He spoke very, very quietly.

Hannah stared at him.

A cold sensation stole over Beatrice. "What do you mean?"

"This situation has become somewhat complicated," he said.

"What are you talking about?" Hannah demanded.

"I do not have all the answers yet, but I can tell you that the scent of the incense that the killer used last night to drug Beatrice was very familiar. I believe it may have come from the laboratory of a former associate of mine."

Beatrice frowned. "What do you mean?"

But Hannah was staring at Joshua, appalled. "Josh, are you certain?"

"I believe that the formula for the incense was originally concocted by Clement Lancing, yes," Joshua said. "It bears all of his hallmarks. What I do not yet know is who employed it tonight. It's possible Lancing's notebooks have fallen into someone else's hands—someone who has the scientific skill that would be required to re-create his formulas. But there is another possibility."

Hannah clasped her hands together very tightly. "Do you really believe that Lancing might be alive, after all?"

"I must assume that is the case until I can prove otherwise," Joshua said.

Beatrice frowned. "Will someone kindly tell me what you are talking about?"

Hannah sighed and rose to her feet. "I will leave it to Josh to explain. It is his story, after all. I shall go upstairs to supervise the packing. I'll have Sally pack your things as well, Beatrice."

"Thank you," Beatrice said.

Joshua made his way across the room to open the door for Hannah. She paused on the threshold, clearly troubled.

"I do not like this, Josh," she said.

"Neither do I, but I must discover the truth. I have no other choice now."

"No," Hannah said. "I suppose not."

She went out into the hall. Joshua closed the door very gently behind her.

Beatrice looked at him. "Well, sir?"

Joshua did not answer immediately. Instead he went to stand at the window. He stood quietly for a moment looking out into the gardens.

After a time he began to talk.

"Clement Lancing was a brilliant chemist who had a passion for archaeology, specifically Egyptian antiquities. He was convinced that, in their quest to discover a perfect way of preserving the bodies of the dead, the ancient Egyptians made a number of scientific discoveries that have been lost over the centuries. His goal was to find the lost secrets."

"How did you come to know Lancing?"

"We were friends at one time," Joshua said. His hand tightened around the steel hilt of the cane. "We met at Oxford and discovered that we had a great deal in common. We were both recruited as spies for the Crown by Victor Hazelton."

"The mysterious Mr. Smith."

"Yes. Clement Lancing and I conducted a number of investigations together." Joshua paused. "We were very good at what we did."

"I see," Beatrice said.

"Lancing's scientific interests, his knowledge of languages and his passion for Egyptian antiquities made him extremely valuable to Hazelton. As an archaeologist, Lancing possessed an ideal cover for traveling abroad. He made connections in several capitals with all sorts of people, from street vendors to high-ranking officials. He was able to provide Hazelton with a great deal of information. He also gave me intelligence that I needed to pursue conspirators and traitors in London."

"And all of this was coordinated through Victor Hazelton?"

"Victor trained us and gave us our assignments," Joshua said.

"When did Clement Lancing become a dangerous criminal?"

Joshua concentrated on the gardens outside the window. "There was a woman."

"Of course," Beatrice said. "I should have guessed."

"Her name was Emma. She was Victor Hazelton's daughter. She was very beautiful and quite brilliant."

"And you and Lancing both desired her."

Joshua's mouth twisted in a faint smile. "As I said, she was beautiful and brilliant. And she was Victor Hazelton's daughter."

"Right. And Hazelton was your mentor and your employer. I suppose that says it all."

"Victor was more than a mentor and an employer," Joshua said quietly. "He was the man who saved me from myself. I will always be grateful to him. But in the end, I failed him."

"I don't understand."

"Never mind. It doesn't matter now." Joshua gripped the windowsill. "In the end, Emma chose Lancing. And while I was disappointed, I understood."

Beatrice raised her brows. "Indeed?"

"There was a passion between those two that simply did not—

could not—exist between Emma and me." Joshua paused. "I am not a man of strong passions."

Beatrice gave a ladylike sniff. At least she hoped it was a ladylike sniff and not an unladylike snort of laughter.

Joshua turned his head to look at her over his shoulder.

"You find that amusing?" he asked.

"No, merely misguided."

"What the devil would you know about my temperament?"

"Evidently a good deal more than you do, sir, but that is neither here nor there at the moment." She waved the issue aside. "You were in the process of giving me some background material that relates to our investigation. Pray continue."

Joshua looked briefly torn, as if he wanted to argue about his passions or lack thereof. Beatrice waited politely.

In the end he abandoned the topic.

"Emma shared Lancing's fascination with chemistry and Egyptian antiquities," he said.

"Go on," Beatrice said quietly.

"In the course of an excavation in Egypt they discovered a tomb. Inside they found a most unusual sarcophagus. There was no mummy inside. They also discovered a statue of Anubis. The eyes of the figure—presumably two gemstones—were missing. There was a papyrus inside the sarcophagus. When Emma deciphered the hieroglyphs, she and Lancing realized that they had found an ancient formula designed to preserve human bodies. They both became obsessed with the possibility of re-creating it."

"Why on earth would they want to create an embalming formula?" Beatrice asked.

"According to the papyrus, the chemicals had astonishing properties. In fact, the formula had the power to awaken the dead."

"Magic." Beatrice tut-tutted. "I cannot believe that two intelligent people of the modern age—people with an extensive understanding of science—could believe in such nonsense."

"They were both skeptical at first," Joshua said. "But their experiments on rats led them to believe that the Egyptian Water, as they called the formula, actually might work. They were convinced that the preservative fluid had paranormal properties."

"Don't try to tell me that they actually succeeded in bringing some dead rodents back to life," Beatrice asked. "That's absolute rubbish."

"They never succeeded in reviving a dead creature but the Egyptian Water did have some astonishing properties. If you looked at a rat that had been preserved in the fluid you would swear that it was in a state of hibernation. It was—" Joshua hesitated, searching for the word. "It was uncanny."

"But the rats that were preserved in that fashion stayed dead," Beatrice insisted.

"Yes. Emma and Lancing, however, were convinced that they were only a step away from success. They believed that the secret lay in the paranormal properties of the eyes of the Anubis statue they had discovered."

"The gemstones that you said were missing?"

"Right," Joshua said. "They began an intensive search for the eyes."

"I'm surprised they believe that there would be anything left to revive," Beatrice said. "After all, the traditional Egyptian manner of preserving the dead involved removing most of the organs and the brain."

"This was an entirely different process. According to the papyrus, time was of the essence. The newly deceased were to be immersed immediately in a chemical bath that supposedly plunged them into a state of suspended animation. They remained in the Egyptian Water until healed of whatever disease or injury had caused their death. Later they could be revived with the energy infused in the Anubis statue."

Beatrice shook her head. "Madness."

"Yes." Joshua turned back to face her. "Their obsession with the Egyptian Water did become a form of madness, at least as far as Lancing was concerned. He began carrying out human experiments."

Beatrice flinched in shock. "Dear heaven."

"He selected his victims from among the poorest and most wretched of street people. When Emma discovered that he was murdering innocent people in his quest, she was horrified. She made the mistake of confronting him. He made her a prisoner in his mansion. Victor finally realized that his daughter was in grave danger. He sent me to rescue Emma. I arrived too late."

"What happened?"

"Emma tried to escape on her own," Joshua said. "Lancing caught her. In his madness he thought that she was running to me, that she loved me. He thought she had betrayed him. He strangled her. I found her body on the floor of the laboratory. Lancing appeared. He said Emma was dead because of me. He said he had been waiting for me, that we were all going to die together. He set off the explosion."

"It was a trap," Beatrice whispered. "But you survived."

He looked at his cane. "To this day, I'm not sure how I made it into that stone hallway in time. The walls protected me to some extent from the full force of the explosion. But the blast was followed by a fire."

"How did you escape?"

"My memories of what happened after the explosion are more in the nature of fever dreams. Lancing kept a lot of powerful chemicals in his laboratory, including that incense you encountered last night. The blast and the fire released fumes into the atmosphere. I used my shirt to cover my mouth and nose but by the time I got out of the house I was hallucinating."

She studied his scar. "And losing blood, as well. The combination would cloud anyone's memories. Were the bodies ever recovered?"

"Yes, at least we assumed so at the time. My injuries kept me from returning to the scene for weeks. Victor Hazelton went to the site with a crew of laborers, but they had to wait days for the rubble to cool down. In the end they found the bodies. Both were burned beyond recognition. The doctor who examined the corpses declared one was male and the other female. That was the end of the matter. Hazelton grieves to this day. He will for the rest of his life."

"That was why he retired from his role as Mr. Smith?"

"He was the Lion, defender of the empire," Joshua said, his tone almost reverent. "But after Emma died he said he no longer cared about the future of England. As far as he is concerned, it is buried with Emma."

"He blames you for her death?"

"Not in so many words. But, yes, we both know that I failed him. The last time I saw him was at Emma's funeral. We have not spoken or communicated with each other since that day."

"An obsessive grief can drive a man mad into despair," Beatrice said. "In such a state he will shut out even those who are dear to him."

Joshua looked out at the gardens. "I know."

She got to her feet and went to stand beside him.

"But still you blame yourself," she said.

Joshua said nothing.

Unable to think of any words that might comfort or console him, she did the only thing she could think of. She touched the hand he used to grip the cane. She felt the now-familiar whisper of awareness that stirred between them and wondered if he felt it, too.

Joshua looked down at her hand on his as though not sure what to make of the small, intimate gesture. She could almost feel him pulling himself out of the past and back into the present.

"Now you are wondering if it's possible that Lancing survived the fire," she said.

"It's a remote possibility but it has to be considered. It's more likely that someone has found his notebooks and used them to create that incense drug. Whatever the case, I have no choice but to discover the truth and the search starts here at Alverstoke Hall."

"I assume you will talk to the staff and examine the guest list?"

"Perhaps. But first I'm going to take another look around the great hall. I did not have time to make a thorough job of it last night."

"I'll come with you," she said quickly.

"I do not want you involved in this affair."

"You said, yourself, I am involved."

"I'll make arrangements to keep you safe in London while I pursue the investigation," Joshua said.

"We are not in London at the moment," she said, keeping her voice steady and cool. Joshua would not respond to passionate demands or a hot argument. Only logic would get through his stubborn head. "You have said before that I have exceptional powers of observation. Where is the harm in allowing me to go back into the antiquities chamber? Who knows? I may see something that will bring back a helpful memory."

Twenty-Five

I was not hallucinating, after all," Beatrice said. She looked at
the seething footprints on the floor. "The man who murdered Roland was, indeed, here last night. He waited there,
behind that large statue. When the blackmailer arrived he crossed
the room to the altar and murdered him."

"But first he probably used the incense to incapacitate his victim," Joshua said. "He used it again when you arrived."

They were standing near the sarcophagus in the great hall, attempting to piece together a picture of what had transpired during
the night. The lamps were illuminated but at Beatrice's request
they were turned down low. Joshua had not argued when she had
explained that it was easier to see the wispy traces of energy in the
shadows. She knew he did not believe that she could actually make
out the paranormal prints of the killer and his victim, but he was
willing to let her handle her side of the investigation her way.

She glanced at him and saw that he was examining the alabaster bowl that contained the remains of the incense.

"I have been meaning to ask you two questions," she said. "First, how is it that you were not affected by the smoke last night?"

"I did the same thing that I did when I escaped from the burning laboratory last year. I covered my nose and mouth with a cloth and tried not to breathe any more than absolutely necessary. It did not take long to find you and remove you from this chamber. A matter of two or three minutes, no more."

"You make it sound so simple."

"When I entered the room I could smell traces of the stuff. That gave me time to take precautions."

"It affected all my senses," Beatrice said. "I got dizzy and I started to hallucinate. It was as if the statues were coming alive."

"If you ever smell the stuff again, cover your nose and mouth and try to get down low to the floor."

"Why?"

"The fumes are carried in the form of smoke, which rises."

"Yes, of course. I should have thought of that."

"You were caught by surprise," he said very seriously. "And there was the shock of finding the body. That sort of thing can be disorienting."

She smiled to herself. "Thank you for your understanding. If you had not found me when you did, I suspect we would not be here chatting today." She looked at the bloodstains on the altar and shivered. "That brings me to my other question."

Joshua moved across the space to examine the altar.

"What?" he asked.

"How did you know that I was in danger? No one came or went from this chamber. The blackmailer was killed before I arrived and the assassin was already inside when I entered the room. What alerted you to my situation?"

"Sometimes one gets a feeling that things have gone wrong with a plan."

"Yes," she said. "I know the feeling. It's called intuition."

"If you are about to inform me that intuition is a psychical talent, you may as well save your breath."

"You don't think it's paranormal in nature?"

"No, I do not," he said. "It's merely a combination of observations—some of which are so small that we are not even consciously aware of them—and unconscious awareness of the connections between those observations."

"Some might call that psychical awareness," she said.

He paid no attention. "Last night while I was watching the door to this chamber I noticed a faint but detectable draft in the hallway outside. It was coming from this room."

"A draft, hmmm? And what does that tell us?"

"It tells us that there is another door in here, most likely a set of servants' stairs."

She glanced around. "I don't see another door."

"Walk me through the events of last night from the very beginning."

She did as he asked. When she finished the short narrative she came to a halt in front of the altar.

"This is where I was standing when the fumes overcame my senses," she said. "I had just seen the body and noticed the killer's psychical prints. I sensed another presence in the chamber. I thought I saw one of the statues coming toward me."

"Which one?"

"It was the jackal-headed god, Anubis, in his partially human form." She wrinkled her nose. "I know, it sounds ridiculous now, but at the time I could have sworn it was a statue come to life."

"Or a man wearing a mask," Joshua suggested.

"Why would the killer wear a mask?"

"Two reasons, first to protect him from the incense."

"Yes, of course. And the second reason?"

"To cast terror into the hearts of his victims. He knows that the incense is causing them to hallucinate. The mask would generate more fear. Some professionals enjoy that aspect of the kill."

She drew a breath. "I see."

"What else did you observe?" Joshua asked.

"Nothing very helpful, I'm afraid. I saw Anubis coming toward me. He spoke in a Russian accent. Something about *Did you think you could escape me, little whore?* And then I saw the light you struck. The killer realized he had been discovered and he fled. That's all I remember."

"Now we must find the source of the draft that I detected. You say the voice came from behind you?"

"Yes."

"The killer did not go past me on his way out, so the second door must be here somewhere."

Joshua started toward the nearest wall. She knew he intended to conduct a methodical search for the source of the draft. She cleared her throat.

"I think I can save you some time," she said.

He glanced at her. "How?"

She looked down at the trail of seething footsteps. "I believe you'll find the door over there behind that granite figure."

He raised his brows. At first she thought he would ignore what she had said and continue to search in his own fashion. To her surprise, however, he crossed the chamber to the large stone statue and disappeared behind it.

"There is a servants' door back here," he announced. "Excellent observation, Beatrice."

"Thank you," she said. "I made it with my paranormal senses."

He reappeared from behind the granite figure. "It's far more likely you felt the draft yourself last night and registered the approximate location using your normal sense."

"You are very good at concocting normal explanations to explain the paranormal."

"That is because the normal explanations usually suffice."

"Mmm."

She walked through the maze of antiquities to join him. When she rounded the granite figure she saw that the door had been designed to be as unobtrusive as possible. Its location behind a jumble of relics made it virtually undetectable from anywhere else in the chamber. A large portion of a tomb painting stood directly in front of it.

"The killer knew about this door," Joshua said. "That means he has more than a passing familiarity with the hall. Clement Lancing moved in a circle that included a number of collectors. He would have known Alverstoke."

"Do you think Lancing is the killer?"

"No," Joshua said. "Lancing had no skill with a knife. He would have used other methods. Poison, most likely."

Joshua wrapped one hand around the doorknob and twisted. The door opened easily enough. Beatrice found herself peering at a flight of stone steps that disappeared into a sea of night. The killer's footprints burned on the steps.

"He was in a rage," she said. "Furious because he had been interrupted before he could finish whatever it was he came here to do."

Joshua contemplated the darkness for a moment.

"I'll get a lantern," he said. "We will find out where this leads."

Twenty-Six

A short time later they started down the ancient steps. Beatrice held the lantern. The light splashed on old stone as they made their way downward into the depths of the old house.

"I can see the killer's footsteps in the dust," Joshua said. "He entered the mansion using this passage and he left the same way."

Beatrice heightened her talent and studied the hot prints. "Yes, it's the same man who was waiting for me last night, the assassin who murdered Roland. I'm sure of it."

"It's an obvious enough conclusion."

"It's a good thing I have long been accustomed to having people question my abilities," she said. "Otherwise I might take offense at your constant skepticism."

"I do not mean to offend you." There was genuine apology in his voice. "It is just that I think you have a rather vivid imagination."

"Do you ever allow your imagination to get carried away by fanciful thoughts, Mr. Gage?"

"I do my best to guard against those sorts of distractions. They rarely yield any useful results."

"But on occasion?" she prompted.

"I'm only human."

"You say that as if it were a serious character flaw."

They descended a few more steps and rounded a corner into another dank passageway. Beatrice's heart sank. The corridor that stretched before them was narrow and filled with unrelenting darkness. She felt the old, familiar edginess spike higher. She held the lantern aloft, hoping to cast the light farther into the shadows.

"Last night," Joshua said.

The words came out of nowhere. Beatrice wondered if, in her struggle to control her nerves, she had missed something in the conversation.

"Sorry," she said. "What about last night?"

She forced herself to breathe slowly and evenly. She could do this. She had a lantern. Joshua was with her.

"Last night when we kissed in that alcove," Joshua said. "That was the last time I got distracted by fanciful thoughts."

"Oh, I see." She was not sure what to say to that. She knew she was blushing again and for a few seconds she was grateful for the flood tide of darkness that surrounded her.

She was trying to come up with an appropriate response when Joshua stopped abruptly.

"What's wrong?" she asked, shivering a little.

"The air has changed. You can smell the sea."

She breathed in cautiously, paying close attention to the atmosphere. Then she caught it, the unmistakable whisper of salt-tinged air. There was a muffled roar in the distance. The pounding of waves on a rocky shore, she thought.

"This passage must lead to the sea." She looked down at the traces of energy on the stone floor. "By the time he got this far he was calmer, more controlled. But he was still frustrated and angry. No, it's more than just anger. It's a kind of obsessive rage."

"A logical assumption based on our knowledge of him," Joshua said. "He is a professional in a bloody business. But like any professional, he prides himself on his expertise. Naturally he would have been in a fury because he was unsuccessful tonight."

"You can't bring yourself to admit that I might be able to see some traces of paranormal energy that he left behind, can you?"

"You arrived at your conclusion with logic and intuition, whether you know it or not."

"Mrs. Flint and Mrs. Marsh were certainly right when they said that clients were always the most difficult part of the business."

"Are you implying that I'm your client?" he asked.

"That is exactly what you are, sir. You are paying Flint and Marsh for my services. That makes you a client."

"The hell it does. We will sort that out some other time."

He went forward more quickly now, his stick creating a steady drumbeat on the stone. Beatrice picked up her skirts, relieved to be moving faster. Physical motion helped suppress the oppressive sensation that gnawed at her.

The sound of the crashing waves grew louder. So did the dampness around them. The stone walls of the tunnel ended suddenly, giving way to the interior of a large cave. Restless seawater filled the lower portion of the cavern, churning and sloshing around a small wooden dock that was designed to rise and fall with the tide. The outside entrance was not visible from where Beatrice stood but she could feel the currents of fresh air that flowed into the space.

"This is an old smuggler's cave," Joshua said. He took the lantern and held it aloft to examine the dock. "The bastard had a boat waiting here. The question is, did he come alone or did he bring someone else along to handle the oars? It is not impossible that a skilled assassin from London would also be a competent oarsman who happens to be familiar with this coastline, but it seems unlikely."

"If we go down to the dock, I might be able to answer the question," Beatrice said.

She felt a little steadier now that they were no longer within the close confines of the passage. The salt air and the movement of the water helped dispel some of the oppressive atmosphere.

Joshua looked at her with a considering expression. For a short time she thought he would refuse her offer. But after a second or two he simply nodded once and started down the short flight of steps to the dock.

When he reached the bottom he stopped, turned and held his hand out to assist her. "Careful," he said. "The steps are wet and slippery."

In spite of the situation the small act of gallantry charmed her. Their relationship thus far seemed to lurch back and forth from a state of prickly suspicion to a wary partnership. She knew that the heated kiss last night had been an aberration, a brief interlude that had surprised both of them. She wondered if Joshua would allow himself to be distracted by fanciful thoughts again.

For a second she hesitated to take his hand, afraid that if she slipped on the wet steps she might pull him down, too. He had, after all, only his cane to help him maintain his own balance. Then she remembered how he had come to her through the noxious incense last night and carried her to safety.

She gave him her hand. His fingers closed like a manacle around hers. She knew then that he had sensed her slight hesitation.

"I won't let you fall," he said grimly.

She stifled a sigh. They were back to the prickly phase of their association.

"I know," she said.

At the bottom of the steps, she tugged her hand free and tried to affect a brisk, businesslike air. She heightened her senses and looked at the hot tendrils of energy that writhed in the prints. In addition to the killer's footsteps she saw another set.

"Two people were here," she said.

"Yes."

Joshua's swift agreement made her turn to look at him. He had walked partway out along the old dock and was leaning down to examine a small, narrow object.

"What is it?" she asked.

"A cigarette." Joshua straightened. "The oarsman smoked while he waited for the assassin to return."

"The oarsman must have been a local. No one else would be likely to know the location of this old smuggler's lair."

"It would not be difficult to hire an able-bodied man with knowledge of the shoreline," Joshua said. "We are on the coast. I'm sure every man and boy in the area can handle a boat and knows the local terrain. The problem lies in ensuring that the oarsman keeps his mouth shut. News of the murder at Alverstoke Hall will be all over the village by now. Sooner or later it will come out that someone from the village was hired to row a stranger to the old smuggler's cave near the hall on the night of the murder."

She caught her breath. "We must find the oarsman."

"I doubt that will be much of a problem," Joshua said. "Dead bodies have a way of washing ashore."

Twenty-Seven

The old smuggler's passage?" Lord Alverstoke's bushy brows and sideburns twitched in a scowl. "I'd forgotten all about that tunnel to the cove. It was originally constructed as an escape route in the event of a siege. Later it was used for contraband. But that was years ago."

"Who else knows about the tunnel besides yourself, sir?" Joshua asked.

He was having a hard time keeping his attention focused on Alverstoke. He kept glancing at the clock. Beatrice was upstairs with Hannah and the maid, finishing the preparations for the journey back to London. Logically he knew she was safe enough for the moment but he did not like letting her out of his sight.

"Well, as to who might know about the passage, that's hard to say." Alverstoke snorted. "Many of the servants have been with me for decades. I expect they are all aware of it. Not as if it's a secret, you know. The house is riddled with passages and stairwells that are no longer used."

"I understand. But can you think of anyone in particular—a visitor, perhaps—who took an interest in the tunnel and its history?"

Questioning Alverstoke was probably pointless, Joshua thought. It was clear the old man knew nothing about the murder. He did not even know how Hannah had gotten on his guest list for the house party. *Leave that sort of thing to my secretary.*

There was no time to talk to every member of the household staff, Joshua decided. Right now his first priority was to get Beatrice out of reach of the assassin. Nevertheless, it would be extremely helpful to discover how the killer had obtained such a thoroughgoing knowledge of the mansion and the secret entrance to the antiquities chamber.

"Afraid not," Alverstoke said, very firm this time. "Can't think of anyone who showed an interest in that old smuggler's tunnel."

"What about antiquities experts? Have you invited any colleagues or other collectors to visit for an extended period? Long enough to have discovered the tunnel by accident, perhaps?"

"I've certainly allowed other experts to examine my collection from time to time but they never stayed here for more than a day or two and I always accompanied them when they viewed the objects in the great hall." Alverstoke pursed his lips. "Except for that lovely young lady who asked to study the artifacts so that she could write a paper for one of the journals. But that was over a year ago. I can't see how her visit could be linked to the murder last night."

A chill of knowing swept through Joshua. "You allowed a woman to study your antiquities?"

"I know what you're thinking." Alverstoke chuckled. "One doesn't expect a female to possess a sound knowledge of antiquities. But this lady was the exception. She was astonishingly well informed. She had actually done some fieldwork in Egypt."

"Sir, this is very important. How did this female antiquities expert contact you?"

"She wrote to me requesting permission to study the artifacts. Signed the letter as E. Baycliff. I assumed she was a man, of course. When she arrived on my doorstep I was shocked to see that she was a female."

"But you invited her to stay?"

"I was going to send her away but she pleaded with me to show her some of the antiquities before she took the train back to London." Alverstoke winked. "Very attractive young woman. So intelligent and quite charming. I saw no harm in taking her on a tour of the great hall. In the end I relented and agreed to let her study some of the artifacts."

"How long did she remain here at Alverstoke Hall?"

"Not long. A few days. She was called back to London before she could finish her research. Something about a death in the family, I believe."

"Did she ask to view your catalog?"

"Yes, of course," Alverstoke said.

"Did she express any special interest in any items in particular in your collection?"

"As I recall, she was very keen to view two rather odd obsidian jewels. Not terribly important antiquities, really. We both agreed they had no doubt once been the eyes of a statue. Someone had removed them at some point, most likely to sell them."

"She found the damned eyes," Joshua said. But he was speaking to himself, mentally rearranging pieces on an invisible chessboard in his head. "That explains a great deal."

Alverstoke scowled. "I say, what's this about eyes?"

"I think I can save you some time with your inventory," Joshua said. "Start with those two obsidian jewels. You will discover that they have gone missing. They disappeared a little over a year ago, in fact. About the time that the woman who called herself E. Baycliff got that telegram informing her of a death in the family."

"You believe Miss Baycliff stole them? Nonsense. She was a lovely young woman, I tell you. Very charming."

"Yes," Joshua said, remembering. "Beautiful, charming and an expert in antiquities."

"Even allowing for the outrageous possibility that she was a thief, why would she take such unimportant relics? Those stones are not particularly valuable."

"If I'm right, those jewels were the Eyes of Anubis."

"What of it? A large number of Anubis figures have been discovered. I've got several in my own collection. Why would Miss Baycliff want the eyes of a particular statue?"

"To raise the dead."

Twenty-Eight

I don't understand, Josh," Hannah said. "Why are you and Beatrice leaving the train here in Upper Dixton? We won't reach London for another hour and a half. This is nothing more than a small village."

Beatrice looked out the rain-streaked windows as the train pulled into the small station. There were only three people waiting on the platform. They were all huddled under umbrellas. The rain was unrelenting. It was late afternoon but the storm had brought on an early twilight.

The news that the body of one of the local fishermen had been discovered on the beach had reached Alverstoke Hall just as she and the others were preparing to leave for the railway station. Lord Alverstoke and almost everyone else had been shocked by word of another mysterious death in the vicinity coming, as it did, on the heels of the murder in the antiquities chamber.

Joshua was the only one who had not exhibited surprise. *"He got rid of the oarsman"* had been his only comment. It was clear that he had been expecting the news.

"Miss Lockwood and I are stopping here because I am convinced that there is a high probability that we are being followed," Joshua said to Hannah.

He was on his feet, pulling his black bag down from the luggage rack. Beatrice waited in the aisle outside the private compartment, her large satchel gripped in one hand, an umbrella in the other. Joshua had informed her that they could not afford to be burdened by her traveling trunk.

She had been as surprised as Hannah and Sally by Joshua's sudden announcement a few minutes earlier. He had not informed them of his plan to depart the train in Upper Dixton until shortly before they arrived. She wondered if he had made his plans before they even boarded at the Alverstoke railway station forty-five minutes ago. Really, the man needed lessons in communication.

But she concluded that this was not the time to lecture him on the subject. The icy intensity that swirled around Joshua had set her own nerves on edge. She knew that he believed that she was in danger. He was no doubt convinced that his conclusion was founded on cold logic and his knowledge of his opponent. But she suspected it was his intuition, not sound reasoning, that was riding him so hard. Either way it all came to the same end. If Joshua feared that someone was planning to snatch her at the first opportunity, it was best to assume that he was right.

"I beg your pardon, sir," Sally said. "But how does a person follow a train?"

"Think about it from the follower's point of view," Joshua said. "If someone watched us buy tickets for London, as I suspect, that individual will be convinced that he knows our destination. He will lower his guard and tell himself that he can simply pick up the trail at the other end—in London."

"Yes, I see what you mean, sir," Sally said. "What a chilling thought."

"I sent a telegram to Nelson before we boarded," Joshua said. "He will meet you at the station in London. He has instructions to watch for any indication that someone suspicious is waiting there or if a suspicious person alights from the train."

Alarm sparked in Hannah's eyes. "Do you suppose the watcher is even now on this very same train?"

"It's possible," Joshua said. "Which is why Beatrice and I will wait on board until the last possible moment. If he does attempt to get off at that point to follow us, he will expose himself immediately. It will be easy enough to spot him in this small railway station."

"He will know that," Beatrice pointed out. "This is a very tiny village, as Hannah said. Very few people will get off here. Strangers in town are bound to stand out."

"Precisely," Joshua said. "In his shoes, I would stay on board until the next stop and then try to work my way back to Upper Dixton by private cab. By then, we will be gone."

"Where are you going?" Hannah asked.

"We will hire a cab to take us to the next village, and from there we will go on to London." Joshua smiled his cold smile. "It will be interesting to see if we pass him on the road."

"It all sounds very complicated," Hannah said uneasily.

"*The trick to losing a watcher is to put yourself in the one place he cannot watch,*" Joshua said. "*His blind spot is always behind him.*"

Beatrice raised her brows. "Is that another quote from Mr. Smith?"

"Sorry, I'm afraid so," Joshua said.

Hannah's mouth tightened in grim disapproval. "That dreadful Victor Hazelton."

"I am aware of your opinion of the man," Joshua said. He looked at Beatrice. "Are you ready?"

"Yes," she said.

He gripped his cane and started to move out of the compartment. Hannah put a hand on his arm to stop him. Her eyes were very serious.

"You do realize what you are doing by leaving this train alone with Beatrice," she said in low tones. "I am aware that you are taking measures to ensure her safety, however—"

"Do not concern yourself, Hannah." His voice was equally soft. "I know what I am about."

Hannah looked at him a few seconds longer and then glanced once more at Beatrice. Evidently satisfied, she sat back against the cushions.

"Be careful, both of you," she said. "We will be waiting in London."

Beatrice got the feeling that she had just missed something in the conversation, but there was no time to analyze the situation. Joshua was urging her to move quickly along the narrow corridor. He followed her to the door.

"Now," he said.

She descended the steps just as the conductor turned to put them up and jump aboard. He regarded her and Joshua with surprise.

"I beg your pardon, ma'am, sir, but this isn't your stop," he said. "You're for London."

Beatrice summoned up a reassuring smile and raised her umbrella against the rain. "Change of plans, I'm afraid."

"But your luggage, ma'am."

Joshua put on his hat and came down the steps. "Arrangements have been made to collect the rest of our bags in London. My wife and I have decided to do some sightseeing here in Upper Dixton."

The words *my wife* sent a small shockwave through Beatrice. By the time she had collected herself she and Joshua were on the platform, the conductor was on board, the door was closed and the train was pulling out of the station.

Beatrice turned to Joshua in disbelief, alarm stirring as it dawned on her just what that last exchange between Joshua and Hannah might have been about. None of her previous clients had ever been concerned about her reputation. She was a private inquiry agent, after all, not a high-ranking lady. The goal was to get her out of the house as soon as the investigation was completed.

But Joshua was not paying any attention to her. He was watching the doors of the railway carriages, waiting to see if anyone else elected to get off at the last possible moment.

Steam hissed. The train gathered speed. It rumbled out of the station and disappeared into the heavy mist.

"It appears that the watcher, if there is one, remained on board," Beatrice ventured.

"So it seems," Joshua said. He looked at the lone cab waiting in the street. The driver was hunched under a heavily caped coat and low-crowned hat. The horse stood stoically, one hoof cocked, head lowered against the steady downpour. "With luck this cab will take us to the next village."

The driver looked down from the box. "Can I help ye, sir?"

"The motion of the train was making my wife ill so we wish to travel to the next town by cab."

"Sorry, sir, afraid that's not possible." The driver sounded genuinely regretful. "The roads are rivers of mud. No one's leaving Upper Dixton by cab until this rain stops. Next train is tomorrow morning."

"In that case, we'll need an inn for the night," Joshua said. "Can you suggest one?"

"There's two in town, sir. I recommend the Blue Fox. It's clean. Decent food."

"The Blue Fox it is."

Joshua opened the cab door and tossed both bags inside. Then he ushered Beatrice up the steps. She folded her umbrella and went through the small door. Joshua followed and sat down across from her. The cab rolled forward down the village's only street.

Joshua looked at Beatrice.

"I'm sorry about this," he said brusquely. "I should have anticipated the possibility that the weather would interfere with my plans."

"As a professional investigator myself, I am well aware that one cannot plan for every contingency."

She was astonished by her own calm demeanor. But then, she was a professional, she reminded herself.

Joshua exhaled slowly and looked out the window. "You do realize that this means we will have to share a room tonight."

"The inn might have two rooms available," she ventured.

"We are posing as a married couple," he reminded her. "It will not look right if we stay in separate rooms. Regardless, I do not want you out of my sight tonight."

"I understand that you are very concerned for my safety, but that assassin has no reason to kill me."

Joshua looked grim. "Perhaps not, but it is obvious that he is intent on kidnapping you."

"It is difficult to believe that someone is still obsessed with Miranda the Clairvoyant after all this time. It makes no sense."

"Lancing or whoever has his notebooks wants you because he is convinced that your paranormal talents are real."

"What do my talents have to do with this?"

"I have a theory," Joshua said. "It is only a theory at this point but everything thus far indicates that it is correct. I believe that Lancing or someone else has succeeded in re-creating the formula for the Egyptian Water."

"Even if that is true, why would this madman want me?"

"When I told you the story this morning I did not explain one aspect of the case. Lancing and Emma were convinced that the statue of Anubis was the key to activating the special properties of the Egyptian Water."

"I understand, but what does that have to do with me?"

"They believed that only a woman with a paranormal talent

could channel the power of the statue into the preservative formula to ignite it."

"Good grief."

"At the time they planned to use Emma to focus the energy of the statue," Joshua said. "They were both convinced that she had paranormal talents. But she is dead, so Lancing is looking for another woman he believes possesses psychical powers. For some reason he has fixed on you."

"But why me and why now? A full year has passed. Why hasn't he settled on some other practitioner? There are any number of them."

"I expect he has tried to find a replacement." Joshua smiled grimly. "But no doubt they all proved to be frauds. For whatever reason, he is convinced that you are genuine."

She shuddered. "He is truly mad, isn't he?"

"There is no doubt. Which is what leads me to believe that it is Lancing we are dealing with. What are the odds that a second madman found his notebooks?"

"I have no idea. I've never been good at probability theory."

She knew she sounded tense. She could not help it. The knowledge that a madman was intent on kidnapping her was disturbing enough. The realization that she would be spending the night in the same room with Joshua was almost as unnerving. But the trepidation was laced with a stirring of excitement. What would happen? she wondered. Perhaps the more pertinent question was, what did she want to happen?

"Please believe me when I say that I never intended to put you in this position," Joshua continued quietly. "I realize that the thought of spending the night in the same bedroom with a man who is not your husband must be extremely alarming, but I give you my solemn oath that I would never—"

"Oh, for pity's sake, do stop apologizing," she said briskly. "I am well aware of how things can go wrong in the course of an investigation. And I know that you would never take advantage of me. You are an honorable man, sir, a true gentleman. I do not fear for my virtue."

For all the good my virtue has done me, she added silently.

"Your reputation will be safe, as well," he continued, as though he had not heard her. "No one will know your true identity tonight. Naturally I will sign the register with another name."

"Not a problem, sir. I am quite accustomed to playing a role."

"Yes, I know," he said.

This new, excruciating politeness between them was as brittle as glass, Beatrice thought. She was not the only one who was on edge because of the prospect of sharing the same room tonight. For some reason, the knowledge that Joshua was uneasy about the plan was oddly reassuring, almost amusing.

There followed another uneasy silence. Beatrice searched for a safe topic of conversation.

"The rain appears to be getting heavier," she ventured. "One cannot even see as far as the end of the street."

"True," Joshua agreed. "But on the positive side, this sort of weather is bound to complicate life for whoever is following us."

She watched the rain for a time. "If Lancing is alive and if he is going to all this trouble to find me, including taking the risk of bringing you out of retirement, he must have a very good motive."

"Yes."

She clasped her hands together. "You believe that he managed to preserve Emma Hazelton's body in the Egyptian Water and that now he plans to revive her, don't you?"

"I think that is exactly what is going on," Joshua said.

She shuddered. "Sheer madness."

Joshua said nothing. He watched the falling rain for the duration of the short ride to the Blue Fox.

Twenty-Nine

S he awoke with a start. She was breathing too quickly and
her heart was pounding.

"Beatrice, wake up. Make no sound."

Joshua's urgent voice was a low, dark whisper in her ear. She
became aware of his hand on her arm. It was his touch that had
jolted her awake. She opened her eyes and saw that he was bending low over the bed. But he was not looking down at her. His
attention was fixed on the window that overlooked the street.

Her first thought was that the world around her had gone
strangely still and silent. There was an unnatural hush in the atmosphere. She was vaguely aware that it had stopped raining.

Her second thought was that she was astonished to discover
that she had fallen asleep in the first place. After the evening
meal, which had been served in the inn's private dining room, she
had climbed the stairs with Joshua. She had requested a spare

sheet from the innkeeper's wife. When it had been sent up to the room she had draped it around the washstand, attaching two corners to wall hooks, to provide some privacy. Joshua had made no comment.

She had anticipated spending the night lying wide awake on one side of the bed until dawn. The only articles of clothing she had removed were her wet overcoat, her hat and her boots. She had set everything to dry in front of the small fire on the hearth.

Joshua had arranged his own, much heavier boots, his long black overcoat and his hat next to her things. She had been aware of a sensual intimacy in the atmosphere as they went about the task of arranging their damp garments. *As if we were a pair of lovers caught in the rain,* she thought.

She had firmly reminded herself that they were in reality a pair of professional investigators who had been caught in the rain.

When they had at last turned down the lamp, Joshua had made no attempt to use the far side of the bed. Instead he had settled into the room's only chair and contemplated the night.

Now he was standing over her, watching the window with the focused attention of the hunter.

"What's wrong?" she whispered.

"I'm not sure yet," he said. "Possibly nothing at all. But a moment ago I saw someone strike a light in a doorway across the street."

"No honest person would have a reason to be hanging about in a convenient doorway at this hour of the night. You think someone is watching this inn, don't you?"

"It's a possibility." Joshua moved away from the bed. "I'm

going outside to take a look. I want you to stay here and I want you to keep your stocking pistol in your hand until I return. Do you understand?"

"Yes, of course, I understand." She sat up and swung her legs over the side of the bed. The action hiked up her skirts. She removed the small weapon from the holster strapped to her leg. "Please be very, very careful, sir."

"You have my word on it." He went to the now smoldering fire to collect his coat. "Lock the door behind me."

"I will."

"Do not open it for anyone except me."

"No," she said.

She stood and followed him to the door. He let himself out into the hall. She closed the door very quietly and slid the bolt into place.

She waited there, listening intently for a moment. She thought she heard the faint thump of his cane in the hall but she could not be certain.

In spite of his old injury, Joshua could move very quietly when he chose.

Thirty

A heavy fog had followed hard upon the rain. It choked the street. The reflected light of the village's two streetlamps caused the murky stuff to glow as if infused with an eerie energy. The cold moonlight added an additional, seemingly unnatural radiance.

There were times, lately, Joshua thought, when he could almost bring himself to believe in the paranormal. But it wasn't the strange effect of the gas lamps and moonlight on fog that made him wonder about the existence of psychical energy. It was the sensation he experienced whenever he was near Beatrice; whenever he thought about her. Which was most of the time, he realized. Even when he was concentrating on murder and a madman, she was always there at the edge of his awareness.

The unfamiliar sense of intimacy between them went beyond sexual attraction, beyond admiration for her spirit and intelligence, beyond anything he had ever experienced with another woman. When he had kissed her last night it was as if he had unlocked a door somewhere inside himself and walked through it into a realm where things were different. The world on the other side of the door was somehow brighter and more interesting in every way.

For the first time since the wildfire of his young manhood he acknowledged that he was capable of strong passions.

At the start of his relationship with Beatrice he had told himself that if she was not involved in the blackmail scheme she might be in serious danger and he had a responsibility to protect her. But something inside him insisted that what he felt was more than a responsibility—it was his right to take care of her.

Which was nonsense, of course. He had no rights at all when it came to Beatrice. But there was a part of him that was not convinced of that.

He pushed aside his fanciful thoughts and watched the opposite side of the street from the shadows of the narrow stone walk alongside the inn. The figure in the doorway extinguished the light and started toward the inn, drifting like a ghost through the glowing fog. It was impossible to make out his features in the heavy mist but it was clear that he was tall and thin and that he moved with the long, easy stride of a predator.

He crossed the street and came swiftly toward the Blue Fox. The sound of his footsteps echoed faintly in the deep silence. He was dressed in a long overcoat and a low-crowned hat pulled down over his eyes. He carried a pack that was slung across one shoulder.

Instead of going up the steps to the front door of the Blue Fox, he veered toward the narrow walk where Joshua waited.

For a few seconds it appeared that he would not risk striking another light before he entered the deep shadows that drenched the walk. That would make things simple and efficient, Joshua thought. The man would not see that there was someone else nearby.

But just before the newcomer started into the passage, he paused. Evidently sensing that all was not right, he took a step back and reached into his pocket.

Circumstances were far from ideal but Joshua knew that he had no choice other than to move as quickly as possible. The man with the pack would see him as soon as the light flared.

Joshua went forward as swiftly and silently as possible but in spite of his great care the cane thumped softly on the stone walk.

"Who's there?" The thick accent was unmistakably Russian.

He lowered the pack to the ground and produced a knife from his pocket.

"You're the one he warned me about, aren't you, the one with the cane? He said you were dangerous. I told him a lame bastard would not be a problem for the Bone Man. I owe you for interrupting my work last night."

He swept forward in a low rush. The blade in his hand glinted in the odd light.

Joshua flattened his palm against the wall of the inn to brace himself and swung the cane in a slashing arc aimed at the Bone Man's knife arm. He did not have the leverage he needed for a bone-breaking blow but he did have the element of surprise. The assassin was not expecting the cane to be employed as a weapon.

The stick struck the assassin's forearm with considerable force. He grunted, dropped the knife and leaped backward with the fluid grace of a dancer.

In an instant he whirled and swept forward again, intending to retrieve the blade.

Joshua kept one hand flattened against the wall and used the cane to sweep the knife aside into the bushes, out of the Bone Man's reach.

The assassin retreated a second time. Joshua expected him to produce another knife. Instead, he grabbed the pack, dragged it out into the street and reached inside.

Joshua started forward again.

The assassin removed an object from the pack and hurled it to the ground at Joshua's feet. Glass shattered. A smoky mist erupted. Joshua instinctively held his breath and retreated out of range of the vapors. But he could not avoid all of the effects. His eyes burned and his throat tightened. He could only hope that he had not breathed in some lethal poison.

The sound of a window being yanked open somewhere above the street reverberated in the night.

"You down there," Beatrice shouted. "Stop or I'll shoot."

Another window slammed open. "Sound the alarm. There's a villain in the street."

Joshua pushed through the vapors into untainted air but the sound of running footsteps told him that his quarry was escaping. There was no chance of overtaking him. A lame bastard had to accept his physical limitations.

In that moment it was all he could do not to slam the damned stick against the nearest wall. But he knew even as the searing anger and frustration threatened to overwhelm him that such a blow would likely destroy the cane. If that happened he would be even less able to protect Beatrice.

And protecting her was all that mattered.

More windows opened. Joshua looked up and saw the innkeeper, garbed in nightshirt and cap, peering down into the street. Beatrice and several other guests were watching from their windows.

"What's going on down there?" the innkeeper demanded. "Shall I summon the constable?"

"Feel free to do so," Joshua said. "But I doubt if he'll find the villain."

"A burglar, eh?"

"A would-be burglar," Joshua said. "I spotted him in time to send him running off."

"I thank you for the effort, sir, but you shouldn't have tried to go after him on your own," the innkeeper admonished. "You should have alerted me. What chance does a man with a cane have of stopping a member of the criminal class?"

"An excellent question," Joshua said.

He grabbed the pack, slung it over his shoulder and limped back toward the inn.

Thirty-One

T his is more of Lancing's work," Joshua said. "The plan was to smoke us out—literally."

He was in his shirtsleeves, the cuffs rolled up on his forearms, the collar undone. His coat and boots were once again warming in front of the rekindled fire. The edgy sensation that always followed in the wake of violence was heating his blood. The knowledge that Beatrice was anxious and concerned about him added fuel to the fires inside. *Lame bastard. You're not much good to her but you're all she's got.*

He forced himself to concentrate on the three unexploded canisters that he had removed from the pack. He positioned them on the small table and turned up the gas lamp. The smoke devices were made of heavily tinted glass. Each was fitted with a rubber stopper.

"No wonder he handled the pack with such care," he said. "The gas is released when the glass is shattered."

"He meant to burn down the inn in an attempt to grab me?" Beatrice asked. She looked and sounded horrified. "So many people could have been killed, including us. That makes no sense unless the person who is after me wants me dead. Maybe we were wrong to assume that he needs me for some crazed reason."

"No." Joshua held one of the glass balls up to the light. "I'm sure he intended to kidnap you tonight. These devices generate unpleasant fumes and a thick vapor that resembles smoke. The effect simulates a fire but there are no flames. If he had been able to smash all four of these things inside the inn, there would have been a great deal of panic. Everyone would have run out into the street, thinking the place was on fire. He planned to take advantage of the confusion to grab you."

"But he must have known that he would have had to deal with you before he could get to me."

"He said he had been warned about me." Joshua put the glass ball down on the table with great care. "But he did not think that I would prove to be much of a problem."

"Because of your cane?"

"Yes."

"I expect that he has revised his opinion of you by now," Beatrice said. "I saw how you used the cane. In your hands it was a weapon."

The cool satisfaction in her voice had a surprising effect on him. The knowledge that she had such deep—albeit probably misplaced—faith in him elevated his mood somewhat.

"Every object has the potential to be a weapon," he said. *"It only requires that one views it in the right light."*

"Another Mr. Smith adage?" she asked, smiling a little.

"I'm afraid so," Joshua said. "I don't know if the encounter tonight changed the Bone Man's opinion of me. It was your threat to shoot him that sent him away. But he will certainly be better prepared the next time we meet."

"I do not even want to consider the possibility that you will encounter him again."

"It's only a matter of time."

"What a dreadful thought." Beatrice's brows snapped together. "How do you think he found us?"

"He and I did not hold an extended conversation but I think it is safe to say that he anticipated that we would leave the train before the last stop in London. Or, more likely, someone who knows how I think anticipated that maneuver."

"Clement Lancing?"

"Lancing and I worked together for a long time," Joshua said. "We trained together. We each know how the other thinks. I knew there was a risk stopping here in Upper Dixton until the storm cleared but there was not much choice."

"Yes, I know," Beatrice said. "That's why you insisted on keeping watch tonight, wasn't it?"

"Yes."

"And because you did keep watch, you were able to stop the assassin," she concluded crisply. "You saved me. For the second time."

Joshua said nothing. He did not want to tell her how close they had come to disaster tonight. The knowledge would only make her more anxious.

"Where do you suppose the Bone Man acquired the smoke devices?" Beatrice asked. "His original plan was to kidnap me at

Alverstoke Hall. It doesn't seem likely that he would have carried those heavy glass canisters around on the off-chance he might need them."

"I doubt if it was his idea to have a backup plan in the event the first strategy failed. But Lancing knows me. He would have anticipated just such a possibility."

"What is our next step?" Beatrice asked.

"It is time to stop evading the enemy. I must take the battle to him. I know Lancing as well as he knows me. The one thing I am absolutely certain of is that if he is alive he will be in a laboratory somewhere. I want Mrs. Marsh's opinion of the contents of these smoke devices."

"You said they are Lancing's work. What can Mrs. Marsh tell you that you don't already know?"

"I am hoping she will be able to direct me to the shops that stock the sort of chemicals that are used to construct such devices."

Understanding lit Beatrice's eyes. "Yes, of course. The formula for the smoke no doubt requires some unusual ingredients."

"As do the formulas for the incense and the Egyptian Water. There cannot be a great many apothecaries and chemist shops in London who can supply the rare and exotic chemicals that Lancing needs."

"You think the apothecary will lead you to him."

"I think that is our best hope at the moment. But there is another strategy I intend to implement as well."

"I take it we will be traveling to London on the morning train?" she asked.

"The answers we need are there."

"In that case, you must get some sleep."

"I can do without it."

She looked at him with eyes that were both brilliant and very serious. "You have gone more than a full day without sleep, sir. You need rest."

Anger spiked somewhere deep inside. "Just because I'm forced to use a damned walking stick, it doesn't follow that I can't survive a few hours without sleep."

"I'm sure you can, but there is no need. I will keep watch while you rest."

"I will take care of you, Beatrice," he promised. His voice sounded rough, more like a growl, even to his own ears.

"I do not doubt that," she said. "But in addition to lack of sleep, you were recently in a fight for your life. It does not require psychical talent to know that you need time to recover and fortify yourself for whatever lies ahead."

He opened his mouth to argue but closed it again without speaking. She was right. Logic and common sense dictated that he ought to try to get some rest.

"You are correct when you say that I need to fortify myself," he said. "A short period of waking sleep would not be a bad idea."

"What is a waking sleep?"

"It's a form of meditation—a self-induced trance—that will allow me to gain some of the benefits of sleep without shutting off my senses."

Her expression softened. "You can trust me to keep watch while you rest."

"I know," he said, without stopping to think.

It was only after the words were out that he registered their full meaning. He *could* trust Beatrice. Hell's teeth, he *did* trust her; he had trusted her almost from the start even though logic told him that was not wise. He had broken one of his own cardinal rules—never trust anyone involved in a case. Everyone was hiding something.

But somewhere along the line he had made an exception with Beatrice, an exception that could not be justified by logic and cold reason. He had allowed himself to be ruled by his passions and he did not give a damn.

It was a stunning discovery, definitely one he wanted to think long and hard about, but this was not the time to contemplate such a significant event.

Belatedly he realized that Beatrice was watching him very intently.

She cleared her throat. "Excuse me, I don't mean to intrude, but are you in some sort of trance at the moment? You appear quite transfixed."

He pulled himself together. "Yes, I am transfixed. But I'm not yet in the trance."

He limped to the bed, sank down and stretched out on the quilt. He closed his eyes and started counting backward from one hundred.

Thirty-Two

He surfaced from the trance, aware that he felt refreshed and invigorated. Beatrice had been right. He had needed rest.

He opened his eyes and looked toward the window. The fog was thicker than ever but now it was illuminated with the first light of dawn.

Beatrice was sitting in the chair, watching the street. She had taken down her hair. It tumbled around her shoulders. How was it possible, he wondered, for a woman to appear at once innocent and delicate but simultaneously infused with spirit and feminine power? The combination was enthralling and deeply arousing.

And this was not the time to be distracted by such fanciful thoughts.

He sat up on the side of the bed. "I'm awake."

He spoke quietly, not wanting to startle her.

But she was already turning in the chair. She gave him a

searching look. Whatever she saw in his face must have satisfied her because she gave him an approving smile.

"You look much more fit," she said.

He leaned forward and rested his forearms on his thighs. "I take that to mean that I looked very unfit before I went into the trance?"

She glared. "Must you always twist my words?"

He winced. "I will try not to be so touchy on the subject of my physical limitations."

"I would suggest that you try not to be so melodramatic, instead. By the way, how is your leg?"

"It's fine," he said, aware that he sounded touchy again.

"Do you have some of Mrs. Marsh's tonic left?"

"Yes."

She jumped to her feet. "Is it in your bag? I'll get it for you."

"Stop," he ordered. "Do not move."

She halted, eyes widening in alarm. "What is it? What's wrong?"

He pushed himself to his feet and gripped the cane. He went forward, putting himself directly in front of her.

"If you take one more step toward that bag," he said evenly, "you will collide with me, in which case one of two things will happen."

She blinked. "Yes?"

"The impact will either cause me to lose my balance and topple to the floor—"

"Unlikely," she said. Her eyes were very bright. "What is the other possibility?"

"I will grab hold of you in a desperate effort to steady myself."

"Oh," she said.

She looked at him for what seemed like an eternity. His blood heated. The atmosphere in the small space was charged as if a thunderstorm was gathering. He dared not move.

"I might not be able to let go of you," he said.

Beatrice took two very small, very cautious steps forward. When she stopped she was mere inches away. The skirts of her gown brushed his bare feet. She lifted one finger and pushed gently against his chest.

He got the deep, thrilling, breathtakingly intimate shock of awareness that he always got when she touched him. He knew the sensation was a product of his overheated imagination but it felt very, very good, nonetheless.

"Do you think you might be feeling somewhat unsteady on your feet?" she asked, smiling her mysterious smile.

"When I am near you I always find it hard to keep my balance," he said. It was the simple truth, he thought.

She put her hand on his shoulder. "Then perhaps you should hold on to me, sir. I would not want you to fall."

He raised his free hand and touched her hair. The silky stuff was irresistible. He twisted his fingers in it. "I do not think I have any other choice."

He tightened his grip on the cane and wrapped his free arm around her. He pulled her slowly, deliberately against him. She was so light and so soft. She put her other hand on his shoulder and looked at him with her incredible eyes. He knew she must have felt the shudder of need that went through him.

He breathed in her scent and then he took her mouth.

He tried to use the kiss to ignite a slow-burning fire. He would go slowly, he vowed to himself. It had been a very long year in the country—a long time without a woman. But he could control himself. He wanted to seduce Beatrice, to please her, to make her want him as much as he wanted her.

She responded as she had last night, with curiosity and a sweet passion that set fire to his blood.

She sighed and pressed closer. Her fingers tightened around his shoulders. He realized that she was shivering a little. He moved his mouth to her ear.

"Are you cold?" he asked softly.

She rested her forehead against his shoulder. When she answered, her voice was a tight little whisper.

"No, I am not cold," she said.

He lifted her hair and kissed the curve of her neck. "Are you frightened of me?"

"Of you? Never."

"You're shivering."

She raised her head and gave him an uncertain smile. "I have heard that passion can generate a sort of fever but I have never truly believed it. I have always assumed such claims were so much romantic nonsense. Poetic license at best."

"I have always assumed that as well," he said. "But now I know the poets are right. There is a great deal of fire involved."

"I do hope you are not going to stop now to analyze the sensation in a logical manner."

"The only force on the face of the earth that could make me stop now is you, my sweet Beatrice."

She wound her arms around his neck. This time her smile was less shaky. It held, instead, the glowing wonder of a woman who has made the decision to abandon herself to passion.

"I have no intention of stopping you, Mr. Gage. Indeed, I have been waiting a lifetime to experience a passion such as this. I had begun to fear that I might never know such fierce emotions. If I were to stop you now, I know I would regret it for the rest of my life."

He smiled. "I assure you, I would regret it even more and for just as long, Miss Lockwood."

Sensual laughter and heated excitement illuminated her eyes. When he drew her to the bed, she came willingly.

He set the cane aside, braced his good leg against the edge of the four-poster and began to unfasten the small hooks that closed the front of her gown. The process of opening the bodice proved to be a challenge. It was not that he had not had some experience, he thought, amused by his own awkwardness. The problem was that this time was different. Beatrice was different.

He eventually got the gown undone. He eased the sleeves down her arms. The skirts crumpled around her ankles, leaving her in her chemise, petticoats and stockings.

She untied her petticoats and they, too, fell away. In the dim glow of the early light he could see her flushed face. Her small, firm breasts were tight and full beneath the thin chemise.

"You are so perfect," he whispered. He drew his hands down her sides to her hips and then slid them upward to cup her breasts. "As if you were made for me."

"You make me feel beautiful," she said.

Her blush deepened. He could have sworn that there was a

radiance in her eyes. A trick of the light, he thought. But what a beautiful trick.

Gingerly she went to work unfastening the front of his shirt with trembling fingers. He thought he would lose his control before she finally finished. But when she flattened her palms against his bare chest he concluded the sweet torture had been worth it.

"I can feel the strength in you," she said. She gazed at his chest as if fascinated. "Not just your physical strength but the other sort, the more important kind of strength that comes from the inside."

"Ah, Beatrice, you are the strong one."

He sat on the edge of the bed and drew her down beside him. When he pulled her close she came to him with an enthusiasm that warmed everything inside him that had been cold for so long.

He kissed her until she softened against him, until she was making hungry, desperate little sounds in the back of her throat.

The hem of the chemise was crumpled high above her knees, revealing the dainty holster strapped to her thigh.

"I have never before considered guns to be a sensual enticement," he said. "But this one has an oddly stimulating effect on me. Something to do with where you carry it, I believe."

She gave a small, choked laugh.

He unstrapped the holster and the small gun very slowly and set both aside on the table beside the bed. Then he rested one hand on the silky bare skin above her stockings.

She took in a sharp, startled breath at the intimate touch but she did not pull away.

"So soft," he said against her throat.

"You are so strong but you handle me as if I were made of crystal. I'm not fragile, sir."

He touched the corner of her mouth. "I know that you have your own kind of strength, but a man could easily crush you if he were not careful."

Laughter gleamed in her eyes. "You underestimate me, sir. Not your fault. It happens all the time. Indeed, my appearance of timidity and naïveté is my stock-in-trade. It is one of the reasons I am such a successful investigator. But you, of all people, should know that appearances are often deceptive. I am not the innocent you seem to think me."

"Are you trying to tell me that you are a woman of the world?"

"Trust me when I say that my various careers have combined to teach me more about the world than most ladies will ever know in a lifetime."

He kissed her shoulder. "Is that so?"

"Yes," she said. "And I assure you that I know what I am doing now."

"Then you are aware that I'm seducing you?"

"I know that I am *allowing* you to seduce me." She brushed her mouth across his. "And doing my best to seduce you in return. I do hope I am having some success."

A rush of exhilaration swept through him. He groaned and fell back across the bed, his arm around her waist. She sprawled on top of him, her stocking-clad legs entangled with his.

"Can I take that as a yes, Mr. Gage?" she asked.

"Yes, you can, Miss Lockwood." He framed her face with his hands. "What of my own seduction efforts? Can I assume they are having some effect?"

"Oh, yes. Indeed, I would say that you have a psychical talent for seduction, but as you do not believe in the paranormal, there wouldn't be much point."

He touched her nose with the tip of his finger. "It's true that I do not believe in paranormal talents. But I am a great believer in the merits of practicing a skill until it is perfected."

"So am I."

She kissed him again, exploring and tasting him. When she had finished with his mouth she nibbled on his ear and then her warm lips were on his throat.

"You smell good," she whispered.

He grimaced. "I must smell like a man who has recently been in a fight and had to make do with a sponge bath."

"Perhaps I should have said you smell interesting." She kissed his chest. "Hot. Exciting. Manly."

"Manly?" The word surprised a husky laugh from him, a low rumble that came from deep in his chest.

Beatrice laughed, too, but her laughter was light, ethereal, enchanting. She raised herself on her elbows and looked down at him with a mockingly stern expression.

"I do believe you are growling at me, sir," she said.

"Never."

He shifted abruptly, rolling her to one side. He pinned her beneath him and opened the front of the thin chemise. Deliberately he kissed the tips of her apple-shaped breasts.

"You are the one who smells good," he said. "You are a drug to my senses."

"I do believe that you are the most romantic man I have ever met."

"I am not a romantic but I am hungry for you in a way I have never hungered for any other woman. I do not believe in the paranormal but there may be such a thing as magic. I believe you have put a spell on me, Titania."

She speared her fingers through his hair. "If that is true, then I am well and truly caught in the same spell."

"For which I can only give thanks."

He moved one hand down to her leg again and stroked his palm up the inside of her thigh. When he reached her core he found her wet and hot. She was ready for him but he wanted her more than merely ready. He wanted her aching for him, the way he was aching for her.

He thrust his fingers through the curling hair that guarded her sex and found the sensitive bud. It was already tight but he teased it until it was even more swollen and taut. Beatrice gasped and clung to him, one leg twining around his thigh.

He caressed her until his hand was slick and the coverlet beneath her hips was damp; until he was the one who could not take any more. He was walking a tightrope when it came to his self-control. One false step and he would be lost. But he longed to take the fall.

Beatrice clutched at him, her nails digging into his shoulders. "I cannot bear this pressure inside me any longer. Do something."

He sat up on the side of the bed long enough to get out of his trousers and then he came back to her. He used one hand to guide himself to her entrance. He eased into her until he felt the delicate barrier.

"So much for your worldly experience," he said.

She caught hold of his face with both hands and looked at

him. In that moment he was certain that her eyes burned with the fire of a raging fever. He wondered if his own eyes appeared equally hot. Most certainly a trick of the dawn light, he told himself again. That was the only reasonable explanation.

"Finish this, Mr. Gage," she ordered, "or I will never forgive you."

"As you command, Miss Lockwood."

He gathered himself, withdrew slightly, and then thrust hard and deep into her tight body.

He felt the shockwave that went through her because it slammed through him at the same time. For a few seconds he was dazed and disoriented. It was as if he had tumbled into a surging, seething sea of raw energy.

Impossible.

He became aware that Beatrice had stiffened under him. Her lips parted and her nails sank deep. He covered her mouth swiftly, muffling her cry of astonishment, pain and outrage. It took everything he had to hold himself very still. He was sweating hard.

When the outrage seemed to have subsided into a grumble, he raised his head and smoothed her hair away from her damp forehead.

"I'm sorry," he said. He rested his damp forehead on hers. "I'm sorry. I did not want to hurt you."

"Yes, well, it was my own fault." She took a steadying breath. "I believe I did insist. I thought I knew what to expect but I suppose no one can truly be prepared for something that one has never experienced."

"No," he said. "I realize you are not in the mood to hear this but things will be much more comfortable the next time."

She relaxed a little more and put her arms around his neck. "And just how would you know that, Mr. Gage?"

"Logic tells me that," he said. "And do you think you might be able to call me by my first name now?"

She giggled, moving a little beneath him. He winced and caught his breath.

She stopped laughing at once. "Are you all right?"

"I'm not sure," he said. He was speaking through his teeth. "But it would be extremely helpful if you would not move."

"Then what is the point of all this?"

"That is an excellent question." He sucked in a breath. "The thing is, if you keep moving, I will be forced to move, too."

"I see." She wriggled experimentally. "You may be right. Things are somewhat more comfortable now. You are awfully large down there, aren't you? Do you think that is normal?"

He groaned. "I did warn you, Beatrice."

The heat returned to her eyes.

"Yes, you did," she whispered. "It's all right, Joshua. I will not shatter in your hands."

He withdrew slowly and then forged carefully back into her. Tentatively, she raised her hips to meet him. It was too much. He began to move more quickly because he could not do anything else. The need to climax inside her was riding him hard now. Nothing short of the end of the world could stop him. He had to stake his claim on Beatrice, had to make her know that they belonged together.

"Joshua." She clutched at him. *"Joshua."*

Her body shivered. And then she convulsed in his arms. Her head tipped back. Her eyes squeezed shut.

He wanted to savor the thrill of her release but the small pulsations deep inside her were pulling him into a vortex. It was unlike anything he had ever known. He rocked into her one more time and then he poured himself into her, gritting his teeth against the low howl of exultation that welled up inside.

When it was over, he collapsed on top of her. His last semi-coherent thought was that maybe he had been wrong all along. Maybe there really was something to the notion of paranormal energy, after all. Nothing else could explain the startling sense of connection that he experienced in that moment.

All his adult life he had worked to maintain balance in all things, especially when it came to the darker passions.

Another rule broken for the sake of Beatrice. He knew there would be more.

Thirty-Three

He came reluctantly out of the luxurious aftermath and sat up on the side of the bed. A glance out the window told him the fog was lifting. He reached for his trousers and took out his watch. They had two hours until the morning train to London stopped in Upper Dixton.

On the far side of the room, Beatrice was moving about behind the sheet that she had strung around the washstand. He heard water slosh in the bowl and knew that she was washing away the physical evidence of their passion.

For a moment he sat quietly, trying to think of the proper thing to say. He had never before been intimate with a virgin. He pulled on his trousers and fastened them. Then he grasped the cane and pushed himself to his feet.

"Are you . . . all right?" he asked.

"What?" Beatrice put her head around the edge of the sheet. Her hair was pinned up rather carelessly and what he could see of her shoulders indicated she was partially nude. Her brows were scrunched together in bewilderment. Then her expression cleared. "Yes, of course I'm all right. Perfectly fit. I have always enjoyed good health."

He smiled to himself. "How very fortunate for you."

She frowned in concern. "What about you? Is your leg bothering you?"

He held up one hand, palm out in a silencing gesture.

"Sorry," she said quickly. "I was merely concerned that perhaps all that exercise might have caused your old injury to flare up."

He gave her a hard look.

She broke off, flushing. She ducked back behind the sheet and resumed her washing. "Right. When do we leave?"

"Soon."

"Very well," Beatrice said. "My chief concern at the moment is obtaining fresh clothes. I can't wait to get home."

She was rustling around behind the sheet now. He knew that she was getting dressed.

"Beatrice, there is something I have wanted to ask you since the moment I met you."

There was a slight pause on the other side of the sheet.

"Yes?" she asked. There was a great deal of caution in the single word.

"I understand how you wound up working as an agent for Flint and Marsh. But how did you come to find yourself in Dr. Fleming's Academy of the Occult?"

There was another short pause. He got the impression that his question was not the one she had anticipated.

"You know how it is when a woman finds herself alone in the

world," she said airily. "After my parents were killed I landed in an orphanage. My career opportunities were quite limited, as you can imagine."

"Yes," he said. "I know. The world is a hard place for a woman on her own."

"I was sent to my first post as a governess when I was sixteen. I'm afraid I was not a very good governess. My employer's two young sons were little monsters and I lacked the skills to keep them under control. So, I was let go. I managed to obtain another position in the household of a handsome widower. He seemed to take an interest in my well-being. I'm afraid that, in my naïveté, I mistook his kindness for a stronger, more intimate emotion."

"You fell in love with him."

She put her head around the sheet again. "I was sixteen, Joshua. All I knew of love was what I had read in novels and books of poetry. But it was not long before I realized the foolishness of my ways. During the two months that I was concocting romantic fantasies he was occupied with finding himself a suitable wife."

"You were not aware he planned to marry?"

"No." Beatrice emerged from behind the sheet, fully dressed. She gave him a rueful smile. "Imagine my surprise when he announced his engagement to a very wealthy, very lovely lady whose family moved in the best circles."

"I assume you left your post because of his marriage?"

"Well, I would have done so, because I was utterly devastated. I told myself I could not live in the same house with him and his new wife. But as it happened, there was no need for me to take such a drastic step. My employer's fiancée made it clear that she wanted me dismissed before she would move in. I was let go immediately. My employer was kind to the end, however. He offered to set me up in a small house in a quiet neighborhood."

"In other words, he intended to make you his mistress."

"Yes."

He glanced at the stains on the coverlet. "Obviously you rejected the offer."

"It was bad enough that he had broken my heart. The insult was too much. I was furious. I hurled the contents of a vase of flowers at him. I quite ruined his jacket, I'm sure. I have something of a temper."

"You're a redhead," Joshua said. "You're entitled to a temper. You should have cracked the vase over his head."

"Yes, well, they tend to arrest people for inflicting that sort of bodily damage. I was angry but I'm not a complete idiot."

He smiled slightly. "A wise decision under the circumstances. Did you ever see the bastard again?"

Beatrice was amused. "He wasn't a complete bastard, just a wealthy man who was acting in accordance with the conventions of his station. In fairness, I think he was truly fond of me, but naturally he could not marry a governess. He realized that even if I did not at the time. And yes, I did see him again. We passed each other on the street one afternoon about a year later. He was with his new bride. He never noticed me."

Joshua was stunned. "How could he have failed to see you?"

Beatrice giggled. "You really are a romantic at heart, Joshua Gage. He didn't notice me because by that time he had forgotten all about me."

"I find that impossible to believe."

She gave him a whimsical smile. "Do you?"

"Even if I never saw you again, I would not forget you. And I will always know if you are near."

Her eyes darkened into fathomless pools. "As I said, you are a true romantic."

Annoyed, he tightened his grip on the cane. "You did not tell me how you came to land at Dr. Fleming's Academy of the Occult."

She blinked. "Oh, right. There really isn't much more to the story. I changed careers and became a paid companion. Not at the Flint and Marsh Agency, though, a different one. I was fortunate enough to obtain a post in the household of a woman who was fascinated with the study of the paranormal. I shared her interest."

He smiled. "Naturally."

"One afternoon I accompanied her to the Academy to observe Dr. Fleming's demonstrations. My employer booked a private appointment during which Roland recognized that I had some genuine talent and offered to hire me as a paranormal practitioner. My employer urged me to take the position. She said it would give me a far more comfortable life than a career as a companion. She was right, at least until the night that poor Roland was murdered."

"After which you reinvented yourself as a professional investigator."

"Well, not immediately," Beatrice said. "I had no idea that such a profession even existed. However, when I concluded that I had no choice but to return to my former career as a paid companion, I began making the rounds of various agencies. I heard rumors of an exclusive agency in Lantern Street that paid very well. The proprietors were said to be extremely selective when it came to hiring companions. I decided I had nothing to lose so I applied. Mrs. Flint and Mrs. Marsh offered me a position immediately. They said I had a certain talent for the work."

He smiled. "I know I have told you this before but I will say it again. You are an amazing woman, Beatrice."

"One does what one must to survive," she said.

He reflected briefly on all the times he had stood very close to the edge of the cliffs at his country house and looked down into the roiling sea. Always, he had limped back to the house again, telling himself that he could not take that way out because he had responsibilities.

But now he wondered if the real reason he had turned away from the sea was simply because deep down inside, a tiny flame of hope still burned.

"Yes," he said. He made his way across the room and stopped in front of her. He caught her chin on the edge of his hand, bent his head and kissed her lightly on the mouth. "And I assure you that I am very glad that I survived long enough to make your acquaintance, Beatrice Lockwood."

She smiled. Her eyes brightened. "The feeling is mutual, Mr. Gage."

That was not quite what he wanted to hear but this was not the time to pursue the subject. He released her and went to where his coat hung on a hook in the wall.

"Let's have some breakfast and then we will catch the train to London. I will send a telegram to Nelson advising him to meet us and take us directly to the offices of Flint and Marsh. I am very eager to chat with Mrs. Marsh," he said.

He saw that she was still smiling but now there was a sparkle of amusement in her eyes.

"Have I inadvertently managed to entertain you again, Miss Lockwood?" he asked.

"It's nothing," she assured him.

He winced. "Like hell."

"Very well, then, if you must know, I cannot help but notice that you appear to thrive on these clandestine plots and counterplots. You were born for this sort of work, Joshua. Really, you should never have retired."

Thirty-Four

Nelson met them at the railway station in London. They all watched the rest of the passengers exit the train. None appeared unduly suspicious.

"Doesn't mean he wasn't on board," Joshua said. "But in this fog he'll find it impossible to follow us."

Nelson escorted them through heavy mist to a nearby lane where a closed carriage waited. When Beatrice briefly heightened her talent she could see the heat in his footsteps.

"I have news, Uncle Josh," he said, opening the door for Beatrice.

"Excellent," Joshua said. "Save it until we are on our way."

He handed Beatrice up into the cab and followed her into the shadowed confines. He sat down beside her. Nelson vaulted up into the small space and took the opposite seat.

Joshua used his cane to rap the roof of the cab twice. The vehicle rolled forward at a fast clip.

One look at Nelson told Beatrice that—a few minor differences aside—she was looking at a younger mirror image of Joshua. This was how he had appeared in the days before the scars, both physical and emotional, had changed him.

The men of the Gage line were not handsome in the classical sense but they were fascinating in their own way. Perhaps it was the masculine strength in their auras that compelled a woman's attention, Beatrice thought. Whatever the case, Nelson's barely suppressed excitement combined with the intensity of Joshua's more mature aura of controlled power infused the atmosphere of the small cab with so much heat that she wanted to fan herself.

"Don't worry, Miss Lockwood," Nelson said. "Our driver, Henry, has had a great deal of experience, thanks to my uncle. He will ensure that no one follows us to the offices of your employers."

"I don't doubt that," Beatrice said.

"And as Uncle Josh pointed out, the fog will make it all the easier to evade detection," Nelson added.

Beatrice slanted a quick, speculative glance at Joshua. "Was this the cab you used to remove Mr. Euston from the garden the night we met?"

"As a matter of fact, it was," Joshua said. He looked at Nelson. "Tell me what you have learned."

"I did as you asked," Nelson said. "I spoke with everyone I could find who had lived and worked in the street where the Academy of the Occult was located at the time of Fleming's death."

"What's this?" Beatrice glared at Joshua. "You never told me that you were making inquiries into Roland's murder."

"Did I neglect to mention it?" Joshua frowned. "Sorry. I have had other things on my mind of late."

"Why did you ask Nelson to conduct such an investigation?" she demanded.

"Because this affair has its roots in what happened that night," Joshua said, not bothering to conceal his impatience with the distracting questions. He fixed Nelson with a fiercely intent expression. "What did you discover?"

Nelson took out a notebook and flipped through it. He stopped at a page. "There were, as you predicted, a number of inconsistencies in people's memories of the events at the time but there were a few things everyone agreed on. Several suspected that paranormal forces from beyond the grave were involved in the murder. Naturally I discounted that theory."

Joshua dismissed that with a short, brusque movement of one hand. "Of course. What else?"

Nelson gave Beatrice an apologetic look. "I'm sorry to say that many of the residents of the street concluded that the woman they knew as Miranda the Clairvoyant was the killer."

She sighed. "No need to apologize. I read the papers at the time. The knowledge that the police were looking for me was one of the reasons I changed careers. No one ever expects a woman to do that."

"Right." Nelson turned another page. "But here's the interesting material. Two shopkeepers and a baked potato vendor who do business in the neighborhood recalled an unusual man who loitered in the vicinity for a couple of days before the murder. He made them uneasy, they said. The shopkeepers wondered if he might be a thief who was making observations in preparation for a burglary."

"They were on the right track," Joshua said. "But he was planning a murder and a kidnapping, not a burglary."

"The interesting fact was that they all gave a strikingly similar description of the man. They said he spoke very little but when he did it was with a heavy foreign accent."

"The people who inhabit small, closely knit neighborhoods always remember outsiders, especially outsiders with strong accents," Joshua said. "Did they give any more details?"

"It was all quite vague," Nelson said. "But the baked potato vendor said the stranger had a face that could keep a child awake at night. Reminded him of a skull, he said. The shopkeepers agreed."

"That confirms my conclusion," Joshua said. "Lancing is using a professional assassin. Now we must locate the skull-faced man."

"How?" Beatrice asked.

Nelson looked interested. "Yes, how do we do that, Uncle Josh?"

"A professional killer—especially one with a foreign accent—will not have gone unnoticed in the criminal underworld," Joshua said. "That is a small, closely connected neighborhood, too."

"But how do we make inquiries in that world?" Nelson asked.

"I have an associate who makes it a point to know everything that goes on in that realm. As it happens, he owes me a favor or two."

"Now, there's a surprise," Beatrice said. She smiled. "I'm shocked to hear that you are acquainted with such an individual, Mr. Gage."

Nelson burst into laughter. After a moment, Joshua's mouth tugged upward in a reluctant smile.

Like uncle, like nephew, Beatrice thought.

"I cannot wait to go home and bathe and put on a fresh change of clothing," she said.

Joshua looked at her. "You're not going home, not yet. It's too risky. There is a possibility that by now the assassin has discovered your address. He may be watching your house. There is only one place in London where I can be assured of your safety."

"Where is that?"

"The home of an old friend of mine. Assuming I can prevail upon him to help us."

"Does he owe you a favor like your associate in the criminal underworld?" Beatrice asked.

"No. I am the one who owes him," Joshua said.

Thirty-Five

"What is going on between you and Mr. Gage?" Sara asked.

She was sitting on a chair in the small bedroom watching Beatrice dress in clean petticoats and a fresh gown.

"What do you mean?" Beatrice said. "I told you what happened at Alverstoke Hall and afterward." She finished fastening the bodice of the dress and sat down in front of the fire to dry her hair. "Mr. Gage believes that a madman named Clement Lancing is intent on kidnapping me."

She was feeling refreshed and invigorated from the bath. Shortly after their arrival at the back door of Flint & Marsh, she and Joshua had been ushered upstairs to the private quarters of the town house. George had been dispatched to the house Beatrice shared with Clarissa. He had been given instructions to tell the housekeeper that Beatrice had been called away on a special assignment for Flint & Marsh and required a change of clothing and some toiletries. He had returned with a bag packed with the requested items and a few additional things that Mrs. Rambley had thoughtfully included—a hairbrush, hairpins, a nightgown and fresh underclothes.

Mercifully, Sara and Abigail had asked few questions when they found Beatrice and Joshua at the door. Food and baths had clearly been the first priorities. Beatrice had given Sara a summary of events but it was obvious now that Sara was not entirely satisfied.

She regarded Beatrice with a stern air. "You know very well that I am referring to your personal relationship with Mr. Gage."

Beatrice braced herself. "I thought I explained that Mr. Gage has more or less appointed himself my bodyguard until he can find Clement Lancing. I would not call that a personal relationship."

"Rubbish. It is evident from the way he looks at you that Gage has appointed himself your lover as well as your bodyguard."

Beatrice winced and picked up the hairbrush. "Is it that obvious?"

Sara's expression softened. "Yes, I'm afraid so. Under other circumstances, I would not dream of interfering in your private affairs. You are a woman who has been on her own for quite some time. You are not a naïve innocent. More to the point, you are a Flint and Marsh agent, a lady possessed of considerable talent. You can take care of yourself or you would not be working for us. But Mr. Gage is a man unlike any other you have had occasion to encounter."

"I am well aware of that, Sara."

Sara exhaled slowly. "I suppose that is part of the attraction."

Beatrice smiled. "I suppose it is."

Upon reflection, Sara's diagnosis might be the correct one, Beatrice thought. She had been struggling with the question of the attraction she felt for Joshua ever since she had risen from the bed they had shared at dawn.

All morning she had been trying to tell herself that the passion that had flared between them had been fueled, in part, by the excitement generated by danger. In addition she was attracted to Joshua. For his part, there was the factor of that very long year spent rusticating in the country. The two of them had found themselves alone in a bedroom. Those factors had combined to create a volatile brew. The sexual encounter that had taken place at the inn had, in hindsight, been entirely predictable.

But she was not sure that all of those reasons explained the powerful metaphysical bond that she sensed between Joshua and herself this morning. It was as if the lovemaking had established an invisible link between the two of them. She reminded herself that if such a connection actually did exist, it was quite possible that she was the only one who felt it.

Then again, the sensation of an intimate bond might simply be a fantasy that her fevered imagination had concocted to explain her reckless passion. There was no doubt but that she had been struck by a fever of the senses.

"Make no mistake," Sara continued, "I have always had the greatest admiration for Mr. Gage. But he comes from a very different social world, as I'm sure you realize. He is not yet married but it will not be long before he is obliged to wed for the sake of his family name."

"I know all this, Sara." Beatrice tightened her grip on the hairbrush. "As you pointed out, I am not naïve. I am well aware that there is no future for me with Joshua. But I also know that I will never again have an opportunity to experience these feelings and sensations with another man. He is . . . unique."

"As are you, Bea." Sara got to her feet and went to the door. "Under normal circumstances, I have no objections to passion. But in my experience, Flint and Marsh agents who make the mistake of falling in love with a person who is connected to a case usually regret it. I advise you to protect your heart while Mr. Gage is protecting you from this madman."

Thirty-Six

"I am well aware that at the moment you have Miss Lockwood's best interests at heart," Abigail Flint said.

Joshua had been about to reach for another small sandwich. He paused and cocked a brow at Abigail.

"*At the moment* implies that at some future time and place I might not have Miss Lockwood's best interests at heart," he said.

Abigail fixed him with a grim look. "I do not mean to imply anything of the sort. But I do want to make it clear that Miss Lockwood, although an experienced agent, is, nevertheless, a young woman with very little experience of the sorts of strong emotions and passions that can be generated when two people find themselves confronting danger together."

"In other words you are trying to warn me not to take advantage of her."

"In most cases Flint and Marsh agents go about their investigations unnoticed by others, including gentlemen," Abigail said. "In their role as paid companions they are generally invisible in a household. But there have been exceptions. You are not the first man to assume that a Flint and Marsh agent is, by virtue of her career, experienced in the ways of the world."

"One would assume that one of the ladies of Lantern Street could take care of herself."

"Our agents all have one thing in common, Mr. Gage. They come to work for us because, for any number of reasons, they find themselves impoverished and on their own. They do not have families to protect them. We both know that leaves them vulnerable in some ways."

"So you and Mrs. Marsh take it upon yourselves to look after your agents." Joshua picked up the sandwich and took a bite. "That is very commendable of you."

"We do not care to see any of our ladies seduced and abandoned. That sort of thing complicates our business."

He could feel his temper sparking. He could not decide whether to be amused or offended by the interrogation and the warning that he was receiving. Very well, he was guilty of seducing Beatrice, but he had no intention of abandoning her. Not that he had given much thought to their future together, he realized. During the past year he had gotten out of the habit of making any sort of long-range plans. He had been living life day-to-boring-day.

"Does it happen often?" he asked. "The seduction and abandonment of one of your agents, I mean."

"Mrs. Marsh and I do our best to keep that sort of behavior to a minimum." Abigail gave him a steely smile. "But I can assure you that I have used information gained in the course of a case to warn off more than one man who thought he could amuse himself with a lady of Lantern Street."

"Ah, yes, blackmail. Always a useful tool."

"As I said, for the most part, Mrs. Marsh and I are all the family our agents possess. As their employers, we have a responsibility to look after them."

"Beatrice carries a gun and some very potent smelling salts, yet you are concerned that she cannot protect herself," he said.

"Passion can make any woman reckless."

"I have news for you, Mrs. Flint. It can have similar effects on a man. Have you considered the possibility that you have misread the situation? What if I am the one who is at risk of having my heart broken? Will you look after me if I find myself abandoned?"

Abigail gave a small snort. "I am not the least bit concerned about you, sir. Mr. Smith's Messenger is quite capable of taking care of himself."

"Do not be so sure of that, madam."

She glared. "I'm serious, Mr. Gage. I am well aware that Sara and I are in your debt. I expect half of London is in the same situation."

"Not half."

She ignored that. "But I want your word that you will not allow Beatrice to dream dreams that can never come true."

"What of my dreams, Mrs. Flint?" he asked.

"I can only imagine what your dreams are like, sir." She glanced rather pointedly at his scarred face and then at his cane.

"Given what I know of your past, I suspect they are not particularly pleasant."

She did not wait for a response. She rose and walked to the door, leaving him alone.

He waited until the door closed behind her.

"My dreams have improved considerably of late," he said to the empty room.

Thirty-Seven

Beatrice waited until Abigail and Sara had disappeared through the door of Sara's laboratory. Then she sidled up to Joshua. He had the pack containing the smoke canisters slung over one shoulder.

"Did you, by any chance, get a lecture on the subject of your honorable intentions toward me?" she whispered.

He gave her a politely puzzled expression. "Why do you ask?"

"Because I got a pithy little talk on the subject of gentlemen who feel free to trifle with an innocent lady's affections. Very annoying, to say the least."

"The gentlemen or the lecture?"

"That is not amusing, Joshua."

"Sorry." He paused at the door to allow her to enter first. "Yes, I got a lecture."

"I was afraid of that. I apologize on behalf of my employers. They do mean well, you know."

"I never doubted it."

She beetled her brows. "How did you respond?"

"I pointed out that you carry a gun and those rather nasty smelling salts and appeared to be quite capable of defending yourself."

She smiled, pleased. "An excellent response."

"How did you reply to the warning about my intentions?"

"I made it clear that as I am no longer innocent, the lecture came too late to do any good."

She swept through the doorway, ignoring his muffled laugh. Really, the man had the oddest sense of humor, she thought.

Sara and Abigail were waiting. Sara was in the process of donning a large leather apron. Her laboratory occupied the basement of the town house. A number of workbenches were covered with a variety of scientific instruments that ranged from delicate scales to an electricity-generating machine. Some of the glass-fronted cabinets along the walls contained ore and gemstone specimens. Others held bottles and small boxes filled with various chemicals.

"Let's have a look at those smoke-producing devices, Mr. Gage," Sara said. Enthusiasm and curiosity sparked in her eyes as well as in her voice. She gestured toward a nearby workbench. "You can set them on that table. You say they are volatile?"

Joshua went to the workbench and slipped the pack off his shoulder. "The man who used one of these against me ignited it by smashing the canister at my feet. There was a great deal of smoky vapor but no flames."

He put the pack on the workbench, opened it and removed the three remaining canisters.

Sara put on a pair of goggles and tied a mask over her nose and mouth. She pulled on some heavy gloves and went to the table.

"Stand back, everyone," she ordered.

No one argued. Beatrice and the others moved away from the workbench. They all watched, intrigued, as Sara picked up one of the canisters and examined it closely.

"Interesting," she said. "Let's see what's inside."

She removed the stopper with great care. A strong chemical odor wafted out of the opening. Beatrice wrinkled her nose.

"Whew." Abigail waved a hand in front of her face and hastily retreated another few steps.

"Hmm," Sara said.

She used a medicine dropper to remove a sample of the contents. The fluid was clear. She placed a few drops in a test tube and repeated the process several times until a number of samples had been prepared. Then she replaced the stopper in the canister.

She looked at Beatrice, Joshua and Abigail.

"This is going to take a while," she announced. "I can't work with so many people watching my every move. Go upstairs and have some more tea. I'll call you when I've got news."

Obediently, Beatrice and the others trooped back upstairs. Abigail led the way into the small parlor. Joshua went to stand at the window looking out into the fog. Beatrice sensed his impatience. Abigail noticed as well.

"You may as well sit down, Mr. Gage," she said. "There is nothing to be gained by watching the street."

"No, I suppose not. Can't see a damned thing in this fog, anyway." Reluctantly he turned away from the window and lowered himself into a chair. "But I have the feeling that time is running out. Lancing would not have taken the risk of pulling me into this affair if that wasn't the case. I must find the source of the chemicals as soon as possible. And then I must find the assassin."

"I understand," Abigail said. "Meanwhile, what are your plans for tonight? You and Beatrice are welcome to stay with us."

"Thank you, but no," Joshua said. "Beatrice will be safer in another location that I have in mind. I need to be assured that she is protected while I pursue my plan to draw Lancing's hired assassin out into the open. The Bone Man is an obstacle that I wish to remove as quickly as possible."

Beatrice looked at him. "It seems to me that the simplest way to draw the killer into a trap would be to use me as bait."

"No," Joshua said. The single word was flat and unequivocal.

"Have you got a better plan?" she asked politely.

"Let's just say it is an alternative strategy."

She did not like the sound of that. "What do you intend to do?"

"It's clear now that Lancing used me to find you, but now I have become a problem for him," Joshua said.

Abigail's brows rose in cool comprehension. "Lancing knows that you are standing in his way. Even if he manages to grab Beatrice, he is aware that you will continue to be a problem."

"Because you won't stop looking for me," Beatrice said quietly.

"No," Joshua said. He met her eyes. "Not ever."

Abigail watched him intently. "You believe that Lancing's first objective is to get rid of you?"

"That is certainly the strategy I would employ if I were in his place," Joshua said. "He knows how I think, but the reverse is also true. I know his ways as well as he knows mine. After all, we were both trained by the same man."

"But it is the assassin you must deal with first, not Lancing," Beatrice said.

"The assassin is Lancing's vulnerable point," Joshua said. "The skull-faced man is the one person who knows how to get to Lancing. The thing about hired killers is that one must pay them on a regular basis. That means there is always a rendezvous point. When I have that, I will have Lancing."

"But first you must draw out the assassin," Beatrice said. "If you don't use me as bait, what will you use?"

"Myself," Joshua said. "He will be in a vengeful mood after two failures. His pride will make him reckless."

Beatrice caught her breath. "Joshua, I must tell you that I don't think that is a good plan—"

The muffled sound of an explosion in the basement stopped the conversation cold.

"Good grief," Abigail said. She jumped to her feet and rushed toward the door. "Sara? Are you all right? *Sara.*"

Beatrice and Joshua followed Abigail out into the hall and down to the first floor. At the top of the basement stairs they stopped. Tendrils of smoke and the scent of powerful chemicals wafted up from the basement.

"Sara," Abigail called anxiously. "Answer me."

Sara appeared at the bottom of the steps. She climbed quickly through the drifting vapors. When she reached the doorway she stripped off her mask and goggles and gave them a triumphant smile.

"Good news, Mr. Gage," she said. "I think I know the name of the apothecary who supplied the chemicals for the smoke devices and very likely for that Egyptian Water you described, as well. There is only one person in London who can be relied upon when it comes to obtaining rare and exotic chemicals like these."

"Only one?" Joshua asked.

"As far as I am aware, Mrs. Grimshaw in Teaberry Lane is the only apothecary I know of who specializes in the preparation of compounds and formulas that possess paranormal properties."

Thirty-Eight

I f you say *I told you so* one more time I may be forced to take drastic action," Joshua warned.

"Your threats do not frighten me in the least," Beatrice said. She waved one gloved hand in an airy gesture. Yes, she was gloating, she thought, but she simply could not resist. "I trust that the next time I inform you that there is evidence of a paranormal nature you will pay closer attention to my conclusions."

They were sitting in Joshua's anonymous carriage. Henry, the driver, had stopped at the entrance to Teaberry Lane because the ancient cobbled passage was too narrow for the vehicle.

The lane was choked with fog. It was impossible to make out the sign above the apothecary shop but there was a faint glow in the window, indicating that the establishment was open for business.

Beatrice was intensely aware of the prowling energy that seethed in the intimate confines of the vehicle's cab. The cold,

tightly controlled anticipation of the wolf on the hunt was emanating from Joshua. She knew that he would not believe her if she
informed him that there was a dark heat in his eyes so she did not
mention it.

"I am not convinced that Mrs. Marsh was able to identify the
apothecary because she detected traces of paranormal energy in
the chemicals," Joshua said. "But I have always respected her scientific talents. I don't doubt for a moment that she observed
something in the fluid that led her to her conclusions."

"But you're quite certain that whatever she detected was not of
a paranormal nature," Beatrice said.

"I believe I have mentioned on more than one occasion that
there is no need to resort to the paranormal for an explanation
whenever one encounters a phenomenon that one cannot otherwise explain."

"Whatever you say," Beatrice murmured. "You are, of course,
the expert when it comes to criminal investigation."

He shot her a quick, suspicious look. She smiled sweetly and
blinked a few times.

"Huh." He shook his head and cracked open the door. "You can
forget the air of innocence. It does not work on me, remember?"

"Oh, right, I keep forgetting that small fact."

"Let's go interview Mrs. Grimshaw," he growled.

He kicked down the steps, seized his cane and got out of the
cab. He turned to give Beatrice his hand. She got the exciting little zing of intense awareness when his powerful hand closed
around hers. She peeked up at him from under the brim of her
bonnet, searching his face to see if he had felt the crackle of energy that flowed between them. But his profile was set in hard,

unrevealing planes and angles. If he did feel anything unusual and inexplicable when they were close like this he was using his formidable powers of self-mastery to conceal his reaction.

Henry shifted on the box and looked down at Joshua. "I'll wait here for ye, sir."

"Thank you," Joshua said. He surveyed the fog-shrouded lane. "You have your whistle, I assume?"

"Aye, sir. I'll keep watch, just as I did in the old days. If I see anything worrisome, I'll blow two blasts to alert you. Are you expecting trouble with the apothecary, then?"

"No, but lately I have miscalculated on occasion," Joshua said. "I'm getting old, Henry."

Henry chuckled. "Got a long ways to go before you're as old as me, sir."

Joshua took Beatrice's arm and started walking toward the door of the apothecary's shop. The sound of their footsteps and the faint *tap-tap-tap* of Joshua's cane echoed eerily in the fog. Beatrice glanced back and saw that Henry and the carriage were already no more than vague shadows in the mist.

The icy chill came out of nowhere just as they arrived at the door of the apothecary's shop. The uneasy sensation stirred the hair on the back of her neck. She knew that Joshua felt her start of alarm because he stopped immediately, drawing her to a halt.

"What is it?" he asked.

"I'm not sure," she said.

She opened her senses and examined the front step of the establishment. The energy deposited by an untold number of people over the years had left a thick, churning miasma of paranormal currents. Many of the tracks were darkened with the taint of illness, pain, addiction and impending death. It was an apothecary shop, after all. Most of the people who went through the door were in search of a cure or at least temporary relief either for themselves or for someone else.

But some of the recent prints burned with another kind of heat, the familiar, seething energy she had come to know all too well.

"Joshua," she whispered. "He was here not long ago but he left again."

Joshua did not ask her whom she meant. He tightened his grip on her arm in a silent warning. She looked at him, startled, and saw that he was studying the windows.

"The shades have been drawn," he said very quietly. He glanced at the windows of the rooms above the shop. "They are closed up there, too. Take out your stocking gun."

She did not hesitate. Whipping up her skirts and petticoats, she removed the small weapon from its sheath.

"Go stand out of sight in that doorway," he said, nodding toward the vaulted entrance of the neighboring building. "And do not hesitate to fire that gun if anyone so much as looks twice at you. Do you understand?"

"Yes, but what are you planning to do?"

"Just go. Now."

She hurried into the shelter of the nearby vestibule. From there she watched Joshua wrap a gloved hand around the door handle. She could see that he met resistance. The door was locked.

She wondered if he would try to pick the lock. But his methods proved far more efficient. He slammed the end of the ebony-and-steel cane into one of the windowpanes set into the upper half of the door.

Glass shattered. Joshua reached through the opening and unlocked the door.

He vanished inside.

A few seconds later a large, black glass bottle sailed through the doorway and landed in the middle of the lane. It shattered violently. There was a small explosive pop and a hiss. Flames leaped. They burned white-hot for a brief time before dying out.

There followed a deep silence. Beatrice held her breath.

Joshua appeared in the doorway. "You can come in now." He looked at the gun in her hand. "Would you mind putting that away? Or at the very least stop aiming it at me?"

"Oh, sorry." Beatrice hiked up her skirts and put the small pistol back into the dainty holster.

She hurried to the entrance of the shop and looked past Joshua. The body of an elderly woman was sprawled on the floor. The faint but unmistakable scent of chloroform tainted the atmosphere.

"Dear heaven," Beatrice whispered. "Is she—?"

"She's still alive," Joshua said. "We arrived in time. That firebomb was attached to a timing mechanism. It was set to go off in about ten minutes. He wanted time to make certain that he was well clear of the scene when the fire started."

Thirty-Nine

T hank heavens you came here today," Mrs. Grimshaw
said. "He intended for me to die. He said it would look
as though I had accidentally caused an explosion by
mixing volatile chemicals together. He said the police would
never know what had happened."

There was a shiver in her voice and in her hands. Beatrice put
a cup of hot tea in front of her and surveyed the elderly woman
with concern. The apothecary was still in shock.

"Drink some tea," Beatrice said gently.

Mrs. Grimshaw cheered up at the sight of the tea. She plucked
a small packet from her voluminous apron and emptied half the
contents into the cup. Leaning forward, she inhaled the vapors.
They clearly had a therapeutic effect on her. Her voice and hands
steadied.

She frowned, bewilderment clouding her face. "How did you
discover that I was in danger?"

"We didn't know," Beatrice said. "Not with any degree of certainty." She sat down at the small table and poured tea into Joshua's cup and her own. "But Mr. Gage's intuition guided us here today. He had a feeling that it was imperative we find you immediately."

Mrs. Grimshaw had been badly frightened but she was otherwise uninjured. Beatrice had made tea while Joshua had gone outside to tell Henry what had occurred and to send him on a short errand. She did not know what the nature of the errand was but Henry had taken off at once.

Mrs. Grimshaw gave Joshua a thoughtful look. "I vow, you must have some psychical talent, sir, to know that I was in trouble."

"That's what I keep telling him," Beatrice said. She smiled across the table at Joshua.

He shot her an irritated glance and turned back to Mrs. Grimshaw. "It was not paranormal talent that brought us to your doorstep this morning. It was logic and deductive reasoning, and, I might add, a bit of damned good luck."

Mrs. Grimshaw glanced at Beatrice, a question in her eyes.

"Mr. Gage does not believe in the paranormal," Beatrice explained.

Mrs. Grimshaw's expression cleared. "Ah, that explains it. Well, he's not the first man of talent to deny his own ability, and I daresay he won't be the last."

Beatrice tried to hide a smile but she knew Joshua saw it. He looked pained but he did not pursue the subject.

"I regret that I cannot give you more time to recover from your ordeal, Mrs. Grimshaw," he said. "But there is considerable urgency in this affair. We must move quickly or others may die. Will you please tell me what happened here today?"

"Certainly, sir, but I'm afraid I do not know a great deal about this situation myself. All I can tell you is that shortly before you arrived, one of my regular customers, the one who always buys my special compound of salts, entered the shop and asked me to make up his usual order. I thought nothing of it. I turned away to mix the compound. When it was ready I started to set it on the counter. But he was suddenly behind me. Moved like a cat in the night, he did. He clamped a wet cloth over my face. I remember smelling the chloroform and listening to him tell me that I was going to die in a great fire and then nothing else until you roused me."

Joshua's mouth tightened. "This is my fault, Mrs. Grimshaw. The villain I am pursuing reasoned that sooner or later I would find you and that you might be able to lead me to him. He wanted you dead but not before he got a fresh supply of the salts."

Mrs. Grimshaw's brow wrinkled in confusion. "I don't understand. Who is this villain?"

"The man who tried to murder you and burn down your shop today works for him," Joshua said. "His name is Lancing. He's a scientist who has been using a professional killer to run errands for him for nearly a year."

"Good heavens," Mrs. Grimshaw whispered, stunned.

"Can you describe the man who bought the salts and tried to murder you?"

"Yes, of course," Mrs. Grimshaw said. She collected herself with a visible effort. "He never gave me his name, just told me that he had been sent to buy the salts and some other rare chemicals that only I can supply. I never liked him but he always paid immediately. Never asked for credit. One can't always be too choosy when it comes to customers."

"So true," Beatrice said. "What else can you tell us?"

"Oh, he was quite distinctive. A foreigner, no question about it. Spoke English but with a heavy accent. He was tall. He always wore a low-crowned hat but I could tell that he was quite bald. Had a face like a skull and the coldest eyes you've ever seen."

"Yes," Joshua said. "That description fits the professional assassin."

Mrs. Grimshaw shuddered. "See here, do you think he will come back when he realizes that he failed?"

"No, because he will know that there is no point in taking that risk," Joshua said. "But to be on the safe side, I am going to ask an old associate of mine to send a couple of men to keep watch on you and your shop until this affair is concluded."

Mrs. Grimshaw's eyes widened. "Bodyguards, do you mean?"

"Yes. I sent our coachman off with a message a short time ago. Your watchers should arrive shortly. We will not leave you until they get here."

Mrs. Grimshaw heaved a sigh of relief. "I am very grateful to you, sir. But I really don't understand why this Mr. Lancing you speak of would send his servant to murder me. I told you, I'm the only apothecary in London who can supply him with the chemicals he requires."

"I think Lancing is convinced that he will not be needing a steady supply of the rare chemicals much longer," Joshua said. "He believes that he is nearing the end of his grand experiment."

Forty

"I did not know that crime lords went about in such high style," Beatrice said, marveling at the fine carriage that was approaching.

"Mr. Weaver controls a profitable slice of the London underworld," Joshua said. "He specializes in gambling establishments and taverns. But he also provides financial services to those who cannot obtain such services from respectable banks."

"At rather high interest rates, I expect."

"He is a businessman at heart," Joshua said.

He watched the sleek black carriage pulled by two perfectly matched, high-stepping black horses come to a halt in the street at the top of Teaberry Lane. Two men climbed down. All of Weaver's enforcers had a certain look, he thought. They were big, intimidating, well armed and well dressed. The black ties they wore around their necks were well known throughout the criminal world.

The pair looked at Joshua for direction.

"Please keep watch on the apothecary and her shop in the lane," Joshua said. "Do not let anyone in through the front door or the alley. The establishment is closed until further notice. I am concerned for the safety of the proprietor."

"We'll look after her," one of the men said.

They touched their black caps and went quickly along the lane.

A footman in black livery jumped down to open the door of the carriage and lower the steps. The massively built man seated in the cab looked out through the opening.

"It's been a while, Joshua," Weaver said. He took in the scar and the cane with a thoughtful expression. "I heard there was an accident."

"Word gets around," Joshua said. "Allow me to present Miss Lockwood, a very good friend. Beatrice, this is Mr. Weaver, an old associate of mine."

Beatrice smiled. "Mr. Weaver."

Joshua hid a quick grin. He could not imagine another lady of his acquaintance acknowledging an introduction to a notorious crime lord with grace and charm. It was clear from the surprise that flashed in Weaver's eyes that he was not accustomed to being greeted so cordially by a member of the respectable class.

"A pleasure, Miss Lockwood," Weaver said. He glanced at Joshua, brows slightly elevated, and then gestured with one gloved hand. "I hope the two of you will join me in my carriage while we converse. Standing about in the open affects my nerves."

Joshua handed Beatrice up into the cab and joined her. They sat down on the black velvet cushions.

Beatrice examined Weaver with politely veiled curiosity. There was a lot of Weaver to examine, Joshua thought. The big man took up most of the opposite seat. There was a cool, calculating intelligence in his pale eyes. He was well dressed in the latest fashion. His tailor had done his best to camouflage Weaver's bloated body but there was only so much that could be accomplished. And nothing could disguise the aura of poor health that emanated from Mr. Weaver, Joshua thought. Weaver's color was not good and his breathing was much tighter now than it had been the last time they had met.

"I must admit I am curious to know why you are requesting my assistance after a year of silence," Weaver said.

"It's a long tale and it has not ended," Joshua replied. "It's connected to the accident you mentioned. I think that one of the people believed to have died in the same accident is still alive. He has become something of a problem for Miss Lockwood."

"I see." Weaver inclined his head toward Beatrice. "I'm sorry to hear that, Miss Lockwood." He turned back to Joshua. "I am happy to be able to assist you today but supplying two guards is not sufficient to repay the debt that I owe you. I trust you will let me know if I can be of any further assistance."

"I do have one question," Joshua said. "Have you heard of an independent operator whose services include kidnapping and murder? He is a foreigner and speaks with a thick Russian accent. Witnesses report that he is entirely bald and has a face like a skull. He calls himself the Bone Man."

"Sounds like a character in a Gothic novel." Weaver's eyes narrowed. "But your description is familiar. Nearly a year ago I heard rumors about such a man. It was said that he was recently arrived in London and that he was an experienced professional."

"Professional what?" Beatrice asked.

"Assassin," Weaver explained gently.

"Oh, right," Beatrice said.

"I let it be known that I would be interested in employing such an expert but he never made any attempt to contact me. In fact, he disappeared almost immediately."

"He found another employer," Joshua said.

"I assume this other employer is from your world, Joshua. Because I would most certainly know if one of my competitors had hired him."

"His new employer is a madman named Clement Lancing," Joshua said.

Weaver nodded. "I assume you have a plan?"

"The Bone Man's weakness appears to be his professional pride," Joshua said. "I intend to use that vulnerability to set a trap but I will need your assistance."

"Of course."

Joshua explained the nature of his request. Weaver comprehended immediately.

"That will not be a problem," he said. "I shall make the arrangements as soon as I return to my office."

"Thank you," Joshua said. "Please consider your debt repaid in full."

Weaver grunted. "I will never be able to repay it."

Joshua opened the door of the cab and made his way down to the pavement. He reached up to assist Beatrice.

Together they watched the gleaming black equipage disappear into the mist.

"Dare I ask the nature of the favor you performed for Mr. Weaver?" Beatrice asked.

"His daughter was taken when she was a young girl and held for ransom by one of Weaver's underworld competitors," Joshua said. "I was able to find her and retrieve her unharmed."

"I see. That explains why he feels he can never fully repay the debt."

There was something in her tone that made him realize she was concerned.

"What is it?" Joshua asked.

"Mr. Weaver is a very ill man," she said quietly. "He is dying."

"It's his heart, I'm told. For years he has maintained the truce in the criminal underworld. It will be interesting to see what happens when he is gone."

Forty-One

V ictor Hazelton's library was infused with the dark, somber energy of long-standing grief. There was something else in the mix, as well, Beatrice thought—a quiet, anguished rage. Victor maintained a stoic façade but she could see the dark currents in his footsteps. She suspected that much of his well-controlled anger was directed at himself. He was the legendary Mr. Smith, after all, tasked with keeping the country safe from terrorists and conspirators. But he had failed to protect his beloved daughter from a madman.

Victor was a silver-maned lion of a man with fierce dark eyes and a commanding presence. He appeared to be in his late fifties but he moved with the athletic ease of a much younger person. It was not difficult to imagine him as a legendary spymaster— privy to secrets in the highest levels of government and Society— sending out his trusted agents to track down traitors and crush conspiracies.

He had clearly been surprised to see them when they had been ushered into the library, but he had welcomed them. Beatrice sensed a certain awkwardness between Joshua and Victor but there was also the unmistakable energy of a deep, long-standing bond.

The three of them were seated in the library, Victor behind his massive desk.

The high-ceilinged room was a shrine to Emma Hazelton. One nearby shelf was filled with her notebooks. Another held her diaries. Her framed watercolors were arranged on various walls. Her portrait occupied the place of honor over the fireplace. And all of it was hung with black silk.

Emma had been extraordinarily beautiful, Beatrice thought. She glowed in her portrait. With her fine features, dark hair and dark eyes she would have turned any man's head. But the artist had also managed to capture her intelligence, elegance and charm.

"We must assume that Lancing is alive, Victor." Joshua stacked his hands on the grip of his cane. "He will be quite mad by now."

Victor went very still. His silvery brows snapped together above his aquiline nose. "You believe he survived the explosion?"

"Yes. I know this will be difficult for you to hear, but I think he managed to recover Emma's body."

Victor turned pale. He took a sharp breath. His eyes narrowed.

"Are you certain?" he asked in a hoarse whisper.

"As certain as I can be without actual proof," Joshua said.

"But we found two bodies in the rubble," Victor said. "A man and a woman."

"Charred beyond recognition. Two victims of his experiments,

I imagine. Remember, Lancing lured me there that day with the intention of killing me and destroying all the evidence in a great fire. I think he may have had the two bodies ready before I even got there."

Victor looked shaken to the bone. "But what of Emma?"

"I am speculating here," Joshua said. "But I am almost certain that he has preserved her body all this time in the formula."

"Why in heaven's name would he do such a thing?"

Joshua's jaw hardened. "You know why, sir. He is mad. He has convinced himself that he can bring Emma back to life."

Victor exhaled deeply and closed his eyes briefly. His pain was a harsh, sad force in the atmosphere.

"Lancing was a brilliant scientist," he said. He opened his eyes. "He of all people should know what is possible and what is not."

"He is still a brilliant scientist," Joshua said. "But that does not mean he is not also mad. You know that he was obsessed with Emma. When she tried to escape him he murdered her. It is possible that his guilt and grief pushed him over the edge. By the way, I discovered that he has the Eyes of Anubis. Emma found them for him shortly before he killed her. For the past year Lancing has been purchasing the rare salts required to prepare the recipe for the Egyptian Water from an apothecary in Teaberry Lane."

"This is astounding news." Victor rose and went to stand at the window looking out into the garden. "I am in shock."

"I'm sorry, sir," Joshua said. "I know this is painful for you but I fear there is more unpleasant news. Miss Lockwood is in extreme danger."

Victor turned to face them, his strong features tightened into a grim frown. "Why is that?"

"Lancing is evidently convinced that she possesses the paranormal talent required to activate the powers of the statue," Joshua said. "He thinks he needs her to complete his grand experiment. He has made it plain that he will go to any lengths to kidnap her."

Victor looked at Beatrice with frank curiosity. "Do you possess some psychical abilities, Miss Lockwood?"

"Yes," she said. "Although Mr. Gage does not believe in the paranormal, he tells me that Clement Lancing does."

"There is no question about that." Victor clasped his hands behind his back. "Lancing was convinced that there is an entire spectrum of paranormal forces that extend beyond the normal. In fact, he thought that my daughter possessed some talent. It was one of the reasons he was so obsessed with her. He was certain that she had the ability to ignite the reviving effects of the Egyptian Water."

"But with Emma dead, he requires another woman of talent," Joshua said. "He has sent out a professional criminal who calls himself the Bone Man to kidnap Beatrice."

Victor arched one silver brow. "I am pleased to note that the efforts have failed."

Beatrice looked at Joshua. "Thanks to Mr. Gage."

Victor smiled a wistful, fatherly smile. His eyes warmed with memories. "You were always my best agent, Josh. It appears your injuries have not changed that fact. I assume you have come to me because you have a plan?"

"I have set a trap for the assassin," Joshua said. "With luck he will walk into it tonight. Meanwhile, I would be very grateful if you would allow Beatrice to remain here with you where I know she will be safe."

"Of course," Victor said. "Tell me your strategy."

Forty-Two

"I know you don't believe in the paranormal, let alone the ability to sense the future, but we have agreed that there is such a thing as a sense of intuition," Beatrice said.

They were alone, strolling through the large conservatory attached to Hazelton's mansion. On any other night, the scene would have been conducive to romance, Beatrice thought. Moonlight slanted through the glass walls and ceiling, illuminating an impressive array of greenery that ranged from ferns and palms to orchids of all descriptions. It was the only room in the house that was not drenched in gloom. In this space life thrived. Victor Hazelton should spend more time in his conservatory.

Dinner had been a subdued affair. The dark, paneled dining room, like the library, was drenched in the accoutrements of deep mourning. The walls were hung with more billowing black silk. A photograph of Emma dressed in an elegant gown gazed down upon the diners from above the mantel. The somber-faced footman who served them wore a black armband. He had maintained a hushed silence as he came and went from the kitchen.

Beatrice knew that she would not have enjoyed the meal even if the atmosphere had been more cheerful. Her sense of unease had been stirring all afternoon. It had only grown stronger throughout the evening.

"In spite of appearances, I can take care of myself, Beatrice," Joshua said.

"I am well aware of that. But that does not mean that you should not pay attention to intuition. What is yours telling you?"

He stopped and leaned back against a raised bed of ferns. He set the cane aside and pulled her into his arms.

"I've told you, time is running out," he said. "I cannot risk another moment. I must find the Bone Man tonight and use him to find Lancing. There is no time to devise another plan."

She wanted to argue with him but she knew it was no use. Perhaps if she had an alternative strategy to offer she might have been able to convince him, she thought. But she could not think of one.

She gripped the lapels of his coat. "Promise me that you will be careful and that you will come back to me."

"I promise," he said.

He tightened his hold on her and kissed her. Her anxiety and her fear for his safety acted like fuel to a low-burning fire. She clutched at his shoulders and returned the kiss with a sense of desperation, as if she was afraid she might never see him again.

He responded with a rush of desire that swept both of them into a hot torrent of energy.

He pulled her down onto a nearby pile of canvas sacking and

pushed her skirts up to her waist. He found the open seam in her drawers and stroked her until she was wet and aching. He opened the front of his trousers. She closed her hand around him, guiding him into her.

"I cannot stop," he warned against her throat. "Not tonight. You're a fever in my blood."

"It's all right," she whispered. "It's all right, my love."

My love.

And suddenly she knew beyond any shadow of a doubt that it was the truth. She loved Joshua.

If he heard her he did not react to the words. He was consumed with a feverish passion.

He thrust deep and hard, once, twice, and then he was gritting his teeth against an exultant roar. She held him tightly until the waves of his release finally ceased.

He collapsed on top of her for a moment. When his harsh breathing was back to normal, he groaned and rolled to one side on the canvas and looked up at the moon through the glass-and-steel roof of the conservatory. He picked up her hand and kissed her palm.

"My apologies," he said after a while. "I did not wait for you. I could not. That was ungentlemanly of me."

She smiled and levered herself up on her elbow to look down at him. In the moonlight his eyes gleamed with the heat of the aftermath.

"See to it that you come back safely so that you can finish what you started here tonight," she said. She kept her voice light and teasing.

He did not respond to her attempt to lighten the mood. Instead his eyes got very hot. He wrapped his hand around the back of her head and drew her face down until her mouth was very close to his.

"You have my oath on it," he said.

He kissed her once more to seal the promise.

TWENTY MINUTES LATER she watched him go out into the night and climb into the anonymous carriage that would take him deep into the dark streets of London. When the vehicle disappeared into the fog her intuition shrieked in silent warning. But there was nothing she could do.

Victor took her arm and gently guided her back into the house. He looked at her, his eyes filled with understanding.

"Don't worry," he said. "Josh was always my best agent. Even in his present condition, I'm certain that he can take care of himself."

Forty-Three

"This household must strike you as a very morbid place, Miss Lockwood." Victor poured brandy into a glass. "Some of my old friends have hinted that I have been in deep mourning far too long. They feel it is time that I moved forward with my life."

"I know that there are social rules when it comes to mourning," Beatrice said gently. "But I am of the opinion that everyone grieves in his or her own way. Certainly there cannot be any loss more dreadful than that of a child."

They were back in the library. The black-clad housekeeper had brought in a coffee service. Victor had graciously poured two cups and added a splash of brandy to each but Beatrice had not touched her cup.

She had been growing increasingly anxious ever since Joshua had left the mansion to seek a confrontation with the assassin. It was now after midnight. She was struggling to maintain control

of her nerves. Periodically she gave herself a small lecture, remind-
ing herself that Joshua knew what he was about. But the sense of
dread continued to deepen.

"Emma was all I had after her mother died," Victor explained.
He draped one black-clad arm on the white marble mantel and
looked up at the portrait. "Society expects a widower to remarry
within a few months, especially when he does not have any male
heirs."

"Yes, I know," Beatrice said.

"But I loved my Alice and could not find it in my heart to
betray her memory by bringing another woman into this house. I
had my brilliant, beautiful daughter, and that was more than
enough for me."

"I understand."

The rules and rituals for mourning were complicated but the
social burden fell most heavily on women. Everything from the
black-bordered paper used to announce a death to the length of
time prescribed for wearing black and, later, gray gowns was a
matter of great concern for ladies. A woman in mourning was
watched with close, critical scrutiny. But gentlemen usually con-
fined themselves to a black hatband and, at most, a black armband
for a couple of months. Widows were discouraged from marrying
again. A second marriage implied a lack of sensitivity. Men, however, were encouraged to take another wife as soon as possible.

"I also had two young men in my life who were like sons to
me," Victor continued. "Indeed, my happiest hour came when
Emma told me that she wished to marry one of them."

"Clement Lancing," Beatrice said.

"Yes. My daughter was quite beautiful. She could have had any man she chose. I knew that both Joshua and Clement loved her, but in the end I felt that Lancing was the right choice because he shared Emma's fascination with Egyptology." Victor's jaw tightened. "It was one of the few times in my life that I have been wrong in my judgment of a man. The mistake cost me my Emma."

"Were you aware of Lancing's obsession with the formula for the Egyptian preservative fluid?"

"Of course," Victor said. "Emma was equally fascinated. We discussed it on several occasions. They were excited by the possibility that the ancients had discovered a means of preserving the newly dead in a state of suspended animation. Lancing was convinced that in that deep sleep the formula would exert a healing effect on the organs. When the process was complete, the individual could be successfully revived."

"As I told Mr. Gage, I am astonished that a scientist as brilliant as Clement Lancing would actually believe he could awaken the dead," Beatrice said.

"The line between genius and madness can sometimes be difficult to find." Victor's hand tightened around the edge of the mantel. "Mind you, Lancing did not think the Egyptian Water would work on a long-dead corpse, but he was convinced that if the body of a recently deceased person was immersed in the fluid within a few hours after death, there was every hope. He began conducting terrible experiments."

"Mr. Gage told me about that aspect of the affair."

"When my daughter discovered what was going on she was horrified. She confronted him and, well, I'm sure Josh told you the rest."

"Yes."

Victor shook his head, mouth tightening. "It is difficult enough to comprehend that Lancing actually survived the explosion. The possibility that he may have my daughter's body preserved in a chemical bath is shocking beyond belief. All these months . . ."

"I can only imagine how upsetting that notion must be for you."

"Joshua never took Lancing's and Emma's work on the Egyptian Water seriously because he doesn't believe in the paranormal."

"Yes, he has made that quite clear."

Victor's mouth twisted faintly. "We all have our blind spots. With Josh it is his great desire to live by cold logic and reason. He has always feared that to do otherwise means risking his sense of control."

"You know him well, sir. But then, that is no surprise. I understand that you guided him at a crucial juncture of his life."

"I did what I could," Victor said. "I am very fond of Joshua. What happened nearly a year ago caused both of us great pain. I know that each of us has been grieving this past year. In hindsight, we should have talked more." He glanced at the clock. "It's going to be a very long night."

Another flutter of anxiety shifted through her. The faint, panicky sensation brought her to her feet. She suddenly wanted to be out of the funereal room, out of the mausoleum of a mansion. The sad, seething energy of the house was taking a toll on her nerves.

"Would you mind very much if I went upstairs to my room to wait for Joshua?" she asked.

Victor frowned. "Are you all right, my dear? You look unwell."

"I am quite tense. I'm afraid I'm not good company at the moment."

"Yes, of course." Victor studied her with deep concern. "I see you did not drink your coffee and brandy. Would you care for a glass of the brandy alone? It will help calm your nerves."

"No, I'm fine, thank you. Please call me the instant Joshua comes back."

"You have my word on it."

Victor opened the door for her. She hurried out into the hall and walked swiftly toward the grand staircase. The relief she experienced upon escaping the library proved short-lived. Another wave of fear crashed through her when she climbed the stairs. By the time she reached her bedroom she was in a state of near-panic. She was suddenly desperate for a breath of crisp night air.

She had to get out of the house. Perhaps a few minutes in the gardens would ease her tight breathing.

She opened the door of her bedroom, collected her cloak and a candlestick, and let herself quietly back out into the hall. The long carpet runner muffled her footsteps. She did not want to alarm Victor. She knew he would be worried if he realized that she was going outside alone at such a late hour.

The house was very silent. The household's small staff had gone downstairs some time ago.

The servants' stairs at the end of the hall were the closest route to the gardens. She opened the door to the stairwell, trying to make as little noise as possible.

She heard Victor's footsteps on the main staircase just as she shut the door. She lit the candle and started down. The close confines of the back stairs caused her heart to beat faster. The need for fresh air was overwhelming. It was as if the house was trying to suffocate her.

There was no logical reason for the sparks of raw panic that shot through her, but she had survived on her intuition far too long to ignore the sensation.

She reached the ground floor and paused to blow out the candle. The wall sconces had been turned down low but there was sufficient light to reveal a door that looked as if it served as the tradesmen's entrance.

There was a muffled squeak of floorboards overhead. Victor was moving down the hall toward the master bedroom. The faint groans of the boards should not have terrified her, but they did. The memories of the night she had stood beside Roland as he lay dying and listened to his killer returning to the scene of the crime slammed across her senses. The choking fear welled up inside.

But it had not been Victor Hazelton who had killed Roland, she thought. Why was she so frightened tonight? Perhaps the events of the past few days had been too much for her nerves. She was strong but everyone had a breaking point. She was jumping at shadows now.

She crept silently toward the tradesmen's entrance. Her talent was sparking in reaction to her fear. In the dim light she could see the psychical fog created by the prints of the many people who had come and gone through the door—deliverymen bringing provisions for the household, carpenters and painters who had been summoned to perform repairs, coachmen, gardeners and all those who had come to the door in hopes of gaining a post in the mansion.

The decades of tracks had formed a layer of murky energy that swirled on the floor. But one set of footsteps stood out above all the rest. They glittered with a terrible iridescence. She recognized them instantly.

The man with the skull for a face had come through the door—not once but on several occasions in the past few months.

The fact that he had used the tradesmen's entrance told her all she needed to know. He worked for Victor Hazelton.

There was another creak from the floor above and then a nerve-shattering silence. It was impossible to be certain from where she stood but intuition told her that Victor had stopped at her bedroom door.

She took out her stocking gun and opened the tradesmen's door, half expecting to come face-to-face with the assassin. But there was only moonlit darkness on the other side.

Joshua thought that he had set a trap, but he was wrong. He was walking into one.

Forty-Four

She hurried through the empty streets, her senses skittering. Every doorway and every alley was filled with ominous darkness. She dared not take shortcuts through the parks. Her small pistol would be useless against a gang of footpads.

It seemed like an eternity before she managed to hail a hansom cab. She knew what the driver thought when she hiked up her skirts and stepped up into the small vehicle. Respectable ladies did not go about in hansoms. Only fast women allowed themselves to be seen in the swift little cabs. And only a prostitute would have a reason to be out alone at this time of night.

"Lantern Street," she said crisply. "Hurry, please."

"Got a customer waiting, have ye?" the driver asked genially.

But he obligingly snapped the whip. The horse lurched into a hard trot.

Twenty minutes later they arrived at the door of Flint &

Marsh. Beatrice navigated the narrow cab steps down to the pavement and paid the driver. The hansom rolled off into the darkness.

She went up the front steps of the agency. Not surprisingly, the lights were off. She banged the knocker several times but there was no answer.

Instinct made her take out the stocking gun. Cautiously, she tried the door and was shocked when it turned easily in her hand. Mrs. Beale never forgot to lock up for the night.

She knew she had made a terrible mistake but by then it was too late. The subtle scent of incense wafted out into the night air.

"I've been waiting for you, Beatrice," Victor said from the shadows of the front hall. "It took you long enough to get here. Always hard to find a cab at this hour, isn't it?"

She started to step back, intending to whirl and run.

"If you don't come inside, I will kill all of them," Victor said. "I have nothing left to lose, you see. At this point I can guarantee you that they are all still alive."

He turned up the lamp. She saw Abigail and Sara sprawled on the floor behind him. Both were in their nightclothes. Both were unconscious.

"The housekeeper is in the other room," Victor said. "I have no wish to kill all three women but their lives are in your hands. I will do whatever it takes to obtain your cooperation tonight."

"Dear heaven," Beatrice said. "You truly do think that Clement Lancing can bring your daughter back to life, don't you?"

"She is all I have," Victor said. "I will do anything to save her."

"Including sending the man you say was like a son to you to his death at the hands of an assassin?"

"Take heart. Joshua may survive the encounter. At one time he possessed considerable skill in such matters. It's true, he has lost much of his speed and agility, but he is still formidable. If I were a betting man, I might place a wager on him. But in the end it does not matter which of them survives."

"Because what matters is making sure Joshua is occupied while you kidnap me."

"Indeed."

"He will survive," Beatrice said. "And he will come looking for me. He always finds what he sets out to find."

"Eventually he will find you. But it will take some time for him to track you down—a couple of days, at least. By then I will no longer need you. Our business together will be concluded by dawn this morning. Now put that ridiculous little gun on the console and turn around."

"Why should I turn around?"

"Do it."

She put the stocking gun on the table and turned slowly. Victor moved with terrifying speed. He came up behind her, secured her with an arm around her throat and clamped a cloth over her nose and mouth.

She smelled chloroform and tried not to breathe but in the end she had no choice.

Darkness swallowed her whole.

Forty-Five

The first wave of rumors rippled through the Red Dog Tavern shortly after midnight. Joshua was alone in a booth at the back. He was dressed like the other patrons, in the rough clothes and heavy boots typical of a man who made his living in dark and dangerous ways. The scar had proven to be an asset in places like the Red Dog and the other establishments he had visited that evening.

He caught some of the low voices in the next booth and was certain he heard Weaver's name but he could not hear the details. The crime lord's name was always spoken in a whisper.

He had made the rounds of the gaming hells and taverns near the docks, setting the stage for the trap. There was some gossip about the killer called the Bone Man, but no hard facts. No one seemed to know the identity of his current employer, but there was speculation that he was working for an up-and-coming crime lord who intended to challenge Weaver and the others in the old guard who controlled the criminal underworld.

When the barmaid, an attractive, hard-eyed blonde, approached with his ale, Joshua took out a few extra coins and set them on the table. The woman glanced at the money, interested but wary.

"What do I have to do to earn that much money?" she asked.

"Tell me the news about Weaver."

She glanced around uneasily and then leaned down to set the ale on the table. She lowered her voice. "No one knows for certain yet but there is word on the street that he's dead."

Joshua went cold. "Someone killed him?"

"No, that's the odd part. They're saying his heart failed him."

Joshua thought about what Beatrice had said that afternoon. *He is dying.*

"Do the rumors say when he died?" Joshua asked.

"It's very strange. According to the story, he went out to meet someone earlier in the day. When he returned to his office his footman opened the door to his carriage and found him slumped over, dead as you please. Word is his enforcers kept it quiet as long as possible so that they could make one last visit to all of his businesses tonight to collect their protection fees."

"Which the enforcers will now keep for themselves." Joshua pushed himself to his feet and grabbed his cane.

He had wasted an entire evening. Weaver had not lived long enough to set the trap.

"What about your ale, sir?" the barmaid called.

Joshua did not respond. He made his way through the crowded room, desperate to get to the door. His hand was a fist around the hilt of the cane. He had to fight the frustration and cold anger that spilled through him. He was vaguely aware that people scrambled to move out of his path but he paid no attention, intent only on getting outside.

He knew that Lancing's tentacles were closing around Beatrice at that very moment. So much time lost.

Hazelton will protect her, he thought. But even as he tried to reassure himself, he knew that he could no longer be certain of anything. He had been wrong too often in this case, and Beatrice would pay the price.

He finally made it outside onto the street. The chilly night air and the stench of the river helped him focus. He forced himself to control his breathing, slowing it down, reining in his emotions. He could not think clearly when his brain was consumed by thoughts conjured up by his feverish imagination.

There was no point dwelling on the hours that had been lost. His original strategy lay in ruins. He had to craft a new one immediately or there was no hope. Everything inside him was shouting that time had at last truly run out.

He made his way down the street, heading toward the corner where Henry waited with the carriage. The soft thud of his cane and the echo of the hitch in his stride were the loudest sounds in the night.

He was so intent on formulating a new plan that he did not sense the presence of the killer until the skull-faced man lunged toward him from the alley.

It should have been a killing blow—it would have been a killing blow—but at the last instant he heard the assassin's sharp intake of breath.

Old habits and long training took over. Instinctively, Joshua whirled to confront the attacker. The action sent him spinning off balance. His bad leg gave way beneath him and he tumbled to the ground—and accidentally saved his own life in the process.

The sudden change in the position of his intended victim threw the assassin off his mark. Carried forward by his own momentum, he stumbled a few steps past Joshua, caught himself and swung around to make another attempt.

Joshua struggled to get to his knees. He realized he was still gripping the hilt of his cane. He swung the stick in a slashing arc to fend off the killer.

The Bone Man was ready for the move. He lashed out with one booted foot and connected with the cane.

The bone-jarring blow sent the steel-and-ebony stick flying from Joshua's hand. It clattered on the pavement.

The killer glided forward in a low rush. His eyes were pools of empty night. The blade in his hand glittered darkly in the light of the nearby gas lamp.

He did not notice the small throwing knife that Joshua had drawn from the cane until the blade sank straight into his throat.

He grunted and stumbled to a halt. Blood boiled in his mouth. He looked at Joshua in disbelief.

He sank to his knees, toppled onto his side and collapsed faceup.

An acute silence filled the street. Joshua gathered himself and got to his feet. He limped to where the cane lay on the paving stones. Stooping low, he picked up the stick.

He made his way to the body and used the cane to send the

Bone Man's blade skidding away from the limp hand. There was no such thing as too many precautions.

Bracing himself with the cane, he leaned down and pulled the small throwing knife from the dead man's throat. He wiped the blade clean on the Bone Man's clothes and slid the weapon back into the top of the cane.

He went toward the small, fast carriage on the corner, thinking about one of the maxims he had learned from Victor. *Everyone has a blind spot.*

"You were mine, Victor."

Forty-Six

Nelson was in his small study, a glass of brandy on the table beside him. He had long ago lost interest in the book he had been reading and had moved on to his favorite subject: the contemplation of his boring future. The small taste of the investigation business that he had gotten recently had whetted his appetite. It was as if he had found a calling. But he was not fool enough to believe that Josh would ask him to assist in that sort of thing in the future. His uncle had retired, after all.

He was considering a visit to the American West, where, according to the press, adventure awaited, when the clang of the door knocker shattered the late-night silence of the house.

He debated whether to answer the summons. The visitor would be one of his friends who would be thoroughly drunk by now and wanting companionship for a trip into the more dangerous neighborhoods. For the first time in months the prospect of an evening of heavy drinking and gaming hells did not seem to be the answer.

The knock sounded again, louder this time. He groaned and got to his feet. He went down the hall and opened the front door.

"You're on your own tonight," he said. "I'm not in the mood—" He broke off when he saw Joshua on the step.

The sight of his uncle rendered him speechless for a few seconds. There was a terrible light in Joshua's eyes. Nelson wondered if he was burning with fever. But that did not explain the dark energy that seemed to emanate from him. It was as if Joshua had just returned from a trip to hell and expected to make a return visit quite soon.

"Uncle Josh." Nelson swallowed hard. "Are you all right?"

"He's got her," Joshua said. "It's my fault. I violated the first rule in an investigation. I trusted someone connected to it."

"Hang on, are you talking about Miss Lockwood? Who has her?"

"Hazelton. He was working with Lancing all along. They're going to attempt to revive Emma and they believe they need Beatrice to do it."

"Bloody hell. They've both gone mad, then?"

"It's the only explanation," Joshua said. "I need your help."

"Yes, of course, but how do you know that Victor is in league with Lancing?"

"Get your pistol and come with me. I'll tell you everything on the way."

It took only a moment to retrieve his pistol from the desk in his study. Nelson grabbed it and raced back down the hall. He climbed up into the small cab and sat down beside Joshua. He was aware of a fire in his own blood now. Excitement, resolve and a sense of purpose energized him as nothing else ever had. He wasn't going out on another pointless round of drinking and gambling tonight. He was going to do something important. He was going to help rescue a lady.

Henry cracked his whip. The horse leaped forward.

"First, tell me how you learned that Hazelton is involved in this affair," Nelson said.

"He sent the assassin after me tonight," Joshua said. "He assumed that if I survived, I would credit my own plan and never suspect him. He had no way of knowing that Weaver did not live long enough to help me bait the trap. Hazelton was the only other person except Beatrice who knew that I would be at the Red Dog tonight. He is the only one who could have sent word to the Bone Man."

"He brought in a foreigner to do his killing and kidnapping—someone he knew from his years as Mr. Smith—because he knew that if he used a man from the London underworld, one of your acquaintances in the criminal class who owes you a favor would either warn you or take care of the problem himself."

"Right," Joshua said. "Victor wanted me out of the way but he did not want to take the risk of trying to kill me. If he failed, there would be no hope of reviving Emma."

"He's the one who trained you," Nelson said. "He still respects your ability, in spite of your injuries."

"So it seems. But in the end, it didn't matter if I lived or died tonight. All he cared about was distracting me long enough to allow him to snatch Beatrice."

"But we are going to find her, aren't we?" Nelson said.

"Yes. But first we will stop at my town house for some equipment that I put into storage a year ago."

"Uncle Josh, I don't mean to be pessimistic about our prospects of success, but you can't possibly know where Victor took Miss Lockwood. How are we going to find her?"

"We look for her in the right place."

Forty-Seven

She awoke to the essence of death and the smell of strong chemicals. For a moment she lay still, afraid to move, afraid to open her eyes, fearful of what she might see.

"I think our guest is awake."

The masculine voice was unfamiliar but there was no mistaking the whisper of unwholesome excitement that was woven through it like a dark thread.

"Yes, she is," Victor said. "The least we can do is offer her a stimulating cup of strong tea to help her overcome the effects of the drug."

She realized that she was lying on a cot. A strange lethargy weighed heavily on her senses. She felt vaguely nauseous. A hazy scene fluttered through her head like an image from a dream. She caught a glimpse of Mrs. Flint and Mrs. Marsh sprawled, unconscious, on the floor of their front hall. She remembered the overpowering smell of the chloroform.

Instinctively she pulled hard on her senses, struggling to overcome the dazed ennui that held her in its grip.

She opened her eyes and found herself looking up at the night sky through a glass-and-steel dome. An icy white moon, partially obscured by clouds, shone down. The dome was modern in design as were the gas lamps that illuminated the chamber, but the stone walls around her were very old.

A figure appeared between her and the view of the night sky. She had never met him but she knew it could only be one man.

"Clement Lancing," she said. She had a hard time getting his name out. She knew she sounded half asleep or perhaps slightly inebriated.

"Your tea, Miss Lockwood," Clement said. "You have given us a great deal of difficulty. We were forced to go to extreme lengths to find you, but you, are here at last and in time. That is all that matters."

Clement Lancing was a striking figure of a man—tall, broad-shouldered and endowed with an athletic physique. His dark brown hair was unfashionably long, as if he had not bothered to go to his barber in many months. He wore it brushed straight back from a sharply defined widow's peak. The style framed a high forehead, aristocratic nose and piercing gray eyes.

"How odd," she whispered in her drug-thickened voice. "You don't look mad."

She had expected the remark to send him into a rage. Instead, he startled her with a sad, knowing smile.

"Is that what Gage told you?" he asked. "That I was insane? Well, he would say that, wouldn't he? He is the madman in this affair. He murdered my beautiful Emma."

"Rubbish. You're the one who killed her."

Clement's eyes flared with an unholy light. "That is a lie."

"Enough, both of you," Victor snapped. "We do not have much time. We must conclude this business tonight."

Beatrice sat up cautiously and eased her legs over the side of the cot. Instinctively she searched for the source of the strong chemical odor and saw the massive sarcophagus on the far side of the chamber. She knew at once that the smell was emanating from it. An icy thrill of horror spiked through her. Death leaked from the ancient quartz box. She could feel it all the way across the room.

A tall statue of Anubis with a human body and the head of a jackal stood next to the sarcophagus. A length of gold wire was wrapped around the god's throat. The obsidian eyes glittered in the glary light. She could sense the paranormal energy infused into the statue.

With the horrible exception of the ancient burial box and the statue, the rest of the chamber was unsettlingly similar to Mrs. Marsh's basement laboratory. Workbenches covered with an assortment of chemical apparatuses were arranged around the room. The shelves set against the walls were lined with boxes and jars that she knew very likely contained chemicals.

She pulled hard on her talent and some of her unnatural lethargy receded. The skirts of her gown were crushed and someone had removed her cloak, but she was relieved to note that at least she was still fully dressed. When she looked down she saw that her chatelaine with the small vial containing Mrs. Marsh's special smelling salts was missing.

Her talent was flaring and sparking but she could see the hot footprints that covered the floor of the chamber.

She looked at Clement. "You may like to think yourself the sane one in this affair, but it is clear from your psychical prints that you are quite mad."

Another flash of strange fire lit Clement's eyes. But he managed to suppress it to some degree.

It was Victor who responded to her statement.

"I told you, the line between genius and madness can be difficult to detect," he said quietly. "Believe me, Miss Lockwood, I have been attempting to find it for the past year. In the end, it seems, one must go on faith alone."

Clement held out a mug. "Have some tea. It will restore your nerves, Miss Lockwood."

"No, thank you," she said. "You will understand when I tell you that I must assume that any tea brewed by you would be poisoned." She looked at the sarcophagus. "Like everything else in this place."

"You are wrong, Miss Lockwood," Clement said. "There is no poison here. Quite the contrary, what you are going to witness is a triumph of the science of chemistry. Actually, you will be more than a witness to history tonight. You will make a great contribution."

She looked around the room. "Joshua was right. He said that if you were still alive, you would be found in a laboratory."

"Gage knows me well," Clement said. "It has not been easy hiding from him for the past year. I was fortunate in that he chose to become a recluse on his estates after he murdered my beloved, but in a very real sense, I, too, have been in prison because I dared not leave this place. But that is all finished. What matters is that I have you here in my laboratory at last. I have been searching for you for months."

"Why me?" Beatrice asked.

"Because only a woman with genuine paranormal talent can release the energy in the Anubis figure," Clement said.

"There are thousands of paranormal practitioners in London."

"But the vast majority are frauds," Clement said. "I require a true talent."

"How did you identify me as the one you wanted?" she asked.

"That was Victor's doing," Clement said.

Victor touched the top of the sarcophagus with a reverent hand. "We were getting desperate. I knew I had to take some risks. I used Hannah Trafford to locate you."

"I don't understand," Beatrice said.

"Hannah has always considered herself a student of the paranormal," Victor said. "Josh never believed in that sort of thing so he has always dismissed his sister's interests. I, on the other hand, am well aware that the paranormal exists. I have some psychical talent myself."

"A gift for strategy, perhaps?" she asked coldly.

Victor inclined his head. "Indeed. Because of my long and close association with Josh, I knew a great deal about his family. During my years as Mr. Smith I made it my business to learn as much as possible about my agents' personal lives."

"In other words, you spied on your spies."

"Of course. Hannah is something of an expert on the subject

of the paranormal, although I'm not sure she knows that. I wouldn't be surprised if she has a touch of talent herself. After she attended a few of Fleming's seminars at the Academy of the Occult and booked some appointments with you, she informed the members of her little society of researchers that you were the genuine article, a woman endowed with true psychical ability."

"You hired the Bone Man to kidnap me," Beatrice said. "Why in heaven's name did you order him to murder Roland Fleming?"

"Fleming's death was regrettable but I had no choice. I knew that if you simply disappeared, Fleming would go to the police and demand an investigation."

Beatrice pushed herself to her feet. "So you told the Bone Man to silence him."

"But you slipped away that night," Victor said. "At first I did not think it would be difficult to find you, but eventually I realized that you had literally vanished. It was . . . astonishing, to tell you the truth."

"The Bone Man found Roland's stash of blackmail material that night, didn't he?" Beatrice said.

"Yes. He brought it to me. I had no interest in the items at the start of the affair but later, when I realized I could not find you, I took the biggest risk of all."

"You blackmailed Hannah and made it appear that I was the extortionist. You knew that would draw Joshua into the hunt."

Victor sighed. "By that time I was quite desperate. I feared that I might never find you."

"Was there anything in Roland's collection of extortion material that involved Hannah?"

"No. But Hannah and Josh had no way of knowing that."

"You knew about the man who had died in Hannah's kitchen," Beatrice said. "How did you discover that?"

"Josh kept that a secret, even from me, the one person he trusted outside the family. But as I said, I made it a practice to keep an eye on my agents. There was no way I could get a spy into Josh's house, but Hannah's housekeeper was my unwitting informant. She was there that night and afterward badly shaken. She confided in her sister, who had been on my payroll since soon after I began to train Josh. I had no particular interest in the death at the time."

"But when you realized you had to send Joshua after me, you knew you possessed the perfect bait," Beatrice said. "Blackmailing Hannah yourself, however, would have been far too dangerous."

"It would have drawn Josh straight to me," Victor said. "I required a distraction that would satisfy him."

"You found a cheap, somewhat inept criminal who was more than happy to try to extort money from some wealthy people. You faked a couple of pages from a nonexistent diary hinting at the death in Hannah's kitchen."

"The fool required considerable guidance, but in the end my strategy worked," Victor said.

"You ordered the Bone Man to kill your handpicked blackmailer at Alverstoke Hall."

"I couldn't allow the extortionist to live after he had served his purpose," Victor said. "He knew too much, you see. There was always the chance that, even though I had been careful to keep my identity a secret from the blackmailer, Josh might be able to find me by following the trail."

"You do realize that Joshua will even now be searching for me," Beatrice said.

"Assuming he survives the encounter with the Bone Man," Victor said. "But by then it will be finished. My daughter will have been awakened."

"You cannot run far enough to escape Joshua, you must know that."

"I do not intend to run." Victor looked down at the sarcophagus. "All I care about is Emma."

Clement snorted. "I assure you, Gage will not survive the next twenty-four hours. Even if he escapes the Bone Man's knife, he will die in this house when he comes looking for you."

"You have tried to kill him before and failed," Beatrice said. "What makes you think you will succeed this time?"

Clement's eyes heated with a savage madness. "Things were not entirely under our control on previous occasions. But if Josh comes looking for you again, he will be on my ground."

She glanced around the room again. "You refer to this chamber?"

"The stairs and hallway that lead to this laboratory are set with a number of traps. Each contains a canister of my nightmare-inducing vapor. Only Victor and I know the safe route to this room. Anyone else who attempts to climb the staircase will die a slow and terrible death."

"Why don't you tell me precisely what it is you expect me to do for you?" she said.

"Yes," Victor said, his tone sharpening. "It is time."

"Come with me, Miss Lockwood," Clement said.

He turned and led the way across the chamber to the sarcophagus. She followed him slowly, struggling to suppress her senses. But no matter how she tried to lower her talent she could not entirely escape the traces of decay and death that permeated the atmosphere around the ancient coffin.

Clement walked around the sarcophagus and faced her from the opposite side.

"Behold my beloved," he said. "Tonight you will awaken her."

Beatrice had tried to prepare herself for what she would see when they pushed the lid of the sarcophagus aside. She dreaded the sight but she reminded herself it would not be the first dead body she had viewed.

She was wholly unprepared to discover that the lid of the sarcophagus was fitted with a large panel of transparent crystal. Beneath the clear plate the body of a perfectly preserved woman floated gently in a clear liquid. She was dressed in a prim white nightgown. The hem of the garment was secured to her ankles to keep it from floating up above her knees. Her dark hair drifted around her beautiful face. Her eyes were closed.

Beatrice stopped a short distance away and fought to breathe.

"Dear heaven," she whispered. "This is Emma."

"Yes," Victor said. "She is in a very deep sleep. You see now why I have gone to such lengths to revive her."

Clement looked down at the dead woman. "Beautiful, is she not?"

Beatrice swallowed hard, trying to suppress the queasy sensation in her stomach. It was not just Emma's beauty that had been so artfully preserved. The bruises around her throat were as vivid as if she had been strangled yesterday.

"She was, indeed, quite lovely," Beatrice said quietly.

Clement's eyes heated again. "She *is* lovely."

"She is dead," Beatrice said flatly. "There is nothing I or anyone else can do to bring her back to life."

Victor's eyes darkened with desperation and grim resolve. *"She is not dead."*

"She's asleep," Clement hissed. "A very deep sleep, but a sleeping state, nonetheless. It's called suspended animation."

"I confess I am astonished by the preservative effects of the formula that you have used to keep her body looking so alive, but death is death," Beatrice said.

"Damn you," Clement snarled. He came around the end of the sarcophagus. "You are no scientist. You know nothing about chemistry."

He reached for her throat with hands that trembled with fury. His eyes were on fire.

Beatrice stumbled backward so quickly that her heel caught in the hem of her gown. She went down hard on the floor.

Victor moved swiftly, stepping into Clement's path. "Stop this foolishness. Have you forgotten that we require Miss Lockwood's assistance in this matter?"

Clement halted abruptly. He blinked a couple of times as though dazed, took a deep breath and pulled himself together with a visible effort of will. The fires of madness dimmed in his eyes but not in his aura.

"Yes, of course," he rasped.

Beatrice scrambled to her feet. Clement was not the only one struggling to breathe. Her heart was pounding with terror.

She backed away from the two men and came up hard against a workbench. She heard metal instruments rattle behind her but she ignored the sound, intent on finding a way out of the chamber.

But the only exit was the single door on the far side of the room. Victor and Clement barred the way. Her only real option was to continue buying time for Joshua to find her. That meant not provoking Clement to a killing fury.

Clement had himself in hand once more. "You are right, Victor. I will not kill Miss Lockwood now. That pleasure will come later."

"There is no need for anyone to die tonight," Victor said.

He spoke in soothing tones, as if he were an attendant in an asylum attempting to calm a patient. It was clear this was not the first time he had talked Clement out of a fit of madness.

Beatrice thought about the metallic rattling she had heard when she had come up against the workbench. She glanced over her shoulder to see what had made the noise.

An array of gleaming surgical instruments—scalpels, clamps and syringes—was set out on the workbench. A row of glass jars containing dead rats floating in liquid sat on a nearby shelf.

Victor was still calming Clement. She had to take the chance. It might be the only one she would get. She reached behind herself and groped cautiously. Her fingers closed around the handle of one of the scalpels. She slipped the blade into the hidden pocket of her gown, the one designed to hold a hankie.

Clement straightened his shoulders. He was composed once more but his eyes still burned.

"We have wasted enough time," he said. He went to the statue that stood next to the sarcophagus. "Bring Miss Lockwood to me, Victor."

Victor gave Beatrice an apologetic look. He started toward her.

"It will not be necessary to put your hands on me again," she said in her iciest accent.

Victor stopped, waiting.

She moved slowly toward the sarcophagus.

"I still do not understand what you think I can do to assist you in this madness," she said quietly.

"There are two steps to the awakening process," Clement announced. He sounded like a professor now. "The first requires that the power infused into the statue be released." He picked up the trailing end of the gold wire that was wrapped around the neck of Anubis. "That is your task. The energy will be conducted along this wire into the Egyptian Water. That will cause a chemical reaction that will reverse the state of suspended animation."

She thought about telling him again that he was insane but decided that as he had not responded well the last time, it would probably not be wise to do so.

"What is the second step of the process?" she asked.

"Once the Egyptian Water has been ignited it will be necessary to add fresh blood to the chemicals in order to keep the process going long enough to accomplish the awakening. My beautiful Emma was a woman of talent. It's obvious that the best source of strong blood would be that of another female with strong psychical abilities."

She looked at the surgical instruments set out on the workbench.

"Me," she said.

He smiled. "Yes, Miss Lockwood, you."

Victor frowned. "Clement assures me that the process does not require a great deal of blood, merely a small amount to spark the energy of the Water. You will not be a sacrifice, Miss Lockwood."

She looked into Clement's mad eyes. "You lied to Mr. Hazelton about that aspect of the thing, didn't you? You're going to murder me tonight."

"Nonsense," Clement said. "As Victor said, the process merely requires a small amount of blood."

He was definitely lying but there was no point arguing.

"What if I can't awaken her?" she asked.

"Then I will have no further use for you, will I? You will live only as long as you are useful to me. Enough. It's time. Victor, help me remove the lid of the sarcophagus."

Victor went forward, leaned down and placed both hands on the edge of the crystal-and-stone lid. Clement did the same. Together they pushed the top of the coffin to the side, angling it so that it rested across the foot of the burial box.

The heavy scent of harsh chemicals grew abruptly stronger. Beatrice winced and took a step back. The body floating in the liquid appeared unreal, a beautiful wax doll made to resemble a sleeping woman.

Clement pulled on a pair of leather gloves and picked up the end of the gold wire. He submerged the tip into the preservative fluid.

"Touch the statue's eyes and release the power," he ordered.

Beatrice studied the Anubis. "What, exactly, do you want me to do?"

"I just told you, *touch the eyes*. When you make physical contact with the obsidian stones you will sense the energy locked inside. Even I can feel it. My paranormal senses are not strong enough to release it. Let us hope that yours are because otherwise there is no reason to keep you alive."

Victor scowled. "That's enough, Clement. There is no reason to threaten Miss Lockwood."

Beatrice moved closer to the statue. Warily she raised one arm and touched an obsidian eye with her fingertip. An icy shiver of energy whispered through her. She flinched and quickly took her finger away from the stone.

"This is not a good idea," she said.

"*Do it,*" Clement ordered.

He was losing control again, she realized. Gingerly she put two fingertips on one of the jeweled eyes and heightened her talent. Energy stirred in the stone. Power rose in the atmosphere. Intuitively she tried to find a way to channel it. There was, she discovered, something oddly seductive about controlling the currents. She pushed her senses higher.

She was concentrating so intently on the statue that she did not realize anything was happening to the preservative formula until she heard Victor speak in a hushed voice.

"Look at the Water," he said.

"It's working," Clement said. Fierce satisfaction reverberated in the words. "It's working. It's working."

Keeping her fingertips on the eye, Beatrice turned her head to look at the sarcophagus. The fluid was turning an eerie shade of violet and starting to bubble. She could feel currents of paranormal energy coming from it now.

Clement gave her an impatient glance. "Touch the other eye,

you slow-witted woman. Hurry. Emma's finger twitched. She's coming awake."

"Emma," Victor whispered. "Dear God, Emma. Wake up, my darling girl."

Beatrice looked at the dead woman's hand. The fingers were moving slightly but she knew it was not with the stirrings of a life force. The small motions were caused by the bubbling, frothing water. Clement and Victor were deluding themselves. But some sort of energy was building in the statue and she was quite certain it was dangerous. There was no knowing what would happen if she pushed it higher, but it might prove to be the distraction she needed to escape. She focused on the rising energy in the stones.

Clement gave a startled shout of pain.

Beatrice took her fingers off the statue and whirled around to see what had happened. Clement had dropped the wire into the Water and was peeling off the leather gloves.

Victor looked at him, irritated. "What happened?"

"So strong," Clement muttered. He stared at his fingers. "Too strong. I dare not hold the wire. The gloves are not sufficient protection. I'll leave the wire in the Water and stand aside while the energy is being generated." He stood back. "Again, Miss Lockwood."

This was not going to end well, she thought. But she had nothing to lose.

She put the full power of her talent into exciting the energy in the obsidian. The Egyptian Water churned and roiled and seethed. The body in the tank shuddered and twitched but Beatrice knew the movements did not indicate life. The corpse was being jostled about by the agitation of the fluid.

The energy in the statue was building swiftly now. She was not sure she was still in control.

The explosion did not come from the Anubis, as Beatrice had anticipated. It came from above. A large pane of glass in the dome ceiling shattered inward. Shards rained down.

For a few seconds Clement and Victor did not seem to comprehend what had happened. By the time they realized that the source of the broken glass was from the ceiling, it was too late.

An avenging angel clad in black and carrying a steel-and-ebony sword in the form of a cane was plummeting down into the small antechamber of hell.

Joshua.

Forty-Eight

He had assessed the situation before he made the descent into the chamber. Victor was the first and most immediate threat, Joshua concluded.

He landed hard near one of the workbenches, as planned. He took much of his weight on his good leg and grabbed the edge of the bench to support the rest.

He released the end of the rope ladder that Nelson was paying out from the roof. He had only a split second to catch his balance. In that instant he saw that Victor stood frozen in anguished disbelief. It was, Joshua knew, the only chance he would get.

Victor recovered in the next instant. He reached inside his coat.

Joshua braced himself against the edge of the workbench and swept the cane out in a slashing arc. The heavy length of steel and wood caught Victor on his forearm. Bone cracked. The gun he had just pulled out fell from his hand. He crumpled to his knees.

Nelson shouted from the edge of the dome, "Josh, he's got her."

Joshua turned, using the workbench to keep his balance. He saw that Clement had seized Beatrice. He had one arm wrapped around her neck. He held a scalpel to her throat.

"I see you have not lost your skills while you have been rusticating in the countryside," Clement said. "But I'd advise you to tell your companion up there to stay where he is or I will slit Miss Lockwood's throat."

Joshua looked at Beatrice. Her arms were at her sides. She appeared calm—unnaturally so. No one could remain so composed when a madman had a scalpel at one's throat. Beatrice really was an excellent actress.

"Are you all right?" he asked her.

"Yes," she said, her voice remarkably steady.

She made a small movement with one hand. Her fingers appeared from between the heavy folds of her gown. He glimpsed the sheen of a metal scalpel. She was letting him know that she, too, was armed.

All that they needed was a distraction, Joshua thought.

He looked at the sarcophagus. The fluid continued to froth and churn. He saw that Emma appeared almost alive. Her hair swirled around her face. Her arms undulated gently.

"I would never have believed it," he said. "But I see you have been successful. Her eyes are open. You had better get her out of that fluid before she takes a breath and drowns."

"Emma," Clement whispered. He started to haul Beatrice toward the coffin. His attention was on the dead woman. "Get her out of the Water, damn you, Gage."

"Only if you release Beatrice."

"I'll kill her if you don't get Emma out of the Water, I swear I will."

"It seems that we each hold a hostage," Joshua said. "I suggest that we exchange them."

"If I release Miss Lockwood, you will kill me."

"No," Joshua said. "I will not kill you tonight. If you keep your side of the bargain, I will keep mine. Beatrice and I will leave the same way I arrived, through the dome. You may remain here with your beloved. You know that I have always been a man of my word."

Victor said nothing. He remained on his knees, clutching his broken arm. He gazed in despair at the body of his daughter. Joshua knew that Victor was finally acknowledging the truth. Emma was dead.

Clement's face contorted with anguish and indecision. He gave Beatrice a violent shove that sent her stumbling away from him.

He rushed to the sarcophagus and reached into the frothing liquid to seize the body.

Joshua caught Beatrice. "You will go up the rope ladder first."

She dropped the small scalpel, hitched up her skirts and started climbing.

He followed her up the ladder using his gloved hands to secure his grip. He could put enough weight on his bad leg to make the ascent possible but it was not easy.

When they reached the roof, Nelson helped steady Beatrice at the edge of the dome.

"Are you all right, Miss Lockwood?" he asked.

"I am now, thanks to you and Mr. Gage," she said. "I assume we use the same rope ladder to get down from this roof?"

"Luckily that will not be necessary," Nelson said, reeling in the ladder. "Uncle Joshua found an old stairwell in one of the towers."

"Clement Lancing said that the stairs and hallway that lead to the laboratory were set with traps," Beatrice said.

"I assumed as much," Joshua said. "That is why we came in through the roof. No one ever expects an opponent to approach from above."

"Another Mr. Smith saying?" Beatrice asked.

"Yes, as a matter of fact," Joshua said. "He forgot one of his own rules. But then, everyone has a blind side. Let's get away from here. Inspector Morgan will be waiting to make his arrests."

"But the gas," Beatrice said. "How will the police enter the laboratory?"

"The same way we did, if necessary, but I don't think that will be the case. Victor will let them in. He knows that this is finished."

The screaming started then. Clement Lancing's roar of rage and madness echoed in the night. It was cut short by a single gunshot.

Joshua looked down. Victor was standing over Lancing's body, the gun in his hand. He looked up at Joshua.

"You were always my best agent," Victor said.

Forty-Nine

S eriously, Josh, how did you and Nelson know where to find me?" Beatrice asked. "And please don't give me that line about looking in the right place. I want details."

She and Joshua and Nelson were gathered around the dining table with Sara and Abigail in the cozy morning room in Lantern Street. Thankfully, Sara and Abigail appeared none the worse for their encounter with the incense drug. To all outward appearances, Joshua was his usual cool, controlled self but whenever he looked across the table at Beatrice she detected a little telltale heat in his eyes. For his part, Nelson was still brimming with excitement. He had been the one who had relayed every detail of the rescue to Sara and Abigail.

Mrs. Beale had also recovered from the hallucinogenic fog. She had served up a hearty early morning breakfast of eggs, potatoes and toast. Everyone was drinking a great deal of very strong coffee because none of them had yet had any sleep. Beatrice doubted that any of them except Joshua—who evidently could put himself into a trance whenever he wished—was capable of sleep. They were all still dealing with the edgy energy that followed violence.

"It was simple logic," Joshua said. He reached for another slice of toast and slathered it with jam. "Once I realized that Victor was involved in the affair, everything else fell into place. I knew that if he had established a properly equipped laboratory for Lancing, it would be in a location that Victor deemed safe and under his full control. That location also had to be close to London because Victor would want to make frequent visits to make sure that progress was being made and to be certain his daughter had the appearance of being alive."

Sara looked thoughtful. "It would also need to be a location that was convenient to Mrs. Grimshaw, the apothecary in Teaberry Lane."

"Yes," Joshua said. "I naturally concluded that the most obvious place was Exford Castle. It has been in Victor's family for generations."

Beatrice raised her eyes to the ceiling in a give-me-patience manner. "Naturally."

"Victor knows how I think," Josh said quietly. "That's why he was always one step ahead. But I know him, too. Once I realized that he was the one plotting the strategy, I was able to second-guess him."

Abigail frowned. "What on earth was going on with that statue of Anubis? Did it really have paranormal powers?"

"No," Joshua said flatly.

"Yes," Beatrice said at the same time.

Everyone looked at her. She put her cup down and thought about what had happened in Clement Lancing's laboratory.

"The statue is a kind of engine," she said slowly, "similar to an electricity machine, I think. It requires some psychical ability to activate the forces but the power that is released is just that—raw energy."

"Like the energy released by a steam engine or a generator," Nelson said. "You might be able to use it to turn a wheel or ignite a lamp but that's all."

"Exactly," Beatrice said. "The Anubis energy is certainly not magical in nature. It has no special properties. The currents conducted into the preservative fluid agitated the Egyptian Water but that was all they did."

"I would very much like to examine the statue," Sara said eagerly.

"It's yours," Joshua said. "Consider it a thank-you gift for all that you did for me."

Sara's eyes widened. "That is very generous of you, sir."

Joshua's mouth twisted wryly. "Trust me when I tell you that I have no desire to install that antiquity in my own household."

"I understand." She sighed. "In spite of everything, I do feel sorry for Victor Hazelton. All these months he has been living on a false hope offered up by a madman. In the end his grief drove Hazelton mad, too."

"How true," Abigail said. "And how sad. I doubt that he will go to prison. He will probably be declared insane and likely spend the rest of his life in an asylum."

"No," Joshua said. There was quiet certainty in his voice. "Victor could not endure an asylum. And now that he knows that

Emma has been dead all along he has nothing else to live for, so I do not think that he will survive for long."

Nelson looked up from his eggs, startled. He frowned. "You believe that he will die of grief?"

"In a manner of speaking, yes," Joshua said.

Beatrice understood. She knew from their silence that Sara and Abigail did, too. It took Nelson somewhat longer to grasp Joshua's meaning.

"I see," Nelson said, abruptly subdued. "You expect him to take his own life. But you can't know that for certain—"

"I know him," Joshua said. "I know how he thinks."

Because you believe that Victor thinks a lot like you, Beatrice thought. But she did not say it aloud. At that moment Joshua met her eyes across the table and she knew that he was aware of her thoughts.

"You're wrong, you know," she said simply. "You are two very different men, in spite of your philosophical training and your martial arts abilities. You would never have allowed yourself to believe what you know is impossible—that the dead could be brought back to life by magic. And you would never have murdered people who had done you no harm in order to achieve your objective. You would have found other ways."

Joshua's brows rose. "Because I am a man of logic and reason?"

She smiled. "No, because you are a good and decent man."

Sara chuckled. "She is trying to tell you that you are a hero, Mr. Gage, and I do believe she is correct."

"There are no heroes," Joshua said. "There are only those who try to make the right choice when choice is thrust upon them."

Nelson grinned. "Is that one of Hazelton's sayings?"

Joshua surprised everyone with a smile. "Actually, I made that one up myself."

Beatrice looked at him. "What will you do now?"

Joshua's smile vanished. "I'm going to do the only thing I can for Victor."

"I understand. May I come with you?"

"Are you certain you want to accompany me?"

"Yes," she said. "I want to be with you when you say your goodbyes to both of them."

Fifty

Following breakfast Joshua escorted Beatrice home in a cab and then went off to speak with one of his mysterious associates at Scotland Yard. Nelson accompanied him.

The house echoed with emptiness. Clarissa was still on assignment in the country. Mrs. Rambley had left a note saying that she had gone to visit her recently widowed sister.

Beatrice was in the middle of a bath when the exhaustion finally overtook her. Yawning, she stepped out of the tub, pulled on her wrapper and went to her bedroom to take a nap.

She awoke to the sound of rain on the windows and a knock on the front door. She rose from the bed and went to the window to look down at the street.

Joshua was on the front step. He was wearing a long black coat and a hat against the rain. The cab in which he had arrived was disappearing into the gray mist.

She tightened the sash of her wrapper and hurried downstairs, anxious for a report of his conversation with the police. When she opened the door she knew from the energy that shifted in the atmosphere around him and his fierce grip on the cane that it was only his iron will that was keeping him on his feet.

"Joshua," she said. She stepped back. "Come in."

"I'm sorry if I woke you."

"It's all right. I was just getting up from a nap." She blushed. Her wrapper was entirely modest but she was suddenly aware that she was wearing nothing under it. "You look like you could use some sleep, too."

"I will go home and get some rest after I'm finished here."

After I'm finished here did not bode well. A small shiver of uncertainty lanced across her senses, igniting her intuition. Whatever the reason for this visit, it was a matter of great seriousness to Joshua.

She stepped back. He moved through the doorway and shrugged out of his wet coat. She hung the garment on a wall hook and set his hat to dry on the console.

It was odd to realize that this was only the second time that he had crossed the threshold of her home. Then again, she had never been to his house. They knew so little about each other and yet they knew so much of an intimate nature. But that was the way of the world for those who indulged in illicit love affairs, she reminded herself. The one thing such couples could not share was a home.

A whisper of melancholia twisted her insides.

"What are you thinking?" he asked quietly.

Startled, she summoned her acting talents and managed a bright little smile. "I was thinking that in some ways we are for the most part still strangers. It seems that we have spent the whole of our acquaintance dealing with blackmailers, killers and the odd madman or two."

He watched her with an unwavering intensity. "I have been waiting my entire life to meet you, Beatrice."

She caught her breath. For a few seconds she stood frozen. Her instinct was to throw herself into his arms. But logic reminded her that the darkly passionate energy she sensed in him could easily be explained by the recent excitement and the strong emotions they had experienced together.

To cover her confusion, she led the way into the small parlor. "Would you like tea? My housekeeper is out but I am quite capable of putting the kettle on the stove myself."

"No, thank you."

"Your leg appears to be giving you some trouble today. That is hardly a surprise after what happened last night. I have a bottle of Mrs. Marsh's tonic upstairs in my bedroom. I'll just dash up there and get some for you."

She started toward the stairs.

"No." He paused. "Thank you."

She reminded herself that he had been through a great deal in the past twenty-four hours.

He followed her into the parlor but he did not sit down. Instead, he braced himself with both hands on the hilt of his cane and did not take his eyes off her.

"I stopped here before going home because there is something very important I must say to you," he said. "I want to say it before I sleep."

Dread descended on her. The small parlor seemed to grow

darker. She tried to prepare herself for whatever was coming. Perhaps this was when he would explain in a kindly fashion that he cared for her but that marriage was not an option. Was she willing to commit to the continuation of their affair? she wondered. *Yes*. But such an arrangement could last only as long as he did not take a wife. She would not be a married man's mistress.

But Joshua would never ask that of her, she told herself. He would not deceive a wife. He was above all a man of honor.

"I understand why both of them did what they did," he said.

Consumed with her wild speculations about their future together or lack thereof, she did not immediately grasp his meaning.

"What?" she asked, going quite blank.

"I understand why Victor and Clement did the things they did."

She pulled her jumbled thoughts together. This was about the closure of the case, not about their personal affairs. Really, what had she been thinking? Naturally he would want to tie up all the loose ends before he allowed himself to consider the personal angle.

"Yes, of course," she said crisply. "A father's grief and a lover's sense of guilt are both very powerful motives."

"I don't think you comprehend what I am trying to tell you, Beatrice. I know why they went to the lengths they did, why they allowed themselves to be deluded and driven mad. Why they were willing to kill to revive Emma. I understand those things fully and completely because I am no different."

"What?" Once again she felt blindsided.

"I would do whatever it took to save you," he said.

She took a deep breath and allowed herself to relax.

"Yes, I know," she said. "You were born to protect others. But you would find another way to go about it."

"Perhaps," he said. "If there was another way. But in the end, whatever it took. I love you, Beatrice."

She was so dumbfounded she could only stare at him for a few seconds. She said the first words that came into her head.

"Do you mean to say that you actually believe in love?" she managed. "A form of energy that you cannot see or measure or test?"

"I certainly don't believe that love is a form of paranormal energy," he clarified, very serious now. "And I will admit that until I met you I had never experienced emotions of the sort that I feel for you. But I do not doubt this sense of certainty. It would be like doubting the truth of a sunrise or the tide. Simply because some powerful forces cannot be tested or measured does not mean that one must resort to psychical explanations."

She was suddenly breathless. There was a peculiar roaring in her ears. The world outside the parlor ceased to exist. Frantically she struggled to hang on to reality.

"Well, actually there are other explanations for strong passions," she said carefully. "Physical and intellectual attraction. The stimulating effects of shared danger. Mutual admiration. That very long year you spent in the country—"

"Do you love me?" he asked. "Could you love me?"

With that she tossed aside the tattered remnants of common sense. Laughter did battle with tears. She flung herself into his arms. He staggered under the impact but he somehow managed to move the cane out of the way, catch her and maintain his balance all at the same time. She put her arms around his neck.

"Oh, Joshua, yes, *yes*," she said, joy flooding her senses. "Of course I love you. Surely you knew that."

He took a deep breath and exhaled it slowly. "I have learned that some things require words."

She smiled. "Do you mean to say that not everything can be deduced through logic and observation?"

"Am I going to have to listen to you tease me about that for the rest of my life?"

"That depends. Are we talking about the rest of your life?"

He frowned. "You just said you loved me. I love you. That means we will be married."

"You haven't asked. Some things require words."

He smiled his slow, sensual smile, the one that set all of her senses aflutter.

"Will you marry me so that you will be in a position to tease me endlessly about my way of coming to conclusions?"

"How could I pass up such a spectacularly appealing offer?" She flattened her palms on his chest. "Yes, Joshua, I will marry you."

His eyes were darkly brilliant with something she thought might be joy.

"I will take very good care of you," he vowed.

"Just as I will take very good care of you," she said.

He gripped the cane in one hand and wrapped his other arm around her. He kissed her. It was a binding kiss, a kiss that promised the future.

It was, Beatrice thought, the kiss she had been waiting for all of her life.

Fifty-One

The following day Joshua stood with Victor in the pouring rain. Together they watched as the casket containing Emma's body was lowered into the grave. A clergyman murmured the ritual words.

"Ashes to ashes, dust to dust . . ."

Victor's legs were shackled. His right arm was in a sling. Three constables stood respectfully nearby. A black police van waited at the iron gates of the cemetery. But in spite of it all, Victor stood proud and undiminished, still a commanding presence, still the brilliant and mysterious Mr. Smith.

Beatrice and Nelson waited some distance away. A somber funeral attendant held an umbrella over Beatrice's head.

When the solemn service was concluded Victor reached down with his left hand and scooped up a clod of wet earth. He tossed it down onto the casket. He straightened, closed his eyes in silent prayer and then he looked at Joshua.

"Thank you," he said. "I should have said my goodbyes to her long ago. Now it's done and I am free to seek my own peace tonight."

Joshua did not speak. There was nothing to say.

Victor looked at Beatrice. A melancholy smile flickered at the edge of his mouth. "I congratulate you on finding a woman who will always know your heart. You are a fortunate man."

"I'm aware of that," Joshua said.

"Does it strike you as ironic that you might never have found her if it hadn't been for me?"

"Yes," Joshua said, "it does."

"Your nephew reminds me of you at that age. Smart, fast, with a bit of talent. He is looking to you for guidance now that he is coming into the fullness of his manhood. You have a task ahead of you. I know you will not fail him."

"Everything I know about being a man I learned from you," Joshua said.

"No." Victor shook his head. "You became what you were meant to be. All I did was help you uncover the strength inside you and teach you the discipline and control you needed to handle it. If that strength of spirit had not been there at the start, there is nothing I or anyone else could have done to endow you with those qualities."

"I will miss you, Victor."

"You are the son of my heart," Victor said. "I am very proud of you."

"You came into my life when I needed you. You saved me from myself. I will never forget you."

Victor was quietly pleased. "That is good to know. Goodbye, my son."

"Goodbye, sir."

The constables led Victor to the police van and ushered him into the iron cage. Joshua watched until the carriage clattered away into the rain.

After a while he realized that Beatrice had come to stand beside him.

"We said our farewells," Joshua explained. "He told me that he will find his peace tonight. He will be gone by morning."

"Shackled as he is?"

"He will find a way," Joshua said. "He is Mr. Smith."

He took Beatrice's arm. Together they walked through the rain to where Nelson stood waiting for them.

Fifty-Two

"Nelson told me that he intends to undertake instruction in meditation and the martial arts from you," Hannah said.

She sounded resigned, Joshua thought, but at the same time accepting. They were in his study. He was propped against the edge of his desk, his cane close at hand. Hannah was at the window, gazing out into the small garden. She had arrived on his doorstep a short time earlier. One look at her face had told him that Nelson had spoken to her of his plans.

"I made it clear that he would have to inform you of his decision before I would begin the lessons," Joshua said. "But it is his decision, Hannah."

"I know that. I've always known it. I wanted to protect him."

"I understand. But he has become a man. You cannot protect him any longer."

"You are right, of course." Hannah turned to face him. "Beatrice and I talked. She said that the most generous gift I could give Nelson would be to remove the chains of guilt that I have placed on him. When he told me of his decision, I tried to do that. I said I understood and that he had my blessing."

"I'm sure he appreciated that."

Hannah smiled faintly. "I also told him that I could not imagine a finer mentor and teacher than you."

Joshua hesitated. "I'm surprised to hear you say that."

"Beatrice pointed out the obvious to me. She said that Nelson had clearly inherited the Gage talent and that the most prudent thing to do with such a gift was to learn to control it and channel it in a responsible manner."

"It's not the Gage talent that Nelson inherited. It's the Gage temperament."

Hannah smiled. "Call it what you will, I certainly do not want Nelson to continue down the path he has been following for the past few months, gambling and drinking to excess."

"You knew about that, did you?"

"Of course. He is my son. At the rate he was going he would have come to a bad end, just like Papa."

"Nelson is not like our father, Hannah. He is his own man. He needs to discover what it is that he was born to do."

"But what is that?"

"I don't know," Joshua said. "But in time he will find his own path."

Hannah turned away from the window. "Will you find yours now that Victor Hazelton is gone?"

He tapped his fingers together, wondering how much to tell her. She deserved the truth, he thought.

"I have been approached by the people to whom Victor once reported," he said, "people at the highest levels of the government."

Hannah was appalled. "They want you to take his place?"

"Yes."

Hannah closed her eyes. "I see."

"After discussing the matter with Beatrice, I declined the post. I do not want to return to a life in the shadows. I want to walk in the sunlight with Beatrice and—if we are blessed—with our children."

Hannah frowned. "Somehow, I cannot envision you turning your back on what you do best—finding that which is lost."

He sat forward. "Beatrice said much the same thing. You are both correct, of course. I intend to become a private consultant who specializes in finding people and things that have disappeared. But I will choose my clients with great care. Not everyone who is lost wants to be found."

Fifty-Three

The wedding reception was held on the grounds of Crystal Gardens. It was the second time within the span of a few months that Abigail and Sara had been invited to the nuptials of a former employee. Evangeline Ames—now the wife of Lucas Sebastian, the owner of the Gardens—had been the first bride to be married there. As one of Beatrice's two closest friends, she had insisted on arranging the reception for Beatrice and Joshua. Clarissa Slate, having successfully concluded her recent case, was the bridesmaid.

The day was sunny and warm. In addition to Evangeline and Lucas and Clarissa, Hannah Trafford and her son, Nelson, were among the guests.

The grounds of the mysterious estate looked considerably less ominous than they had the last time they had all gathered there, Sara thought. The level of paranormal energy had definitely been reduced, although Lucas had explained that due to the properties of the ancient underground spring in the center of the gardens, nothing would ever be normal about the plant life that thrived there.

One could not run decades of bizarre paranormal experiments in a garden as Lucas's uncle had done and not expect to come up with some very dangerous results, Sara thought. There was a tremendous amount of psychical energy in the botanical world.

She stood with Abigail near the buffet table and watched Beatrice and Joshua talk with Lucas and Evangeline near a fountain. Joshua and Lucas had obviously become friends. Perhaps it was because they were both so much alike when it came to character and spirit, Sara thought. Both would do whatever was necessary to protect the ones they loved. They shared something else, as well. Joshua was still reluctant to put any credence in the paranormal, but there was no doubt in her mind that he possessed a measure of psychical talent.

"Our Beatrice looks absolutely radiant, doesn't she, Abby?" Sara whipped out a hankie to dab a small tear away from the corner of her eye. "And look at the way Joshua is standing so close to her. One can see the strong bond between them. He would ride into hell to protect her."

"You are such a romantic," Abigail said. She munched a lobster canapé. "But you are right. Joshua's injuries sent him into seclusion for a time but they did not break his spirit. There is steel in that man. It is good to see that the shadows that always seemed to envelop him are gone."

"Thanks to the healing energy of love."

"I am happy for both of them, of course," Abigail said briskly. She picked up another canapé. "But it strikes me that at the rate we are losing our agents to marriage, Flint and Marsh will soon be bankrupt."

"We will find other agents," Sara assured her, unperturbed. "And it is not as though we have lost their services. The four of them have made it clear that they are available for consultation on future cases."

"Bah. Perhaps we should close the doors of Flint and Marsh and go into another business."

"Such as?"

"Matchmaking."

Sara chuckled. "We do seem to be rather good at it, don't we?"

"Evidently, but there's more profit in the investigation business."

"True." Sara looked at Nelson, who was in animated conversation with Lucas's brother, Tony, and his sister, Beth.

"It strikes me that instead of reinventing ourselves as matchmakers, perhaps we should consider expanding the investigative services of Flint and Marsh," Sara said.

"What do you mean?"

Sara tapped one finger against the buffet table. "Young Nelson appears to have inherited talents that are quite similar to those of his uncle. There have been times of late when it would have been helpful to have had a bodyguard available to protect one of our agents who was exposed to danger in the course of a case. I wonder if Nelson would be interested in that sort of work."

Abigail narrowed her eyes. "Why don't we inquire?"

BEATRICE WATCHED HER former employers approach Nelson, Beth and Tony.

"Hmm," she said.

Evangeline, Joshua and Lucas all turned their heads to see what had attracted her attention.

"What do you suppose Mrs. Marsh and Mrs. Flint are up to?" Evangeline said. "They appear to be on a mission."

"Yes," Lucas said. "There is something very determined about that pair."

"If there is one thing I know about Mrs. Flint and Mrs. Marsh, it is that they are excellent businesswomen," Joshua observed.

It was impossible to hear the conversation that was taking place on the other side of the rosebushes, but it was not difficult to see what was happening. Nelson was paying close attention to what Mrs. Flint and Mrs. Marsh were saying. The more they talked, the more enthusiastic he appeared.

"Something tells me that Nelson will soon be engaged in a position with Flint and Marsh in the near future," Beatrice said.

"I believe he is at long last on his way to finding a career," Joshua said. "Hannah will be thrilled."

Beatrice winced. "I doubt it."

"She will understand," Joshua said. "I was very much like him when I was that age."

Fifty-Four

They spent their wedding night in Fern Gate Cottage. The small, cozy house belonged to Lucas Sebastian. It was situated down the lane from Crystal Gardens.

Beatrice put on the beautiful new nightgown that Sara and Abigail had given her. She waited in bed listening as Joshua made his way methodically through the cottage checking locks and windows. She smiled to herself. When he arrived in the doorway he paused to give her an inquiring look.

"Something amusing?" he asked.

"I was just thinking of how careful you are when it comes to the details."

Joshua propped his cane against the bedside table and started to unfasten his shirt. "Details are like small holes in the bottom of the boat. Plug them and the vessel will stay afloat."

She raised her brows. "One of your own quotes?"

He smiled. "I'm afraid so."

"Words to live by, I'm sure." She plumped up the pillows behind her and watched with pleasure as Joshua removed his shirt. "But you can't anticipate everything in life."

"I am well aware of that." Joshua finished undressing, turned down the lamp and got into bed beside her. He gathered her close against him. "For example, I certainly never anticipated you, my love. I broke most of my rules because of you."

She savored the heat in his eyes. "Just most of the rules? Not all?"

"No, not all."

He brushed his mouth across hers and wrapped one powerful hand around her hip.

She felt the energy of joy and love and passion welling up inside her but she pulled back an inch or so and put her fingers on his mouth to stop him from deepening the kiss.

"Wait," she said. "I have to know which rule you did not break."

He smiled at her there in the moonlight, love heating his eyes. "The one that states that simply because something cannot be explained, it does not follow that it does not exist."

"Good heavens, sir, are you telling me that you have at last come to believe in the existence of the paranormal?"

"I will not go that far," he said. "But I promise you that I do believe in love. And I will love you always and forever."

She remembered what Abigail and Sara had said about him the night she told them about her encounter with Mr. Smith's mysterious Messenger—*Anyone who had dealings with him knew that if he made a promise, that promise would be kept.*

She touched the side of Joshua's scarred face with her fingertips. "That will do for now."

He covered her mouth with his own. The promise was there in his searing kiss. Always and forever.

Joshua might not be convinced that love was a form of paranormal energy, but he was capable of love, and he loved her as much as she loved him. That was more than enough for tonight.

More than enough for a lifetime.

From

DECEPTION COVE

By

JAYNE CASTLE

A NOTE FROM JAYNE

Welcome back to Rainshadow Island on the world of Harmony.

In the Rainshadow novels you will meet the passionate men and women who are drawn to this remote island in the Amber Sea. You will get to know their friends and neighbors in the small town of Shadow Bay.

Everyone on Rainshadow has a past; everyone has secrets. But none of those secrets is as dangerous as the ancient mystery concealed inside the paranormal fence that guards the forbidden territory of the island known as the Preserve.

The secrets of the Preserve have been locked away for centuries. But now something dangerous is stirring . . .

One

The two low-rent thugs were waiting for Alice when she left the darkened theater through the stage door. She sensed their presence as soon as she started walking toward the street. They were hiding behind the large garbage bin in the middle of the alley. They were not the subtle type.

"I do not have time for this," she said to the dust bunny perched on her shoulder.

Houdini chortled enthusiastically and bounced a little. At first glance he looked like a large wad of dryer lint that had been decorated with six paws and two baby-blue eyes. He had a second set of eyes—they were a very feral shade of amber—but he only opened them for hunting and other violent activities. He was still wearing the elegant red satin bowtie that Alice had put on him for the night's performance of the Alien Illusions Magic Show.

A born ham, Houdini adored the limelight. He was always up for a performance. Somehow he sensed that they were about to give one here in the alley. True, it would be for an audience of two and neither of the lowlifes had purchased a ticket, but he wasn't particular about the size of the crowd and the concept of money was lost on him. He took a more pragmatic approach to finances. Pizza worked for him.

"I'm glad you're enjoying yourself," Alice said. "We've got an empty refrigerator waiting back at the apartment and a mean landlord who will be expecting the rent tomorrow, remember?"

She did not have the money for the rent. The Alien Illusions Magic Show had folded without notice tonight. That kind of thing happened in show business, but in this case she was pretty sure she knew why the owner of the theater had cancelled all future productions. He had been bribed to dump the act.

She was now towing a wheeled suitcase crammed with costumes, wigs, stage makeup, and everything else she had been able to salvage from her tiny dressing room. A large blue tote filled with props was slung over her shoulder.

It had not been a good day, and the night was turning out to be worse. Not only was she once again unemployed, she'd been experiencing the all too familiar edgy sensation for the past several hours. During the past year she had learned the hard way that the icy little jolts of warning were coming from her intuition. Someone was watching her. Again.

And now a couple of street creeps were about to try to mug her.

"Really, how much can any woman be expected to take?" she said to Houdini.

Houdini chortled again, eager to go on stage.

One of the thugs emerged from behind the far end of the garbage bin. His head, which had been shaved to better display the tattoos on his skull, gleamed in the light cast by the fixture over the stage door. He had a knife in one hand.

The second man popped out of hiding and moved toward her along a parallel trajectory. He wore a stocking cap over his long, straggly hair. The blade of his knife glittered in the light.

"Now what's a nice girl like you doing out here all alone at night?" Tattoo Head asked. "Didn't anyone tell you this is a dangerous neighborhood?"

His voice was high-pitched and over-rezzed with the sort of unnatural excitement that indicated he had been doing some serious stimulants earlier in the evening.

"Get out of my way," Alice said. She adjusted the

weight of the tote on her shoulder, tightened her grip on the suitcase, and kept walking. "I'm not in a good mood."

"Now why you wanna go and talk like that to a couple of guys who just want to party?" the man with the stocking cap crooned. "We're gonna show you a real good time."

"A real good time." Tattoo Head leered. "What's that thing on your shoulder? Some kinda fluffy rat?"

Alice ignored him, closing the distance between the three of them as she trudged toward the alley entrance. No doubt about it, a really bad day was turning into a really bad night.

"Listen up, bitch," Stocking Cap snarled. "Stop right there. First, put that big purse down on the ground. You hear me? You're gonna take out all the money you got inside and if my friend and I like what we see, we'll all have some fun. If we don't like what we see, why then, you're gonna have to give us a reason not to cut you up a bit."

Alice kept walking.

"Hey, my buddy told you to stop," Tattoo Head hissed.

Alice continued walking. She felt Houdini's little claws grip her shoulder. He was no longer chortling. He growled a warning and sleeked out, his scruffy gray fur flattened against his small frame. He opened his second set of eyes and watched the knife-wielding pair closely. He was ready to rumble.

"There's an old saying about dust bunnies," Alice said to the thugs. *"By the time you see the teeth, it's too late.* Turns out Houdini and I have our own little twist on that bit of wisdom. *If you can't see the teeth or anything else, you're in trouble."*

"What do you think you're doing, you stupid woman?" Stocking Cap said. He skipped and danced across the pavement, closing in on her. "You asked for it. I'm gonna have to cut up that face of yours to teach you a lesson."

"Oh, for pity's sake," Alice said. "I've got some real issues at the moment. You shouldn't mess with a woman who has issues. Never say you weren't warned."

She jacked up her senses and pulled hard on her talent. She had never met anyone else with the same kind of psychic ability that she possessed—light-talents of any kind were rare. Those strong enough to do what she could do were considered the stuff of fairytales.

She cranked up her aura and used the energy to bend the wavelengths of normal spectrum light around herself and Houdini. The process was similar to the way a rock diverts water in a stream. To all intents and purposes, she had just gone invisible to the human eye.

She pushed a little harder and extended the shield to her tote and suitcase. It took a lot of power to bend light around not only herself and Houdini but the objects she was touching as well. She figured she wouldn't have to do it for long. She had learned over the years that people tended to freak out when they realized that, in her case, going invisible was not merely a magic trick.

As paranormal talents went, the ability to vanish for a short period of time was not nearly as useful as one might think. Career options were limited. Having concluded that she was not cut out for a life of crime, she had tried various other professional endeavors ranging from the food and beverage business to a job as a clerk in a museum gift shop. The last one had nearly gotten her killed.

This past year she had tried her hand at the magic business. It seemed like the perfect career for a woman with her skill-set. As it happened, however, any halfway experienced magician could routinely make objects disappear on stage. The fact that she used psychic energy to achieve the effect did not impress anyone in show business. She was a one-trick wonder.

Still, the ability to disappear at will along with whatever she happened to have physical contact with at the time did have its benefits.

"Shit," Tattoo Head yelped. He halted abruptly and stared at the place where Alice had been seconds earlier. "Where'd she go?"

"I don't know," Stocking Cap said. He was clearly jittery. "This is too weird. Maybe that last dose of green dust was bad, man. Gotta find a new dealer."

"It's not the dust," Tattoo Head said, edging back toward the entrance of the alley. Fear shivered in the atmosphere around him. "Maybe that magic act of hers is for real. Maybe she's a witch or something."

"No way. Are you crazy? No such thing as a witch."

Alice hurried toward the alley entrance. She could not remain invisible for long, not now. She had used a lot of energy on stage. Psychic energy was subject to the laws of physics, just like any other kind of energy. Use a lot of it and you needed time to recover. But she was sure she would only have to bend light for another minute or two. Stocking Cap and Tattoo Head were starting to panic.

On her shoulder Houdini chortled gleefully. The sound echoed eerily in the night. So did her footsteps and the rattle of the suitcase wheels on the pavement.

"Shit, I can hear her," Tattoo Head said. "It's like she's a ghost."

That proved too much for Stocking Cap.

"I'm getting out of here," he said.

He whirled and fled toward the alley entrance. Tattoo Head was hard on his heels. They nearly trampled Alice in their haste. She got out of the way, hauling the suitcase to one side and stood with her back to the brick wall as the pair thudded past.

They did not get far. A man materialized in the shadows at the front of the narrow passage. Moving with the swift, efficient speed and agility of a specter-cat, he did something fast and ruthless to Tattoo Head and Stocking Cap. Alice could have sworn that she saw a spark of dark paranormal lightning flash in the night but it winked out before she could be certain.

She blinked and saw Tattoo Head and Stocking Cap were on the ground. Neither moved.

The newcomer walked to where his victims lay and collected their knives. Then he crouched and went swiftly through the pockets of the unconscious men.

Just when you were convinced that a day could not get any worse, Alice thought. She stood frozen, her back to the alley wall, suddenly afraid to make any noise. She held her breath and struggled to keep the invisibility shield wrapped around herself, Houdini, and her burdens.

For his part, Houdini no longer appeared concerned. He was alert and watchful but he was back in dryer-lint mode. She was not sure what to make of that. On the one hand, it was reassuring to know that he did not sense another threat. Then again, maybe he was simply relishing the extended performance.

Evidently satisfied with his search, the man who had taken down Tattoo Head and Stocking Cap rose easily to his feet and started walking toward her.

As he came into the full glare of the alley door light, she saw that he was wearing wraparound, mirrored sunglasses.

Mirrored sunglasses. At midnight.

She just had time to realize that the stranger looked somewhat familiar before it dawned on her that he was looking directly at her.

"You must be Alice North," he said. "Your great-grandfather and mine were partners in a seafaring business a long time ago. My name is Drake Sebastian."

That explained a lot, she thought, including the sunglasses-at-midnight thing. The Sebastians kept a low profile but given her personal interest in the family, she paid attention when a member of the clan occasionally appeared in a rez-screen video or in the newspapers. Drake was the heir to the corporate throne—the man slated to take over the helm of the family empire—so lately he had been showing up more than any of the other Sebastians.

Drake was never seen in public without his mirrored glasses. They were his trademark. According to the media, he did not wear them for effect. The unique mirrored lenses had been developed specially for him in a Sebastian company research lab. It was no secret that following a lab accident three years earlier he had developed a severe sensitivity to light from the normal end of the spectrum. Now, without his special sunglasses, Drake was even blinded by a low-watt lightbulb.

For the past year there was only one thing Alice had feared more than her obsessive ex-mother-in-law's unrelenting harassment. Her worst nightmare for months was that the powerful Sebastian family might figure out that something very bad had happened on Rainshadow Island a year ago and that she was responsible.

Now it appeared the clan had, indeed, sent someone to track her down—and not just some low-ranking security agent. It was the next president and CEO of the family empire standing here in the alley. And he was looking straight at her even though she was bending light with all of her talent.

No doubt about it. *This was officially a really, really bad night*, she thought.

"You can see me," she said.

The overhead light glinted on Drake's mirrored glasses. His mouth curved in a mysterious smile, an

edgy combination of masculine satisfaction and anticipation that sent shivers of awareness across her senses.

"Oh, yeah," he said. "I can see you, Alice North."

"Crap."

"Nice to meet you, too."